Poplar Place

by Ellen Butler

Power to the Pen

Reviews & Awards

2014 InD'Tale Crowned Heart Award
2016 Finalist Chanticleer Chatelaine Award
2014 5 Star Readers' Favorite Award

What follows is a work that knows what it wants to be and nicely achieves it. What feels initially like a straightforward romance becomes more interesting when the past intrudes, raising the stakes. Plot, character and setting are each well imagined and nicely executed in a story that moves at a page-turning clip.
~ Publisher's Weekly Booklife Prize for Fiction

Ellen Butler has created a great romantic story! Poplar Place was a wonderful mix of elements; a little mystery with a little romance and the perfect length to finish quickly. Poplar Place provides a great romantic escape from our everyday lives, even if it's just a visit.
~ Readers Favorite

"Poplar Place" is such a wonderful, unique story! The flow is spot on and it keeps the reader riveted to the page
~ InD'tale Magazine

Copyright © 2014, Ellen Butler, Poplar Place Media > Books > Fiction
Category/Tags: Women's fiction, Suspense, Romance, Legal drama, Paranormal elements

Power to the Pen
PO Box 1474
Woodbridge, VA 22198
PowertothePen@ellenbutler.net

Print ISBN 13: 978-0-9984193-4-3
Print release 2nd Edition: May 2018

Cover Design by Calliope-Designs.com
Editor, Judy Alter

Warning: All Rights Reserved. The unauthorized reproduction or distribution of the copyrighted work is illegal and forbidden without the written permission of the author and publisher; exceptions are made for brief excerpts used in published reviews.

This is a work of fiction. Names, characters, corporations, institutions, organizations, events, or locales in this novel are either the product of the authors imagination or, if real, used fictitiously. The resemblance of any character to actual persons (living or dead) is entirely coincidental.

Dedication

To Alex. Thanks for your support.

Chapter One

March

"I think I'm in love," I whispered with quiet reverence. It was a mistake. I knew that immediately. A mistake and irresponsible to fall in love at first glance. After all, what did I know about the inside if all I could see were the beautiful luscious lines on the outside? Besides, I knew better. When you fall in love with a house on the spot, you lose perspective. Heaven forbid the seller realized you loved the home because then you'd lost your bargaining power, especially if you were willing to pay anything to get it. Unfortunately, I didn't have the luxury of paying anything to get it.

The house was built in the style of an old Victorian, but I knew from the price sheet it was only sixteen years old and thus wouldn't provide me with the headaches of a turn-of-the-century home. It was located in a small town called Denton, South Carolina, about an hour northwest of Charleston. The house had quaint gingerbread molding with a wrap-around front porch, a style usually seen more often in the New England area, and it was probably one of the reasons I loved it so much. It felt like a bit of home to me amidst the southern belle-flavored houses normally seen throughout South Carolina. The street appealed to me too. It was quiet and shady with rows of Bradford Pear trees lining the sides like soldiers at attention. In early spring, the trees would bloom with their fluffy white blossoms announcing the end of winter. I could easily envision strolling down the tree-lined sidewalk on my way to work.

A recent transplant to Denton, I had become the newest

librarian at the Denton Regional Library. South Carolina was my new home. Or maybe a better description would be the place I had run to, away from a former life—a life I was doing my best to put distance and the memory of far away. I was looking for a place to reinvest the money I'd received from the sale of my downtown loft. The market was up when I left the steel town of Pittsburgh and the Denton housing market was slightly depressed. Money would go a long way toward buying a house down here. Although, it did seem slightly ridiculous for one person to be thinking of living in a 3,000 square foot home…alone. Dismissively, I shook my head; I wouldn't allow thoughts like that to distract me from this gorgeous dwelling.

To me, the house represented salvation, a new beginning in small-town America. I wished to shed the memories of my old life as a snake shed its skin when it grew. Perhaps I, too, would grow a new skin in Denton. Looking over the front porch, I pictured myself sitting on a rocker watching the neighborhood kids ride their bikes up and down the street.

Perhaps I'll get a cat to keep me company. Great, I'll become the crazy cat lady living alone in the big house. What was I thinking? Shading my eyes with a hand, I turned to look at the upper stories and thought I caught a faint movement in the third-story window on the far right—possibly a curtain fluttering from a draft. Perhaps the owner was inside watching me.

My daydreams came to an abrupt halt as my realtor parked on the street behind my car. Jackie Barnes stepped out of her cream Cadillac with a wave and peachy southern smile aimed my way. As usual, she was dressed to the nines in a deep blue dress and drool-worthy pink stilettos. Her hair was shellacked into a blonde helmet that would take hurricane force winds to displace. The classic style suited her age, I guessed at mid-forties, and her looks. I felt a bit frumpy next to her wearing khaki shorts and a red polo. My realtor was a striking woman and compared to her I blended into the realm of average. Thick chestnut brown hair fell to my shoulders and blew gently in the breeze. I inherited the hair from my mom and loved its natural body and reddish highlights. On the other hand, my eyes were your average brown. Romantics might call them luscious chocolate, but to me they were just boring brown eyes. My figure could best be described as an hourglass.

Jackie arrived at my side, chattering away. "Isn't it fabulous?" She didn't wait for an answer. "It's only sixteen-years-old, but the architect did such a wonderful job with the wrap- around porch and gingerbread accents you'd never know it wasn't designed at the turn of the century." She let out a rush of air. "So, what do you think?"

I liked Jackie for her perkiness and southern accent, which exuded hospitality and charm. She became my realtor when I literally walked off the street into her office with no appointment and very little idea exactly what I was looking for—much like the rest of my life lately. Jackie, with unflappable good humor and what seemed to be inexhaustible patience, showed me home after home for about three weeks. I supposed that was the difference between realtors in the big city versus my new small town. I thanked my lucky stars for it. In Pittsburgh, I have no doubt a realtor would have dropped me like a hot potato or pawned me off on her most junior recruit. Jackie seemed to feel something motherly toward me and kept plugging away trying to find just the right "thang" for me.

I smiled at Jackie. "It looks perfect."

"Oh, I'm so glad you like it." She had a look of relief. "It just came on the market yesterday. I believe it's vacant. The former owner passed away a few months ago and the heirs are just now gettin' around to sellin'. Let's go ahead to see if it looks as good on the inside, shall we? The selling agent said she is going to meet us here and explain some sort of condition to the sale." She rolled her eyes. "I'm not sure what that means. I hope it doesn't mean the interior is a wreck or the foundation is falling apart." Jackie looked back at me as she trotted up to the front door, her heels tapping against the brick walkway, gesturing madly with her hands. "If it's the foundation, let me tell you, honey, it's just not worth it. I have all sorts of horror stories about poorly laid foundations that crack and every time it rains the water pours into the cellah."

All I needed to do was nod and make nondescript sounds of agreement and Jackie would carry on her chattering.

"Now it says in the MLS it has three finished levels and a cellah. Let's see, they list three bedrooms and two and a half baths." With a brief pause, Jackie glanced around. "Isn't this porch just as cute as can be? What you need here are some rockers and a swing right over there and, of course, some sweet tea for sippin' in the evenin'. I just have a good feeling about this one.

Honey, I think it might be you." Jackie stopped speaking for a moment as she punched in the code to the keypad of the lock box hanging on the front door. She slipped the key into the lock, took a deep breath and gave a great swoop of her arm. "Here we go …"

The clacking of Jackie's shoes echoed through the house as we stepped into the foyer. I was surprised by the emptiness; I had assumed the former owner's furniture would still be in place for showings. Shiny hardwood floors seemed to run throughout the first floor and up the stairs directly to my left. A bright lemony scent of cleaning products pervaded my senses as I entered the front parlor on my right. The rooms felt open and airy due to the nine-foot ceilings. Three windows spanned the front of the house showing off a good view of the porch and large cherry blossom tree in the front yard. The rounded portion of house, well known to the Victorian style, was set up as an octagonal office off the parlor, and the front porch wrapped all the way around the circular portion, ending about ten feet beyond the side of the house. I fell in love with the office-study instantly for its odd shape. More windows spanned the front and sides of the octagon, and built-in bookshelves lined the other wall.

I followed Jackie back through the parlor and into the kitchen. It was a modern marvel with quartz countertops, cherry cabinets, a hefty center island and appliances that looked large and brand new. I wandered over to the stove and read Viking along the front. There was a breakfast nook expansive enough to accommodate a table for six. The kitchen was beautiful, but what stopped me cold was the view from the French doors leading out into the backyard. Yard was an understatement. What met my eyes was a beautiful English-style garden with oriental accents thrown in. Jackie's phone rang and she stepped into the other room to answer.

Unlocking the back door, I strolled into the Garden of Eden surrounded by a six-foot brick fence. The garden snaked its way through blooming larkspur and lilies of various sorts. A lilac bush bloomed to my left along with hollyhocks and dozens of other flowers that would open in the summer heat. Laying my handbag on a green cafe table, I stepped off the brick patio onto a gravel walkway. I'd seen gardens like this at European castles and English manors when I backpacked through Europe during a college summer. I walked under an arbor of honeysuckle vines that had spread enough to close out the light from the sun above. On my left a concrete bench sat tucked against the arbor wall, waiting for two lovers. Following the path as it branched to my left, I was instantly charmed by the fountain. A plump cupid stood atop his cement pedestal and waited for water to come flowing out of the arrow he pointed directly at me. Pulling my eyes away from the cupid, I followed the path on my right and walked deeper into the garden, shadowed by an old tree I determined must be an elm, its new leaves bright green in early development. In the far back corner stood a gazebo surrounded by nodding columbines and brightly colored azaleas in pinks, purples and whites. My fingertips dragged lightly along one of the two padded teak chairs inside the gazebo. Leaves rustled in the breeze and a feeling of serenity enveloped me as I pictured myself drinking a morning cup of coffee out here. Something clicked into place and, at that moment, I knew I'd buy this house even if I had to replace the entire foundation.

Once again Jackie pulled me from my reverie. She'd probably been calling for quite some time. I looked back. She balanced unsteadily as she teetered along the pebbly pathway in her stilettos. "Cara ... honey, are you out here?"

I reluctantly walked away from my gazebo oasis and hailed Jackie.

"Oh, there you are." She appeared relieved. "Aren't these gardens just so purty?"

Pretty was the understatement of the year—stunning, spectacular, extraordinary seemed to fit the bill. I nodded. "Yes, they're quite beautiful. I'll buy the house. Let's write up a contract."

"Oh, sweetie, you haven't even seen the rest of the house yet." Jackie laughed. "Let's keep lookin'. The main floor seems fine to me. I took a peep in the cellah and it didn't look like it was crumbling or cracked. We'd better just wait and see what's what. I don't want to put a single, young thang like you in a house with problems. I just couldn't forgive myself. Let's look around a bit more, and don't say a thing to Anne, the selling agent. We wouldn't want to give her the upper hand, would we?" Jackie gave a conspiratorial wink.

In keeping with Jackie's recommendation, we wandered through the downstairs dining and family rooms admiring the crown molding throughout the first floor and the wainscoting in the dining room. After opening every kitchen appliance and closet door, Jackie led the way to the second floor.

The master bedroom faced the front of the house above the parlor, with tall windows that had stained glass transoms along the top. A sitting area was located above the study. The scent of lemons grew stronger as I entered an en suite bath with all the amenities, including a whirlpool tub. Next to the master bedroom sat the guest bath, and two guest rooms took up the back of the house. Both had windows overlooking the beautiful gardens. Gazing out the window, I had a bird's-eye view of the layout; the pathways leading to the left of the house were filled with more leafy trees and an area of roses. I envied an imaginary guest this view.

We left the second guest bedroom, turned right and walked to the end of a short hallway where a heavy exterior door with a dead bolt on it was shut tight.

Jackie flipped the lock. "This must lead to the third floor, which I believe is finished. This dead bolt is kind of ... peculiar."

She swung the door into the hall, and I looked over her shoulder at a small square landing. A generic white exterior door lay straight ahead and on our right stood the same style door. Each had a dead bolt. Jackie crossed to the door straight ahead. The lock snapped with a sharp click and the door swung into the alcove. Muted sunshine lit the small nook highlighting a brown indoor-outdoor rug that had seen better days. Jackie stuck her head out of the opening.

"Well, look at this. I didn't even notice this from the outside." Jackie turned back to me. "The architect cleverly hid a set of outdoor stairs above the carport. They lead down to the back of the house. Maybe it was a fire code or something."

"Mm," I murmured, stepping forward and tilting my head to look over her shoulder.

Sure enough, I could see the top of a set of white wooden stairs hidden by a partial wall. "The other door must lead to the finished attic."

There was minimal space on the little landing with the door open, and I didn't want to crowd Jackie, so I stepped back into the upper hallway. Jackie shut the door to the outside, turned back to the landing, and grasped the doorknob of the third door. It didn't budge. The dead bolt needed a key. Jackie tried the house key to no avail.

That's odd. I was about to say something when we were interrupted by a clattering of high heels and a melodic yoo-hooing.

"Anne, is that you?" Jackie called, "We're up here trying to get in the attic, but it's locked."

"No, no. You can't get into the attic, Jackie. Why don't you come downstairs so I can explain?" Anne sounded a bit panicky.

Seeing the consternation on Jackie's face at being told we couldn't see the attic, I said, "We'll be right down."

We crossed the hall and headed downstairs. Indeed, something must be wrong in the attic.

Perhaps it was full of furniture from the rest of the house. I let my imagination run wild and conjured up the ghost of the former owner who roamed the attic groaning with chains clanking in the night. *Could I live with that?*

We met up with the selling agent in the front parlor. Jackie introduced me to Anne, a pert redhead with hazel eyes and a sprinkling of freckles over the bridge of her nose. I guessed Anne to be somewhere in her early thirties, just a few years older than me.

She smiled, showing her perfectly bleached, porcelain-white teeth as she held out her hand. "I'm pleased to meet you." Her arm jingled with gold bangle bracelets as she shook my hand.

I responded with a similarly inane remark.

Finished with the pleasantries, Jackie got right down to business. "So, what's going on with the attic? Why can't we see it? Is there something wrong with it?"

"Oh no. There's nothing wrong with it. A tenant lives in it."

"That explains the dead bolt."

Jackie and I released a sigh of relief.

"Yes, well, if that's all, maybe we can arrange a time to see the apartment when the tenant can make it available," said Jackie.

"Unfortunately, it's not that easy. You see …" Anne looked apprehensive, "The provisions of the sale of the house state the tenant stays. You can't go into the attic."

Jackie pulled herself to her full height and towered over Anne. "I beg your pardon? What exactly is going on here? I've never heard of anything so ludicrous."

Anne winced.

"Ladies, perhaps we should sit down. There's a small table out back where I'm sure Anne can explain the situation and we'll straighten everything out." I gestured toward the French doors.

Anne nodded gratefully. "Yes, that's a good idea. Let's all sit down."

As we walked out back, I wondered how it would be to own this house and have a tenant. I could certainly use the extra cash, and with the outdoor staircase—its purpose abundantly clear now—I wouldn't have to see whoever it was much at all. I knew I wanted the house badly enough I was trying to justify this strange provision. Once we were all settled around the table, I invited Anne to tell us the story.

"Well, you see, the owner of the house was Jerome Stein, a retired lawyer. He passed away about three months ago, and his son, Max, is taking care of the sale of the house. Mr. Stein gave the tenant a ten-year lease on the apartment upstairs. The lease was written into Mr. Stein's will and anyone purchasing the home must agree to honor the lease. Rest assured we've looked into the lease and the will, and it seems very straightforward. Mr. Stein was a good lawyer and knew what he was doing. It was written like a commercial lease. It's all very technical. I suppose a buyer could go to court, or something ..." She trailed off.

Jackie looked stunned by both Anne's speech and the bizarre arrangement.

"How many years are left on the lease?" I turned my attention on Anne.

"There are four years left, with an option to extend for five more."

"Who can invoke the option?"

"It has to be mutually agreed upon by both parties."

"What do you know about the tenant?"

"His name is ..."

At that, Jackie came out of her speechlessness with a vengeance. "His name! The tenant is male?"

"Well, yes, but he's harmless. As a matter of fact, he's a recluse. You probably wouldn't even notice him. You see, he's some sort of computer programmer and rarely leaves the house. His groceries are delivered once a week." Anne gave a reassuring smile.

"Great. Some creepy computer nerd that plays games all day lives on the third floor," Jackie said derisively.

I looked at Anne. "Is he agoraphobic?"

Jackie looked confused. "Agora-what?"

"Agoraphobic. Does he have a phobia of going outside his home?"

Anne took a moment to respond. "I don't really know. I do

know that twice a week his psychiatrist comes to the house to see him."

"Who's his shrink?" Jackie asked.

"Dr. Nolan from downtown on Bradford Street."

Silence descended as we chewed on this information. I looked at the small wrought iron balcony jutting out from the third floor.

"What's his name?"

"Dr. Jeffrey Nolan," responded Anne.

"No, the tenant's."

"Oh, let me see. It's right here in my file." Anne searched through her files. "Yes, this is it. Daniel Johnson."

"I can't see the apartment at all?"

"I have photos that were taken by Mr. Stein before the tenant moved in. You can at least see what the finished space looks like. It has a small kitchen, two bedrooms, a den, a bath and a large living room. All the utilities for the attic are billed directly to the tenant, except for sewer and water."

"How much does he pay in rent?"

Referring back to her notes, Anne named a price that temporarily stunned me. The rent he paid would completely cover my monthly mortgage.

"There's also an automatic three percent increase in rent every three years."

"Is he ever late?" Jackie jumped back into the conversation.

"No. Never. From what I understand from Max, he pays punctually on the first of the month."

I mulled over this new piece of information. "When can I meet Mr. Johnson?"

"Well, that's the rub. He doesn't see anyone besides his psychiatrist. I understand Mr. Stein met him when he moved in, but Max seems to think he keeps to himself and he's not sure his father ever saw much of him."

"Can I speak to Mr. Johnson on the phone?"

Anne brightened for a moment. "I have his e-mail address. I'm sure I could give you that."

Jackie snorted but I pressed on, "Can I talk to his psychiatrist?"

"Cara!" exclaimed Jackie. "You can't actually be thinking about buyin' the house with this ridiculous condition."

"Yes, as a matter of fact, I am thinking very seriously about buying this house. Obviously, Mr. Stein, a well-known local lawyer, thought enough of Mr. Johnson to give him a ten-year lease. Clearly, the third floor is a full working apartment, quite separate from the rest of the house. Most importantly, the rent from the apartment would provide me a second income."

Seeing a live one on the line, Anne began thrusting documents at me. "Here's the floor plan Mr. Stein used when he had it finished. Here are some color copies of the finished product. I have the full color photos back at the office if you'd like to see them."

"But ... but," Jackie stammered, "he could turn out to be some sort of lunatic that will murder you in the middle of the night. Or maybe ... maybe he has that pack rat illness and the attic is full of newspapers and garbage ... and MICE! The house could turn into a foul-smelling pigsty. Or maybe he's runnin' a meth lab up there!" Jackie pointed one of her pink manicured fingers at Anne. Turning back to me, she continued on her rant. "That's it! Drugs! The police will descend upon you at three in the mornin', guns a-blazin', and the entire house will be blown to bits durin' the raid."

"This isn't a war, Jackie. I'm sure Mr. Stein wouldn't have allowed a drug dealer to live on his third floor. Right, Anne?" I calmly eyed Anne who shrank back into her chair during Jackie's rant.

Slowly she sat forward. "Well, I don't think he's violent or doing anything illegal. I'm sure Dr. Nolan could speak to you about any concerns you might have."

I wasn't so sure the good doctor would speak to me at all about Mr. Johnson. After all, doctors tended to guard their clients' privacy like a mother bear guarded her cubs. However, small towns were known gossip mills, and maybe this Dr. Nolan would be willing to give me a little more information about the reclusive Daniel Johnson.

"Yes, I think you're right, Anne. I'd like to speak with Dr. Nolan. If you could just write his address down for me, I'll pay him a visit."

With a sage nod, the realtor wrote down the information and handed it to me.

Jackie seemed to be holding back strong emotions that would come tumbling forth once Anne was out of the picture.

"If you two don't mind, I'd like to take another look around the house." I rose.

"Yes. Take all the time you need." Anne smiled.

"Well, I don't wish to keep you from your other clients, Anne. I'm sure Jackie can get everything locked up right and tight when we leave." I shook Anne's hand with a smile, knowing perfectly well Jackie wasn't going to stay quiet for much longer.

Anne took her dismissal well and headed through the kitchen.

Jackie waited for the front door to close before she started in. "Honey, have you lost your mind? This whole situation is the most ridiculous thing I've ever heard of. Now, if you're truly interested in the house, I'm sure we can have a lawyer look at the contract and get the tenant evicted."

From my experiences, I was sure Jackie was right. There were always contractual loopholes. I also had a feeling Max, the son, would want to honor his father's memory and wouldn't sell me the property if a lawyer moved into the picture.

"Jackie, I don't want to chuck this poor guy out on the street. This is his home. He's been living here for six years and obviously he has some sort of neurosis that would make it difficult for him to find a new place."

"Well, I'm sure we could arrange for a thirty-day notice which would give him plenty of time to find someplace new to rent."

"The rent he pays would more than cover my mortgage." Some of the money I'd save on the mortgage could go toward a car payment instead. My Honda was twelve years old and had begun nickel and diming me recently. I was getting close to holding a burial for it.

Jackie had trouble giving up. "But, honey …"

"Look. I'm not deciding anything yet. I'll meet with the psychiatrist and maybe talk to Max and then go from there." Gathering my handbag, I stood, effectively ending the conversation. Out of the corner of my eye, I saw Jackie's shoulders slump as she began collecting her things.

Chapter Two

My karma must have been working that day because a few hours later I pulled into a parking spot right in front of Dr. Jeffrey Nolan's office. It was about five, and I hoped to catch Dr. Nolan at the end of his last session. As I stepped onto the curb, a brown-haired gentleman of medium height opened the door to the small brick office building and began to lock up.

"Excuse me."

"Yes?" the gentleman turned. A pair of Caribbean-Ocean blue eyes looked questioningly at me.

For a moment, I lost track of my purpose for being there as I stared at the fabulous eyes. The face smiled and his eyes crinkled kindly.

I finally snapped out of my trance. "Are you Dr. Jeffrey Nolan?"

"Yes. Can I help you?"

"I was hoping to catch you before you closed up. My name is Cara, Cara Baker. I'm considering buying the house on Poplar Place." My cheeks burned, and I didn't quite know how to proceed.

Dr. Nolan had been warned. Comprehension flared across his countenance. "Yes. Anne called earlier and said you might stop by." He smiled again, putting me at ease. "You want to ask me about Danny Johnson, I believe."

"Yes. Well … I wouldn't want to compromise any doctor-patient confidentiality, but I find myself in a peculiar situation …"

"Why don't we step inside?" He unlocked the door and preceded me into a rather vanilla waiting room with a couch that had seen better days and four padded chairs. Dr. Nolan indicated I should sit on the couch and pulled up one of the chairs to sit across from me. A closer look at him revealed a bit of graying around his temples, and smile lines around a straight nose and mouth, leading me to believe he was older than I originally suspected, perhaps in his late thirties.

He was clean-shaven, and once you got past the incredible peepers, what I would consider fairly attractive.

"Now, you want to know about Daniel Johnson?" I nodded and was drawn back into his quiet eyes.

"Normally, I couldn't speak to you about Danny, due to doctor-patient confidentiality. However, Danny also contacted me and is very concerned. He doesn't want to hold up the sale of the house. So, I've been given permission to release limited information about him." Dr. Nolan paused. "Basically, Danny doesn't like person-to-person contact."

"Is he agoraphobic?"

"No, not in the medical sense you mean. He doesn't like to be touched, though."

"Why not?"

"That I cannot discuss with you," he replied gravely.

"Is he a threat to himself?"

"No, he is not suicidal."

"Would he be a threat to me?"

"No. In my professional opinion, he is not a threat to himself or anyone else."

As I let this information roll around in my head, Jackie's tirade on the patio came to mind. "Does he ..." I hesitated, feeling a bit foolish. "Does he keep the apartment clean? It's not full of newspapers or trash? I mean, he doesn't have that pack rat disease, does he?"

Dr. Nolan smiled. "No trash. He's not a hoarder, if that's what you mean. He keeps the apartment very clean, and all the trash gets thrown out."

"When? When does he put his trash out if he never leaves?" I flipped my hand in the air.

Dr. Nolan laughed. "Generally, he puts the trash out once a week, late, after everyone has gone to bed. Contrary to rumors, Danny does leave the house. He rarely goes about town—instead he visits the ocean and other private spots."

"He's not into drugs? There's no meth lab, is there?"

"No, he's not a drug addict, and he is definitely not running a meth lab."

"Have you seen the entire apartment? He could be hiding something in a back room." "Ms. Baker, I can assure you I have seen the entire apartment, and Danny is not making drugs."

"Doctor Nolan." I stopped not quite sure how to put my thoughts into words. "I think I need this house. I have no problem having a tenant. After all, it's a large house. To be honest, it sounds like Mr. Johnson is just an eccentric hermit who obviously got along with a retired lawyer for six years already."

This comment received a minute nod.

"For some reason I feel no threat and only a small amount of hesitancy at buying the house along with Mr. Johnson's rental contract. He sounds harmless." I hesitated. My gaze met Dr. Nolan's. "I feel this house calling to me. Do you think I'm crazy? Am I just trying to justify this strange situation?"

Dr. Nolan patted my hand. "Only you can answer those questions. I think you should follow your instincts. I agree with you. It's a great house, and I'm sure you'll get along just fine with Danny."

"There's just one more question maybe you can answer. Why doesn't Mr. Johnson simply buy the house, or purchase his own home? With the rent he's paying, he can afford it."

"I cannot answer. I don't know the reason."

I rose to take my leave. "Thank you very much, Dr. Nolan. You've put my mind at ease. I suppose I'll be seeing you around."

Dr. Nolan held my hand with both of his. "I look forward to it and please, call me Jeff.

Good luck with the paperwork." He tilted his head. "I think Danny was right when he called me. You'll be perfect for the house. Perhaps we can have coffee together after you get settled."

"I'd like that." I had no thoughts of starting up a romance, but I did have my vanity, and it pleased me that this handsome man was interested in having coffee with me. On my way out to the car, I pulled out my cell phone and dialed Jackie's number.

She answered after the third ring. "Did you see the doctor?"

"Yes, and he assured me the apartment was clean, there are no newspapers gathering, Mr. Johnson is not a homicidal maniac, and he is not running a meth lab."

Jackie let out a sigh on the other end. "Well, if you're sure this is what you want …"

"Yes, Jackie. I've never wanted anything more in my life." It was the utter truth.

We spoke about the contract details, and I told her I'd stop by her office in the morning to sign everything. Happiness welled in my chest, and I think my eyes must have been shining. I could feel it in my bones. An exciting new adventure was beginning. Deciding to see the house again, I drove over and sat out front. I scrutinized the third floor for a lengthy time, waiting to see if there was any movement from my soon-to-be tenant.

Chapter Three

April

Triumphantly, I slipped the shiny brass key into the dead bolt of my new house at 2112 Poplar Place. A month after I fell in love with the house, Max Stein came up from Atlanta to sign the paperwork; the closing was uncomplicated and trouble-free. Max was so pleased the house sold along with the rental agreement he took Jackie, Anne and me out for lunch afterward. It was a celebratory meal for all of us. Jackie and Anne each made a nice commission. Max was thrilled to be able to sell the house and lease so quickly, and I was the proud new owner of a gorgeous house with spectacular gardens ... and one small recluse. Max ordered champagne to toast the happy occasion.

Letting myself into the front door, once again, I pondered what Daniel Johnson might look like. I pictured a homely looking fellow, balding, mousy brown hair, nerdy glasses, probably on the short side. When I was a child, I read a book about Mr. Mole who lived underground. He walked sort of hunched over and had messy hair. I smiled at the memory and began thinking of my tenant as "Mr. Mole."

The move-in went smoothly, and I was on my second week of unpacking, painting and arranging my things. I worked at the library Tuesday through Saturday, and every moment I had off I spent fixing up the house. Today was Monday. I roamed through the first floor debating whether to organize books in the study or begin painting the half bath. The morning breeze ruffled the new curtains as it blew through the open French door. Nature's beauty called.

I meandered through all of the garden paths, admiring the fountain, smelling the flowers, looking at the trailing vines and pulling a few weeds. There were surprisingly few weeds to be seen in a garden this size and I wondered if Max had paid a professional to maintain the property, following his father's death. I made a mental note to contact Max and ask him. Originally, I planned to take care of the garden myself, but perhaps it would be best to speak with a professional since I really had no idea what I was getting into with such extensive landscaping. My wanderings brought me to the gazebo. I sat and watched the dappled sunlight sift through the leaves on the trees and drank my morning coffee. Relaxing in the Zen-like space every morning was a ritual I could readily get used to.

After lollygagging for an hour in the garden, I returned to the house to unpack and organize the library. As I stopped to put my coffee cup in the sink, the velvety roses on the kitchen table caught my eye. Friday afternoon a beautiful bouquet of roses and assorted flowers, varying in colors from pink to red to yellow, sat on my doorstep. The blossoms were now opening up to release their luscious smells. The container the bouquet was delivered in was just as stunning as the flowers themselves. When I picked them up from the front porch, I expected inexpensive glass; however, the weight of the vase led me to believe it was crystal. Intrigued, I held it over my head to see if there were any distinctive markings identifying the maker. Sure enough, a Swarovski Swan was centered in the middle. The card said simply—*Enjoy your new home*. There was no signature or florist name, and I figured they were from Jackie. I jotted down a note to give her a call to thank her.

I set up my computer in the study. I had a work computer at the library with Internet and e-mail access, but it had been over a week since I'd checked my private accounts. Once everything was plugged in, I flipped the computer on and waited for it to boot up. With resignation, I watched the inundation as the messages piled up. Over 300 filled my junk mail, and when it finished downloading, I was pleasantly surprised to find only fifty-two unread in my inbox. I worked my way down the list and my eye was drawn to a new address I didn't recognize. The message was sent five days ago. I clicked on it.

Dear Ms. Baker,

Congratulations on the purchase of your new home. I am sorry if my affliction caused any difficulty in the sale. I will try my best to remain as unobtrusive in your life as possible. Thank you for your understanding. You will receive the rent check promptly on the first of every month.

Sincerely,
Daniel Johnson

I read the message once, twice and then a third time. A number of emotions flooded through me. First, excitement that my reclusive and, until now, unknown tenant had contacted me. Second, I felt a sense of pleasure at his words of congratulations. Then a bit of sadness that he called his phobia an "affliction." The words reminded me of the Middle Ages when mental illness was thought of as deeds of the devil and those who had a mental illness were locked up in the vilest of places. That he felt the need to stay out of my way or pretend not to exist upset me. Perhaps, to him, the world was an unfriendly place and he a misfit. A sense of determination took over. I made it my mission to make Danny feel welcome, at least in my home, and hopefully in more of this world.

Dear Mr. Johnson,

Thank you for your congratulations. I look forward to sharing my home with you. I hope one day you will feel comfortable enough to meet with me. If you ever need to talk, feel free to use this e-mail or the phone number I have listed below.

Cara Baker

I clicked the send button when the doorbell chimed. Jackie stood on the other side of the screen holding a lovely flower and ivy springtime wreath.

"Hello, sweetie. I wanted to stop by to bring you this housewarming gift and see how you're settling in." She leaned in to deliver a peck on the cheek as she strolled into the foyer.

"This is gorgeous! Thank you so much. It'll look perfect on my front door." I took the wreath from her. "Come on into the kitchen and have a glass of tea."

Jackie's heels clicked down the hall as she followed me into the kitchen and sat at the table. "Wow. Look at those roses. They are fabulous?"

"Indeed. I planned to call you this afternoon and thank you. Aren't they blooming beautifully?" I laid the new wreath next to the flowers.

"What makes you think those are from me? I didn't send them. I stick with my standby wreath." Jackie pointed to the new wreath with a red lacquered fingernail. "Any time of year I think they make a front door welcoming."

"There wasn't a signature on the note. It just said 'Enjoy your new home.' Nobody from work knew I was moving. I just assumed they were from you," I said with some consternation.

Jackie let out a low whistle. "Honey, looks to me like you've got an admirer. What about that Dr. Nolan? He knew you were moving. Didn't he ask you out?"

"Yes. Perhaps you're right. Actually, we are meeting for coffee on Thursday morning before work. I'll ask him if he sent the flowers."

I handed Jackie a glass of tea and lowered myself onto a chair across from her. "So, how's life with the hermit?"

"I call him Mr. Mole."

Jackie gave a snort and choked on her tea.

After she stopped coughing and regained control, I explained about the childhood book, which sent her into peals of laughter. Together we chatted for over an hour, talking about the house, her business, my job and whatever else came to mind. I relished our conversation and felt Jackie and I were moving past the realtor-client relationship and into a friendship. I hoped this was true because, I could use a friend in South Carolina. Small towns were friendly, but making friends turned out to be harder than I'd expected since I was considered an outsider. People always wanted to know every detail about your life before arriving in Denton, and I tended to close up like a clam and deflect questions or make excuses to end conversations. Additionally, while I felt comfortable making decisions about painting and decorating the house on my own, there were times I felt the loneliness of being alone and wished for a friend to reach out to who could help me decide between Sea-spray Blue or Cottage Blue or if I should put the love seat against the windows or along the short wall.

After we finished our tea, I asked Jackie's advice about furniture placement in the parlor.

We spent half an hour moving around my grandmother's pieces. I debated whether I should mention the e-mail from Danny Johnson but, in the end, I kept it to myself. Jackie was warming to the idea; however, she and I still disagreed over my tenant and I didn't want to bring tension into our lovely afternoon. It was almost six when Jackie left with an invitation for her and her husband, Beau, to join me for dinner Friday night.

Chapter Four

Wednesday morning found me staring at my front lawn. The time had come to mow. I don't know who mowed the lawn when Jerome Stein was alive. A large shed behind the carport yielded gardening tools, saws, some general household tools, two bags of dirt, a bag of mulch, a ladder and other sundry parts one found in a shed or garage. It was a pleasant surprise to find a lawn mower amongst the many items. I hadn't realize the shed was full when I purchased the house and figured either Max had no need for these particular items and conveyed them with the house or had simply overlooked them. Since he hadn't called to request any of the items, I assumed he left them on purpose and today I appreciated his generosity. I wheeled the lawn mower into the empty side of the carport and checked the gas tank, wincing at the strong smell. It looked full enough to me, so I wouldn't need to stop at the gas station on the way home. Later I'd gird myself to tackle my first lawn mowing experience ... after work, of course ... and maybe after a beer.

One of the things I loved about my new home was its convenience to my job. The Denton Regional Library was a four-block walk from my house, and only three and a half if I cut through the park. In the very hot summer months or when it rained, I'd end up driving. However, weather permitting, I planned to walk, and today the weather was sixty and breezy. I took a travel cup of coffee with me as I headed off to my destination, enjoying the beautiful morning and my commune with nature on the way. The houses that lined the street varied in shape and size. This neighborhood wasn't tract housing constructed by a single builder. Over the years lots were privately purchased and built upon. I loved the street for that very reason; the diverse structures were graceful and original, and yards were filled with shade trees and full-grown landscaping.

I arrived at the library just as Mandy Mosley, one of my coworkers and head of the computer lab, zipped into the parking lot in her bright blue PT Cruiser.

"Good morning. Isn't it a wonderful day?" I chirped.

Mandy returned my smile with a wave as she bounced up the front steps toward me. "Sugar, the days don't get much better than this."

I towered over Mandy and felt like an Amazon. I was average height and weight, but Mandy was a petite, perky blonde who stood all of five feet. She often wore a ponytail, with makeup that highlighted her blue eyes and dimpled smile. Her wardrobe consisted of short skirts, high heels and adorable tops that showed midriff when she reached up to put away books on the top shelves. On me these outfits would look ridiculously slutty. However, Mandy's cheerleader looks and personality allowed her to completely pull them off. All of the men that came to the library stared unabashedly at her when she offered to help them, and I often wondered how any of the males who signed up for her computer courses actually learned anything. Mandy grew up in a small town in Alabama and fit into the slower pace of Denton with ease. Even though I felt like a schlumping oaf around Mandy's petite athletic grace, we were good coworkers and, with a few lunches under our belts, were slowly moving into an enjoyable friendship.

"Did you hear about the fund-raiser?"

We walked into our small office packed with four cubicles.

"No. What are we planning?" I looked over my cubicle wall at her.

She shrugged. "Don't know. That's the main topic of conversation for today's staff meeting. Greta's going to ask for our ideas. I heard we need to raise at least fifteen thousand to upgrade the computer lab and redesign the children's and reference sections. Since those are both of our areas, I think

Greta might be looking to us to come up with good ideas. Ugh. I'm not really a cookie-baking fund-raiser type."

"I think we'll need to do a lot more than bake cookies to raise that kind of money."

My mind started turning over possible fund-raising ideas. Once upon a time I loved organizing parties, and a fund-raiser wasn't much different. You just asked your guests to part with some of their hard-earned cash before leaving. I logged onto my computer. Greta's e-mail stared back at me announcing our staff meeting agenda. Sure enough, the third item listed was the fund-raiser. I glanced at my watch. The meeting would start in twenty minutes, and my fingers flew across the keyboard as I typed my ideas to present.

Greta Baumgartner, the director of our regional library and two satellite libraries, sat with her Cheaters pushed up on her head, looking down the conference table at the staff with an expectant eye. "Okay, people, we need money to keep up with today's technology. Now, as you know, the county has limited funds when it comes to improvements to the library. Our Friends of the Library continue to host their used book sales, which provide supplemental dollars for things such as the children's programs, weekend activities, book clubs and the Symphony Nights."

"However, it's been a dozen years since there have been major renovations and upgrades. We've had blueprints drawn up to redesign the children's and reference sections, to expand the computer lab and to upgrade all the computers. We'd also like to add a tot lot in the unused courtyard. In order to move forward, we need to raise at least twenty-five thousand dollars to supplement the budget. Hanley's GMC car dealership, out on Route 5, has generously offered to match funds raised up to ten thousand dollars." Greta waited a moment for this information to sink in. "So, it's time to brainstorm, folks. What kind of fund-raiser can we host to raise fifteen grand?"

There was silence around the room as I slowly raised my hand. "I have a few ideas."

"Let's hear them."

"What if we held a black-tie night with a silent auction? We could get donations from local merchants. I'm thinking products or gift certificates for services. We could look further afield by contacting companies in Charleston and maybe we can get a rental company to donate a free beach week." I paused for a breath. "I was also thinking the ticket price should be at least one hundred apiece and we should target our wealthy residents and local politicians. Maybe we could get the mayor to say a few words and do some glad-handing on behalf of the library. We can have a bar set up by the door in the special events room where the silent auction can be arranged. A little bit of wine can loosen wallets. We can have food stations with heavy hors d'oeuvres spread throughout the library. Maybe we could see about getting an author to come as well. New York Times bestseller Linda Lincoln is native to Charleston. Perhaps our Friends of the Library can talk some of the symphony members into donating their time to have music over …" My face burned with embarrassment when I realized everyone was staring at me. I was running roughshod over our brainstorming session by hijacking the discussion.

Greta busily scratched my ideas on her yellow notepad and regarded me over her Cheaters. "Where? Where do you think we should have the music?"

I pointed to the area in between the information center and the checkout desk. "Over there."

George Kessinger, a retired college professor from Duke University and our information desk representative, sat forward. "Linda Lincoln, or Linda Poganski as she was known back in college, was in a few of my literature classes. Perhaps I could approach her to participate in our event."

Mandy piped in, "I'm dating a trumpet player from the symphony orchestra. He and the French horn player are also part of a quintet. I could see if the quintet could donate their time to play for a few hours."

Stephanie, a part-timer who worked the checkout desk, leaned in, "I might have a connection to one of the local wine merchants. I can ask him to donate a case of wine for the silent auction and some wine for the bar."

Suddenly the room was a buzz of noise. Side conversations started up about who should cater the event, what night we should host the fund-raiser and what kinds of donations we could get for the silent auction. I sat back and relaxed as the excitement flowed around the room.

****

The cloud I floated on had me practically skipping home. Once Greta called the staff meeting back to order, my original ideas were expanded upon, dates were discussed, a task list was drawn up and staff members began contacting local merchants for silent auction donations.

With a whistle, I bounced up my front walk and smelled the scent of fresh-cut grass. I froze mid-whistle and slowly turned to look at my front lawn. My front lawn was the reason for the fresh-cut smell. The grass looked like a green carpet; all the ragged edges were gone. I walked over to the carport. The lawn mower was missing. I continued around to the shed. The red beast had been returned to its previous location, looking no different from when I wheeled it out this morning.

Who mowed my lawn? I hurried back to my front porch to look for a bill or business card. Nothing. I checked the mailbox. Nothing. I looked around the front yard again, wondering when the bill would arrive and what it would cost. Although I appreciated not having to mow the lawn—seriously, it wasn't an experience I looked forward to—I wasn't sure how expensive lawn mowing services were and if I could afford them.

Chapter Five

Jeff waved as I walked into the coffeehouse Thursday morning. He handed me a cup. "Caramel Latte, nonfat milk, no sugar. Did I get that right?"

"Mm. Delicious." I took my first drink of the warm liquid caffeine that would keep me going for the day.

"How's the move coming along? Are you unpacked yet?"

Every time I looked at the good doctor, his brilliant blue eyes ensnared me. I don't know whether it was due to his training or if it was simply his personality, but when Jeff's eyes focused on you, it gave you the sense you were the most important individual in the world and anything you had to say was vital to him. I was no different from any other warm-blooded woman and felt a gentle tingle flow through my body.

"I am slowly but surely getting unpacked and settled in. Jackie helped me pick out paint for my bedroom, and I have a furniture delivery scheduled for next week. So, I'm pleased at how well things are coming along."

"I'm glad to hear it."

"By the way, before I forget, someone sent me a beautiful bouquet of roses, but the card was unsigned. Did you send them?" I gave a bit of a flirty smile, or what I hoped was a flirty smile. It occurred to me, as I showered this morning, I hadn't had anything resembling a date with a man in more than two years. I began to wonder if I remembered how to act on a date and if I could still flirt.

Jeff looked at me with an apologetic smile. "Unfortunately no, Cara, I didn't send the flowers. I wish I had thought of it, though. I bet I know who gave you the flowers."

"You do? I've already asked Jackie and she said it wasn't her. If it wasn't you, I don't know who it could be. I just told the folks at my office I moved into a new place yesterday, and I received the flowers not long after I moved in."

"Was the name of the flower company on the card?"

"No. That was the strange thing. It was a simple white card."

"I believe the flowers came out of your garden and were left there for you by Danny."

I sat back, drinking in both the coffee and Jeff's statement. That would explain the plain white card and crystal vase. Obviously the vase was one he had around the house. I knew there were roses climbing the walls in the garden, but I wasn't familiar enough with it to notice which roses had been cut.

"Does Danny spend time in the garden when I'm not home?"

"Yes." Jeff smiled and nodded. "Danny designed and planted the garden."

I gaped like a fish opening and closing my mouth for a few moments. "Why didn't anyone tell me?"

"I don't know if anyone besides Jerome and I knew." He shrugged.

"That's why he won't move. The garden is his masterpiece. I don't understand why he didn't buy the house He must be my mysterious lawn guy, too."

"Mysterious lawn guy?"

I laughed at his quizzical gaze. "Yes. I was ready to tackle my first lawn-mowing job, but when I came home from work yesterday, the lawn had already been mowed. I figured I'd be getting a bill from some landscaping company and was starting to worry about what I'd owe them."

"I think your mystery is now solved."

"So, Danny gets out into the yard on a regular basis. He must wait until I leave for work."

"I suppose so."

We'd focused on Danny for a while, and I got the

impression Jeff wasn't comfortable speaking about his patient. So, I turned the conversation on a different track by mentioning the library's fund-raiser and the next half hour flew by. Jeff and I talked about his hobbies, hiking, camping and canoeing. I told him about my childhood, living in Rhode Island and about my parents who were now retired and traveling the country in a decked-out RV. They rented their house for a year while they drove their way through the United States and Canada.

What I didn't tell Jeff, perhaps because he was a psychiatrist, was my parents threatened to return east because, out of the blue, I quit my lucrative career in Pittsburgh and moved my life to South Carolina to become a librarian. I knew traveling the country was their retirement dream and was barely able to assure them I wasn't having a mental breakdown and they should carry on. Little did they know, my mental status had been unsteady due to anger and guilt for at least a year prior to the move. I just didn't want to burden them with my problems. I didn't tell Jeff any of this because I wanted to push it away, be happy in my new home and job, and leave the ghosts behind me.

As we left the coffee shop, I thanked Jeff for a lovely morning and invited him to dinner on Friday with Jackie and Beau.

"I appreciate the invitation. Unfortunately, I already have plans." He frowned and looked disappointed.

"Perhaps another time."

We were on the sidewalk ready to go our separate ways when awkwardness came over me. Did he expect a kiss? Perhaps a peck on the cheek? A handshake seemed a bit cool; maybe a hug would be best.

Jeff must have read the panicky confusion on my face because he took the decision out of my hands by gently leaning in and giving me a peck on the cheek and a light hug.

"Thanks for the coffee and conversation."

"You're welcome, Cara. I hope to see you again soon." Jeff clasped my hand just a little longer than necessary.

What were my feelings for Jeff? I was definitely attracted to him. I'd have to be blind or dead not to be physically attracted. Added to that, he was kind, funny and intelligent. But, yes— sad to say—there was a but—I didn't get that giddy, light-me-up feeling when he was around.

Moreover, although I would have enjoyed his company at Friday's dinner, I really wasn't all that crushed when he couldn't make it. Conceivably this might grow into a romantic relationship. On the other hand, I wasn't sure if I was interested in pursuing such a relationship with him or anyone. Right now I was focused on establishing myself in my new town, job and home.

Romantic relationships could get complicated and I didn't need complications right now. So, I relegated Dr. Nolan to the "let's see what happens" category and happily headed off to work.

****

There were no children's programs at the library on Friday afternoons during the school year. This allowed me to prep for Saturday and the following week's programs as well as catch up on paperwork. Greta had asked me to set up the catering for the fund-raiser. I began by preparing brochures explaining the library's goals and event information then drafted a list of caterers and restaurants in the local area to target and contact the following week.

It was half past four when I left the library. I'd driven this morning so I could stop by the Piggly Wiggly or, as Mandy called it, "The Pig," on the way home to purchase my ingredients for dinner with Jackie and Beau. Baked ziti, salad and garlic bread with olive oil were on the menu tonight. Not very original, but back in Pittsburgh, my Italian meals were celebrated. I decided to stick with a tried and true recipe. On the way to the market, my car started making a funny clanking noise.

Unfortunately, I knew virtually nothing about cars and my old Honda had been around for twelve going on thirteen years.

This meant things such as fan belts, oxygen sensors, catalytic converters and other strange vehicular paraphernalia, I swore the garage mechanic made up, were beginning to need replacing. Of course, these important car parts cost me five hundred dollars or more every time I dropped it off. Usually after looking under the hood for half an hour, the mechanic wandered out shaking his head and with a woeful expression gave me the bad news about whatever was now wrong with my car. However, I refused to allow the Honda to ruin my Friday night. So, like any normal female in my situation, I turned the music up loud enough to drown out the clanking noise and prayed to the car god to get me home from the grocery store.

After an hour of cooking, my kitchen smelled like tomatoes, oregano and garlic. Heaven. I prepared a double batch of ziti and an extra loaf of garlic bread to share with my hermit. It was my way of making contact. About an hour before Jackie and Beau were supposed to arrive, I took my offering wrapped in a towel, along with a note and the Swarovski crystal vase, upstairs. I opened the door that led to the attic stairwell landing and knocked on Daniel Johnson's door.

"I have some dinner here in the stairwell for you, Mr. Johnson. Be careful it's hot. I'm leaving now." I didn't want to freak him out, so I shut my door, snapped the dead bolt into place and walked with a heavy tread back downstairs. The note I left thanked him for the beautiful flower arrangement, for mowing the yard and keeping up the garden. I figured I'd check the stairwell tonight before going to bed to make sure he'd picked up the food. After all, I didn't want to invite cockroaches or mice.

Jackie and Beau showed up about ten minutes late bearing a bottle of Cabernet Sauvignon, which I opened immediately to allow it to breathe. It would be the perfect complement to dinner. While we waited for the second pan of ziti to finish baking, I invited them to sit outside where I had a bottle of Pinot Grigio chilling and antipasto laid out on the table. Beau poured the wine, glasses clinked and Jackie popped a stuffed olive into her mouth. My first impression of Jackie's husband was "Big." Beau stood around 6'4" and was solidly built. His thinning blond hair was almost white and it looked as though he'd spent the day out on the golf course because he was very tan with a bit of sunburn on his nose. His blue eyes displayed the wrinkles of a man who spent time in the sun, but I liked how they crinkled at the corners when he smiled. He and Jackie made a good-looking couple.

"So, what have you been up to this week?" Jackie asked.

"Goodness, I don't know where to start. So much has happened since I saw you last."

"Then you must begin at the beginning. I'm dying to hear about your coffee date with the handsome Dr. Nolan." Jackie's gaze gleamed with excitement. "Since I'm old and married, I must live vicariously through you young people." She turned and gave Beau a peck on the cheek. "Nothing personal, honey."

Beau rolled his eyes. "Of course not, sweetie. Pay no attention to the old man sitting at the table."

"Oh hush, you." Jackie playfully elbowed Beau in the ribs.

Beau gently rested his arm on Jackie's shoulders, winked and smiled while taking a sip of wine.

The playful bantering between the two made me see what a great couple they were and, for a brief moment, I was jealous. One day I wanted the same comfortable camaraderie this couple shared.

I shook my head. "The beginning doesn't start with the good doctor. It starts before that."

Jackie leaned in and popped another olive in her mouth. "Do tell."

"Well, on Tuesday, while I was at work, the lawn fairy came and mowed my yard."

"What's a lawn fairy and where can I get one?" Beau asked.

I smiled mischievously. "At work Tuesday, Greta announced we need to raise fifteen thousand dollars in order to fund the new changes to the library. So, I suggested we hold a black- tie affair at the library with a silent auction to help raise the money. Which, by the way, I expect you two to attend so I'll at least know two people, besides my coworkers. Also, I will be hitting you up for anything you can contribute to the silent auction."

"We have a house on the water in Myrtle Beach. We could donate a week for the auction," Jackie offered. "What else can we donate, Beau?"

"I'll look around work and see what I can find."

"The beach house would be great." I looked over at Beau. "I'm sorry, Beau, I've never asked Jackie where you work. What do you do for a living?"

"Nothing much. I work at a little sporting goods store. You might have seen it out by the highway. It's called Barnes Urban Outfitters. Would you like me to top you off?" Beau held out the wine bottle.

"Yes, please." I handed him my half-empty glass. "I've seen the store. As a matter of fact, I went in it to buy running shoes. Are you related to the Barnes of Barnes Urban Outfitters?"

"I might be," was Beau's cagey reply.

I must have looked at him strangely because Jackie playfully swatted at him.

"Stop messing with her, darlin'. It's not nice." She looked at me. "Beau *is* the Barnes in Barnes Urban Outfitters. He owns stores throughout South Carolina, all the way south to Florida and west to Texas. And yes, I'm sure the store can donate some items for the auction."

I gaped at the two of them for a few minutes. "Wow, uh, I don't know what to say. Thanks. Anything you can donate would be great. When did you start the business?"

"Almost eighteen years ago," Beau replied.

"How did you decide to get into the sporting goods business?"

Beau looked at Jackie. "Didn't you tell her anything about me?"

Jackie shook her head. "I know you think you're the center of my world, sweetie, but when I'm with the girls, we actually don't talk about you. We talk about girl things." Jackie looked at me. "Am I right?"

"Uh, yes, I guess so." I felt as though I'd missed a part of the conversation.

"Go ahead and tell her about the glory days." Jackie smiled.

"These are the glory days, hon." Beau said to Jackie and then turned to me. "Well, the short story is this, I went to college at LSU where I played football and got my business degree. I was drafted out of college to play ball for the Dallas Cowboys."

"Ugh." Jackie rolled her eyes.

"Hey, the Cowboys were a good team," Beau defended.

"They were a bunch of criminals."

"Anyway, I digress. I played with the Cowboys for a year before I was traded to the Miami Dolphins, where I played for some years until I blew out my left knee during a tackle. The doc said that was the end of my football career. So, I came home to Charleston and put my business degree to work."

"Hold on, hold on." I leaned forward with my hand up trying to comprehend the information Beau just dropped on me. "Let me get this straight. You played pro-football?"

"That's right."

"What position did you play?"

"Fullback."

In my college days, I attended football games. I sat with my sorority sisters where there was a lot of alcohol and gossiping involved, but very little watching of the game. When the guys around me actually paying attention to the game cheered, then I cheered. To me, football games were all about tailgating, eating football snacks and socializing. So the intricacies of football rules and player positions were pretty much beyond me. I was sure my face gave this away.

"Fullback? Huh, that's um, very impressive." I probably sounded like an idiot. Jackie and Beau both laughed.

"When did you two get together?"

"We were college sweethearts. When Beau was a junior and I was a sophomore, I had to tutor him in French. I thought he was a dumb jock." Jackie smiled.

"And I thought she was a beautiful know-it-all. It took me a long time to get her to go out with me." Beau kissed Jackie lightly on the head.

"Yes. He was so pathetic I finally gave in. The rest, as they say, is history."

I clapped my hands. "That is such a sweet story. I love it. You two must come to the auction."

"I promise we'll come to your fund-raiser if you feed me dinner tonight." Beau laughed.

"Yipes! Dinner!" I jumped out of my chair and ran into the kitchen, hoping I wouldn't see smoke billowing out of the oven like on cartoons.

Luck was with me. The ziti was cooked to perfection. Beau ate two helpings of the pasta, half a loaf of garlic bread and two pieces of strawberry pie. The three of us talked well into darkness. The night was beautiful, with the moon shining down and the stars twinkling far off in the galaxy. A soft breeze rustled the trees. I went in to get sweaters for Jackie and me because we were enjoying the lovely night too much to move into the house. It was close to midnight when Jackie and Beau drove off in their Jaguar.

I walked through the house turning off lights and locking up. When I got to the second floor, I remembered the pasta dish I'd left for Mr. Mole. Quietly I unlocked the attic door and peered down. Sure enough the dishes and vase were gone. I smiled to myself, relocked the door and headed to bed.

Chapter Six

May

Sunday was the first of the month. *How would I receive my rent check?* Since it was my day off, I was being lazy and didn't go out to get the newspaper until almost ten. When I opened the front door, I found a pleasant surprise. The crystal vase, filled with a varietal bouquet of flowers, including roses, daises and lilies, sat next to the newspaper. An envelope was taped to the side of the vase. Lying next to the flowers was my clean Pyrex dish. The bouquet charmed me, and I recognized some of the flowers currently blooming in my garden. I opened the envelope and pulled out a note and a check for the rent. The note said:

Beautiful flowers for a beautiful lady. Thank you for the pasta dish. It was delicious. Am willing to perform additional tasks of menial labor around the house for food from such a talented cook.
Enclosed is this month's rent check. Sincerely,
Danny

With a grin, I placed the flowers on the kitchen table, grabbed my cup of coffee and skipped upstairs to shower. I needed to get moving. I had a list of items to get from the local hardware store, including paint for my bedroom and bath.

Alas, my trip to the hardware store was not to be. When I turned the key to start my car, there was a thunk and a bang, the car vibrated for a moment and died completely. I turned the key twice to hear nothing but a slight click and grinding noise.

"Crap! Crap, crap, crap and double crap!" While launching

myself out of the driver's seat, I proceeded to mumble profanities at my pathetic vehicle. I slammed the door and kicked the back tire. "Yeeouch!" I yelped. Slowly breathing in and out, I walked around the driveway and counted backwards from ten in an effort to get a grip.

Whatever was wrong, I knew it'd cost me a bundle and, on top of everything else, I'd have to pay to get this hunk of junk towed to the shop. I opened the passenger door to grab my purse. Sitting on top of my handbag was the envelope with the lovely rent check just waiting to be cashed. A rather substantial amount of money. A perfect amount of money for a down payment on a slightly used car. I shook my head to banish those thoughts.

The car needed replacing. It had over 140,000 miles, and I wasn't sure it was worth fixing. I luxuriated in the thought of a new car, with the new car smell. A quiet ride. No more monthly problems that cropped up at the worst of times—most recently being down the middle of Main Street. It was this type of thinking that drove me to call Mandy and ask if she wanted to take me car shopping.

Three hours later, I motored my sporty new convertible Mini Cooper into the carport and parked it next to the broken-down Honda. The Mini was red with white racing stripes. I put the top up and got out to admire my shiny new roadster, slowly running my hand down the glossy front of the hood. The convertible was a year old with only 8,000 miles, and it still had that new car smell. The best part was the dealership was going to give me $400 for the Honda and would come tow it away. I tried not to jump up and down in my chair with joy while Mandy wheedled that part of the deal. Mandy, that woman was a godsend. With my background in law, I had no problems negotiating. However, Mandy's wide-eyed innocence, southern sweet talk and revealing wardrobe probably did more for my cause than any of my smooth lawyer legalese.

The phone rang when I entered the house and I rushed to pick it up before the machine answered. "Hello."

"Cara darling, it's Mom." My mother's loving voice crackled

a bit, as cell phones were wont to do.

"Hi, Mom! How are you? Where are you?" I hadn't heard from my parents in almost three weeks.

"We're in Canada. Somewhere in Saskatchewan. We're planning to be in Victoria by the end of the summer."

"How's Dad?"

"He's fine. His sciatica was acting up last week, so we stayed a bit longer at the campsite until he felt better. He's still mapping out our driving routes." My father was always the vacation planner in the family. Back in the days before Google Maps and GPS systems, Dad visited our local AAA office to pore over the maps they furnished and organize a TripTik that provided precise directions to whatever beach, cabin or hotel we headed. My mother sat in the front seat and navigated as my father drove. Things hadn't changed much in the thirty-five years they'd been married.

"How's everything with your new house?"

Although the question was innocent enough, across the miles the concern was evident in Mom's voice. I'd told my parents about purchasing a new home in Denton but failed to tell them about the hermit I inherited with the house. The story was convoluted, and I didn't want to worry them. I figured I'd tell them about my living arrangements when they chose to come visit. *After all, what they don't know can't hurt them. Right?*

"Everything's fine. I'm completely unpacked and starting to paint. Nana's furniture looks great in the front parlor. I found a perfect home for the antique escritoire."

"That's great, sweetie. Does everything fit?"

"Sure. No problems with space. I've got loads of room. By the way, tell Dad I just bought a new car."

"Mike, she bought a new car." I heard my mother say in the background. "I don't know.

Let me ask." Mom's voice came back to full volume. "Your father wants to know what you bought."

"A convertible Mini Cooper."

Mom turned away from the phone again. "She says she bought a Mini Cooper." She paused. "I don't know. Here, you talk to her."

"Cara." Dad's deep voice came over the line. "Your mother says you bought a new car."

I breathed calmly as the interrogation I'd known was coming began. "Yeah, Dad, I bought a Mini Cooper. It's reliable, is only a year old, has 8,000 miles and is red."

"You do the research on it? How does a tiny car like that do in a crash?"

Actually, I hadn't done any research. The need for a new car came on suddenly, and I was in love with the idea of a convertible, so I bought it. *I think it's safe.* "Sure, Dad. It's safe. You know it has airbags and stuff. It's great on gas mileage." I changed the subject. "So, when will you be coming back east to visit me?"

"We plan to come back in December so we can spend the Christmas holidays with you. Why? Do you need us to come sooner?" Dad's voice sounded worried.

"No, no. Christmas sounds perfect. You can come to South Carolina and help me put up the first Christmas tree in my new home."

"All right. Your mother wants to talk to you again. It was good talking to you. You take care of yourself."

"You too, Dad." I was relieved to have diverted a lecture about car buying. "Cara?" Mom came back on the line.

"I'm still here."

"You call us if you need anything."

"I'm fine, Mom. Don't worry. I have a new car and a new house, and I love my job at the library. Did I tell you we're planning a fund-raiser? A real swanky affair. Black tie with all the trimmings."

"That's what I'm worried about. Everything is all about the 'new.' What about your old friends in Pittsburgh? When was the last time you talked to Angela?"

I paused because I knew Mom was right. I had completely cut myself off from everything in Pittsburgh, including my best friend, Angela. We'd exchanged a few e-mails, but I hadn't returned any of her calls. The only calls I'd returned were to my ex-boss regarding a few of the last cases I worked on before resigning. There had been two calls and they were all business.

Nothing personal. I ended the last call quite abruptly when my ex-boss asked how things were going with my new job.

"Angela and I have e-mailed. She's doing fine. Don't worry about me. Right now 'new' is good for me. It's what I need." I didn't want to allow my mother to dig further, so I came up with an excuse to get off the phone. "Listen, Mom, I've got some things to take care of. I need to go. Love to you and Dad. Drive safely."

"We love you too, baby."

I hung up the phone and put my head down on the table. I loved my parents, but hiding the issues that made me leave Pittsburgh was exhausting. I didn't like lying to them, but I wasn't ready to talk to them—or anyone, for that matter—about my life up north. The euphoria I'd felt from my new car purchase ebbed away and left me feeling low. Determined to throw off the melancholy, I opened my pantry door and began cruising the shelves looking for ingredients to make something yummy. Everyone knows chocolate cures all ailments.

A few hours later my kitchen sink was piled high with pots, pans, bowls and mixing utensils. On the island sat two coconut cream pies and a few dozen chocolate chunk cookies. The sweet aroma of vanilla and sugar hung heavy in the air. I filled a tin with cookies. *What to do with this plethora of calorie-laden desserts?* If I left the sweets here, I'd eat them all and gain a million unwanted pounds. I figured I'd take a pie and a some cookies to work on Tuesday.

Pondering my options for off-loading the sweets, my eyes wandered to the back garden. The lawn would need mowing this week, so I headed upstairs to the attic landing.

I hollered, knocking on the attic door, "Hey, neighbor. I'm leaving a pie and some cookies this time." Following the same routine as last time, I shut the door, locked it, and walked with a heavy tread back downstairs. Before going to bed, I checked the attic landing and, sure enough, the desserts were gone. If anything, my hermit would be well fed, and I might never have to learn how to work the lawn mower. Win-win all around.

Chapter Seven

The last few weeks of May flew by in a blur. Mr. Mole and I conversed via food, left by me, and notes, left by him. The flowers kept coming. When they died, I left the vase, along with an offering of food, and within a day or two, I'd find a new bouquet on my front or back porch waiting for me. There were always at least two bouquets in the house. The notes Danny left were generally humorous, but kind, and a bit flirtatious. I figured he had a small crush on me or he was just being charming. Either way, the flowers and notes boosted my ego and allowed me snippets of insight into his personality. I kept the notes, and they made a small pile on my kitchen counter. The garden in back was regularly weeded and pruned and had become my oasis for relaxing in the evening. Having a live-in gardener sure had its benefits.

His response to cookies said:

Sweets from the sweetest neighbor. Cookies were fantastic. Are you trying to make me fat? Never mind. You only live once. Make more soon, please.

P.S. I like the new ride. A convertible suits you.

When I left Mexican enchiladas, Danny's note said:

Yummy. I love Mexican. Needs more <u>spice</u>. There's a cayenne pepper plant out back which will ripen in July. I'll pick some for you to use next time.

After about two weeks, I made chicken potpies and left one

for Danny. It was probably the sixth time I'd left him food, and his response was different from the earlier ones.

Chicken potpie was delicious. I should probably tell you I do receive groceries weekly and can feed myself. However, you're a much better cook, so I won't tell you to stop.

But please, don't feel obligated to feed me. Even if you don't feed me, I will continue to mow the lawn and maintain the garden. The landscaping activities I do for my own pleasure and to reduce stress. I've been taking care of the yard since I moved in when Jerome was alive. I can tell by your generosity you're a very kind person. It's clear your beauty is not only skin-deep.

You'll never know how much I appreciate your purchasing this house and allowing me to stay.

Your Very Thankful Neighbor, Danny

I'd never thought of myself as beautiful. More like passably attractive, but it was nice to know my hermit thought I was beautiful on the inside, where it counted. Other aspects about Danny were beginning to intrigue me, and I concluded he must make a good living creating computer games. First, the rent he paid was priced high for Denton. A mortgage in that monthly range could afford him a pleasant home. Second, the note cards he used were engraved with his monogram on vellum stationery. Finally, the Swarovski Crystal vase was just the tip of the flower holder iceberg. Danny left bouquet offerings in a variety of vessels, including Baccarat and Lalique, but my favorite vase was a Waterford from the Robert Held Art Collection; the crystal swirled with deep blues and greens and had 24 karat gold leafing. I went searching online to find out more about this piece and almost fell out of my chair when I found similar pieces with price ranges from $2,000 to $4,500. I couldn't believe Danny had actually left this one-of-a-kind artwork sitting on my front porch. When I returned the vase, I left a note requesting he not use the Waterford vase again. The artwork was stunning but, due to its high value, I couldn't afford the risk it might get broken. It was irreplaceable.

Danny's response to my request was to leave the Waterford vase filled with flowers on the back deck the next day with a note:

What's life if we can't enjoy the finer things? It's a vase and should be used. I bought it with you in mind. Consider it a gift. If you break it, I'll buy you a new one.
Yours, Danny

I could have argued with him via notes or e-mail but decided against it. I knew there was no way I could accept such a gift, and honestly, I thought Danny was joking about that part anyway. So, I was very careful with the Waterford and hoped he wouldn't use it often.

In the meantime, Jeff and I had two lunch dates and a dinner date, and we met twice at my house. Both times I was leaving as he was arriving to have a session with Danny. The second lunch date ended with a very nice kiss. It wasn't a bone-melting kiss; on the other hand, it wasn't bad. It was…nice. I knew nice was boring for a kiss, but I hadn't been kissed in a long time, so for now, nice was good.

However, the last date with Jeff left me wondering what the heck was going on. Jeff asked all sorts of oddball questions and made me feel like I was being gently interrogated. Did I think aliens existed? What did I think about people who thought aliens existed? Did I believe in life after death? Heaven and hell? What was my opinion about psychics? Did I think people could have a sixth sense? Never having met a psychic, I really had no opinion one way or another and I didn't even want to think about the alien discussion. It was all rather bizarre and since that lunch, I hadn't heard from Jeff, nor had I contacted him. I left the date feeling a bit turned off and wondering if the psychologist was cracking up.

Organizing the fund-raiser, in addition to our regular duties, kept everyone busy at the library. Jackie came through with her Myrtle Beach donation, but Beau really went over the top and blew us away. Barnes Urban Outfitters donated a His and Hers set of golf clubs, two top-of-the-line tennis rackets, a canoe, a kayak, a treadmill and two mountain bikes. Additionally, the company became a $2,000 Gold Level Sponsor. Beau was going to send the sporting goods over the day before the auction so we wouldn't have to find a place to store everything. Apparently, he was a minor celebrity in Denton and my connection with him made my stock at work go up a couple of notches. He and Jackie purchased tickets, along with the mayor, the deputy mayor and three councilmen. The library fund-raiser was quickly becoming the end of summer event to attend by the wealthy residents of Denton. Moreover, the word had spread to Charleston and we were seeing some of South Carolina's elite purchasing tickets for it. We were even seeing a number of middle-class residents splurging to be a part of the fun. George also came through and Linda Lincoln, the Charleston author, had agreed to attend. Linda donated a box of her most recently released romance novel, which we were going to give out as door prizes, to be autographed by the famous author in person.

    I was able to arrange four different restaurants to sponsor food stations. One station was being hosted by an expensive steak house on Main Street. They planned to bring appetizer favorites, such as stuffed mushrooms and potatoes, hot wings, fried onions with special sauce and coconut shrimp and have a roast beef carving station. The Oriental restaurant was serving various wontons and dumplings, sushi and spring rolls. About twenty minutes outside of Denton, I found an Indian restaurant willing to sponsor a station. They would be offering a variety of kebobs, hummus and Tandoori cuisine.

    My *coup de gras* was getting The Chowder House, a famous Charleston seafood restaurant, to sponsor the last station. Whereas the other three restaurants had chosen their menus, The Chowder House requested I visit to sample their menu and recommend what they should serve at the fund-raiser. The hardest decision I had to make was who to take with me to the tasting. My options were Mandy, Jackie or Jeff. I immediately crossed Jeff off the list after the wacky lunch date. That left Mandy and Jackie. I felt I owed Jackie for the beach house donation. On the other hand, Mandy worked at the library, so I'd appreciate her suggestions. I also felt I owed her for helping me purchase my new car. In the end, Jackie was going to be out of town visiting her daughter at college so the choice was made for me.

Mandy and I dressed up for our girl's night out. It was late May and the southern heat had arrived. Luckily the humidity had yet to stick around, coming and going in spurts. I wore a sassy sundress with my favorite push-up bra and high-heeled sandals. My hair was swept back into a French twist with tendrils strategically hanging down. I added lots of mascara and red lipstick.

As I left, I thought I saw some movement on the third floor, so I waved while backing out of the driveway and headed over to pick up Mandy.

She wore her usual stilettos, short skirt and skimpy top but added some flare with lots of big curls. She looked fabulous. Once Mandy was buckled in, I wrapped a blue silk scarf around my head, á la Grace Kelly, handed a green one to Mandy and put the top down on the Mini. She followed suit, and then we motored onto the open road.

We rolled into Charleston around seven and pulled up to The Chowder House. I handed the keys to the valet as we got out of the car. When I gave my name to the hostess, we were led to an outdoor table overlooking the water. Mandy and I both ordered Mojitos to start the evening, while a musician with an acoustic guitar set up shop on the other side of the deck and started with a musical selection from The Eagles. A few minutes after we placed our order, a tall lanky man with deep chocolate-colored skin and shoulder-length dreadlocks brought our drinks and introduced himself as the chef, Anton.

"You are da ladies from the library, yes?" Anton had a flashy smile and a languorous Jamaican accent.

"Yes, indeed we are. I'm Mandy and this is Cara. We're looking forward to trying some of your savory dishes." Mandy flirtatiously leaned forward, showing an abundance of cleavage.

"No problem, mon. You won be disappointed. I will be

sending out a dozen deefferent dishes for you to try. If you have problems, just ask Janie to sen for ole Anton." He looked directly down Mandy's blouse.

"Thank you, Anton. We look forward to it." I snapped Anton's attention away from Mandy's overflowing flesh.

"I thought you were dating that guy from the symphony," I hissed at Mandy as Anton walked away.

"Eric? Sure, I'm dating him. We're not married, though. Doesn't mean I can't have an innocent flirtation with someone as yummy as Anton. I love guys with accents." Mandy rubbed her hands together. Flirting came as naturally to Mandy as breathing, and I hoped it would never land her in trouble.

Reclining back, I sipped my Mojito and listened to upbeat strains of the latest selection, "Taking Care of Business."

A variety of savory seafood dishes began coming out of Anton's kitchen soon afterward; it became apparent when it came to seafood, Mandy could eat more crustaceans than a Sumo wrestler. I don't know where she put it all for such a tiny person.

Anton strolled out at regular intervals to see how we liked the dishes and to flirt unmercifully with both Mandy and me. At one point he sat down to drink a beer and I caught him scoping out my Wonderbra'd cleavage. He requested the guitarist play a Jimmy Buffett song and led all of the patrons on the deck in a rousing rendition of "Margaritaville." Overall, it was a sumptuous meal and Anton's light and witty flirtations kept Mandy and me amused. After sampling a dozen of Anton's dishes, it was obvious he was a genius in the kitchen and The Chowder House's reputation was well earned.

Once we finished gorging ourselves, we chose steamed peel-and-eat shrimp, Cajun crab cakes, clams and mussels on the half-shell, fried calamari, stuffed lobster patties au gratin and hush puppies. Anton would choose a "catch of the day" fish for a carving station. The cherry on top of our evening happened when we found out Anton had comped our meal.

After tipping the valet, Mandy and I got in the Mini to head home. As she buckled her seat belt, Mandy's phone chirruped.

"It's a text from Eric. He just got home from his performance and wants to see me tonight." She giggled.

"Girlfriend, it's eleven thirty already, and we aren't even back in Denton."

"So?"

"So, when a guy texts you at eleven thirty, it can only mean one thing."

"Oh yeah? What's that?" Her eyes opened wide and innocent.

"A boo-tay call." I laughed.

Mandy shot me a big smile and wiggled her brows. "How fast can you get me there?"

"You're a nut." I shook my head. "So, how is he, you know…in the sack?"

Mandy shivered and licked her lips. "Yummy. Let's just say, all that trumpeting strengthens the lips and tongue to make for a great kisser. He likes to kiss…lots and lots of kisses." She sighed dreamily.

I laughed with a bit of envy.

Mandy proceeded to crank my stereo and sing along at the top of her voice with the latest pop hit as I flew down the highway back to Denton.

It was long past midnight when I zipped into my parking spot after dropping Mandy off at Eric's. The lights were on in Danny's apartment, so I sent up a wave in case he was watching. I breezed into the kitchen and found the answering machine light blinking at me. There were two messages.

"Hi, Cara, it's Jeff Nolan. I'm calling because I need to speak with you about something important. I'll try to reach you tomorrow."

Oh boy, what now? More aliens?

Jeff was starting to give me the jeepers. Perhaps it was time to give him a gentle heave-ho. Unfortunately, that could be tricky considering he was at the house on a regular basis meeting with my mysterious hermit.

If Jeff's message gave me the creeps, the second message

infuriated me. "This message is for Cara Baker. This is Agent Bryant. I hope you remember me. We met during the Colquitt case. I have some information for you. Please contact me at…"

I erased Agent Bryant's message without taking down his phone number. It would be a cold day in hell before I returned any of his calls. Glancing at the caller ID, I noticed the number was blocked. Typical FBI. I made a mental note not to answer any blocked numbers. I didn't want to start thinking about the past and if I went to bed, it would all start swirling around in my head. So, I grabbed a bottle of wine from the fridge and put one of my favorite chick flicks in the DVD player.

*****

The next morning was Saturday, and my doorbell rang at quarter after nine. I debated whether or not to answer it. I was tired and grouchy from a minor hangover and lack of sleep and, needless to say, I wasn't in the mood for company. Since I didn't have to be at the library until noon, I was still in my shorty pajamas and my hair stood on end, sporting a fork-in-the-electric-socket style. After the second ring, I opened the door.

Jeff stood on the other side of the screen.

Geez.

Jeff looked quite nice wearing Dockers and a red polo. *Perhaps I should have brushed my hair before opening the door.* My eyebrows went up in a silent question.

"Good morning." He took in my bedraggled appearance. "I'm sorry if I woke you."

I flapped a hand at him while I yawned. "It's okay. What can I do for you?"

"I'm here because I spoke with Danny last night and again this morning…and he's decided he wants to meet you."

I stood gaping at him for a beat. His statement completely threw me for a loop. "Come on in. I was just making coffee. I'll pour you a cup and we can talk."

Jeff followed me into the kitchen and sat down at the table.

"So, Danny finally wants to meet. That's great. I've been

hoping to make him feel comfortable enough to do so. We've been exchanging notes for a couple of weeks now." My excitement grew.

"Yes. Danny's been keeping me up to date. By the way, your coconut cream pie was delicious."

I gave a wan smile as I poured the coffee. Knowing Danny and Jeff talked about me bothered me. Obviously, I knew as Danny's psychiatrist, Jeff heard plenty of personal information, and clearly I was a part of his life now. However, I had hoped our written conversations would remain private between the two of us. This information made me realize I'd have to be more careful with Danny in the future.

I sat across from Jeff. "So, how does this work? Should I invite Danny down for dinner or something?"

"Actually, he's asked if we could come to his apartment for dinner tomorrow night."

"We?"

"He'd like me to make the introductions. He thinks you'll both be more comfortable if I'm there to smooth the way."

"Okay. I can do tomorrow night."

"Listen, Cara, I know on our last date I asked you a number of rather strange questions."

"Uh-huh." *No argument there.*

"All I can say is there was a reason for those questions. When you meet Danny, please just keep an open mind."

"Why? What do you mean? Does Danny think he's been abducted by aliens? He's not going to ask me to wear a colander on my head, is he?"

Jeff gave a ghost of a smile. "No colanders and no alien abductions." He paused. "Just keep an open mind."

"Sure. What's this all about? Does he have some sort of deformity?" I pressed. After all, I could temper my feelings if I knew exactly what I'd be walking into. I didn't want to embarrass myself by showing shock or disgust over a gruesome deformity growing out of his head.

Jeff sighed, apparently debating with himself, trying to decide what he could ethically divulge. "I know this isn't what you want to hear, but I'm not in a position to disclose Danny's secrets. He doesn't have a deformity. Look, I know he plans to reveal personal information that you might find..." Jeff seemed to search for the right word, "disconcerting. If this meeting goes well, I'm hoping it will be the first step toward Danny's re-entry into society. Right now, I really need you to be understanding. He needs your support."

Well if it was all mental, then I could handle that. I laid my hand upon his. "Look, I like Danny. He's a great tenant and I've enjoyed our written exchanges. Whatever the big secret is, I'm sure it won't change my feelings. You don't have to worry. Everything will be just fine."

"Thanks."

I ran my fingernail around the edge of my coffee cup and stared into the coffee. "So ... what's going on with us? I've been out of the dating scene for a while. I'm a bit rusty."

Heaving a deep sigh, Jeff rubbed his hands over his face. He wouldn't meet my eyes. Instead, he stared over my shoulder. "I'm in a difficult position being Danny's psychiatrist and confidant. You are his landlord. I find you interesting and attractive, but..." More face rubbing. "I probably shouldn't tell you this. Danny has a bit of a crush on you."

"Yeah, I kind of thought he might. He's very flattering in his notes."

Jeff's beautiful eyes came back to mine. "I think it would be better for Danny if we were just friends, for now."

"All right. I can understand that." I felt very little disappointment this "thing" with Jeff would lead nowhere. "Thank you for being frank with me." Relief and regret crossed his features.

I held out my hand. "Friends."

Jeff grasped my proffered hand. "Friends. And, Cara..."

"Hmmm?"

"Thanks for understanding."

Chapter Eight

Sunday evening Jeff rang my doorbell at six thirty on the dot. I couldn't decide if his timeliness was his best or worst trait. I stepped back from the door and invited him in.

"Do I look okay? I wasn't sure what I should wear." Before his arrival I'd tried on and discarded a dozen outfits. My bedroom looked as though a cyclone had blown through. I wanted to dress up a bit but remain casual. Jeff was seeing the latest outfit, a white denim skirt, hot pink sandals and a bright-blue embroidered cotton top.

Jeff looked me up and down. "You look fabulous as always. Frankly, you could make a garbage sack look good."

"Well thank you, Jeff, but plastic was so last season." I tried to sound calm and flippant, but there were butterflies in my stomach.

Jeff must have sensed my nervousness. "Everything will be fine." He repeated my sentiments from yesterday.

This brought a smile. "So, should we go up then?"

"Lead the way."

We headed up my stairwell. I unlocked the dead bolt on the attic door and allowed Jeff to go ahead of me. He knocked twice and then opened Danny's apartment door. I followed him, smelling the savory aroma of saffron and spices. The entrance into the kitchen and a pot on the stove came into view. On the right was the large living room, which housed two leather sofas facing each other and a coffee table in between. Two armchairs flanked the sofas, and in the far corner was a brick fireplace with a large flat screen TV perched above the mantle. Lining the adjoining wall was a technology workstation where two tables housed three computers, two flat screen monitors, a laptop, a printer/fax machine and other various computer components I didn't recognize. Through the open door of the rounded circular turret, home gym equipment sat on rubber matting.

Standing behind a brown leather couch was my hermit, Daniel Johnson. Never before had I been so completely wronged by my preconceived notions. Danny was definitely not Mr. Mole. He was not short, not brown-haired, not stooped, not nerdy. Instead, standing in front of me was a gorgeously tanned and toned six-foot god with blond hair and green eyes. Danny must have spent hours in the garden to gain the tan. His hair was probably closer to a dirty blond in the winter but had bleached to a wheat color women paid hundreds of dollars to attain. It was a tad on the long side and curled up at the nape of his neck. His face was clean-shaven, revealing high cheek bones cut down the middle by a patrician nose. His eyes were jade green and probably darkened depending upon the color he wore. It was clear he used his home gym.

He wore a white polo and his forearms were roped with sinewy muscles. His khaki shorts showed muscular toned legs with a sprinkling of blond hair.

Danny stood silent while I sized him up.

Jeff broke the stillness with an introduction. "Cara Baker, this is Danny Johnson."

I put my hand out and walked forward. "Danny, it's so nice to finally meet in person."

Danny looked at my hand.

I stopped short and my face burned. "Oh, dear. I'm sorry. That's wrong, isn't it? I believe you prefer not to have contact."

Danny didn't move toward me, but his deep voice pulled me in and caressed me. "No, Cara, it's not you. Don't be embarrassed. It's me." He looked over at Jeff.

Jeff nodded. "If you're prepared, you should give it a try."

With a brief inclination of his head, Danny moved from behind the leather couch toward me with his hand outstretched.

Surprised by this invitation, I looked to Jeff for approval. He looked fixedly in my eyes, willing me to do the right thing. I shrugged. If Danny was willing to shake my hand, who was I to deter him? When he stopped across from me, I firmly took his hand and gave it a gentle shake.

His warm callused hand returned the pressure. "Thank you for agreeing to come."

There was a quick zip up my arm and a crackle of static electricity sparked between our hands. The hair on the back of my neck rose and there was a slight ringing in my ears.

I could swear Danny's green eyes brightened, but he quickly removed his hand from my grip and dropped his eyes. "Sorry."

I looked briefly at my hand, still tingling from the contact, and stuck it in my pocket. "No problem. All your equipment must increase the static electricity in here." I gave a weak laugh. "I've been looking forward to meeting you since I moved in." I paused at a loss. "Do you, uh, need to wash your hand now or something?"

Danny quirked an eyebrow and looked at his muscular digits. "Why would I need to wash my hand?"

"I guess ... I thought you might ... you know, have issues with germs." I stuttered, feeling like a prize idiot.

Realization dawned. "Oh. No, I'm not a germaphobe."

I felt uncomfortable and out of my depth. I looked over to Jeff for guidance.

Jeff must have interpreted my look. "Why don't we all sit down? Danny, I know you planned to address this after dinner. However, for Cara's comfort, I think it best if we talk now."

Danny looked at me. "Yes, I think you're right. Would you like something to drink before we get started?"

I let out a deep breath and nodded. "Sure, what do you have?"

"How about a glass of wine?"

"That would be great."

"Red or white?"

"White, please."

He looked over his shoulder at Jeff. "What would you like?"

"White wine is fine for me too." He gestured toward the

couch.

Jeff and I took seats as Danny went to the kitchen to get our drinks.

I was too restless to sit; I got up and walked over to the French doors that led out to the small wrought iron balcony. Danny had a fabulous bird's-eye view of the garden. How many hours had it taken him to build such beautiful landscaping? The dahlias were starting to bloom. The hair on my arms stood on end as he approached. I took a wineglass. Danny handed the other glass to Jeff and then offered me a seat. Deciding quickly, I chose an armchair rather than sit with one of the gentlemen on a couch.

I took a sip of wine. A light crisp Pinot Grigio with flavors of peach and vanilla rolled down my throat. Danny had good taste in wine, something we shared. "Danny, may I ask you a question unrelated to my being here?"

"You can ask me anything."

"Why didn't you just buy the house from Max? I mean, not that I mind. I'm thrilled to be living here. I just thought Max would give you right of first refusal since you already lived here."

"He did. I asked him to try and sell it first. If it looked as though no one was going to purchase the home with me living in it, I would have eventually purchased it. Frankly, I didn't want the hassle of taking care of a house this large, but I wasn't ready to leave the gardens behind either."

"Why didn't you purchase the home and rent out the downstairs?"

"At first I didn't think of doing that ... because of my situation. Then, lucky for me, you came along and everything worked out for the best. I don't regret not buying the house. It was meant for you. You love it, don't you?"

He was right on the mark about that. I did love it. The house was meant for me. "Yes, I do love the house, but the gardens were the reason I bought it. I think if it had been a two-room shack with those gardens, I would have purchased it all the same. You've done a stunning job. If you ever give up your day job, you could do it professionally."

Danny flashed a lovely white smile that made my stomach clench. "Thank you. Maybe someday I will."

Wow. He really was drop-dead gorgeous. I think I stared. Before I made a complete fool of myself, I forced my eyes to look away. The fruity wine slid down my dry throat as I glanced around the room waiting for someone to start the conversation about the real reason I was here.

With a deep breath, Danny took the plunge. "Well, you're probably wondering what this is all about. Why I'm known as the neighborhood freak."

"Freak is a little harsh," I protested. There was no way this beautiful specimen of mankind could be a freak.

"Nonetheless, I'm strange. You see, I have this ability." He looked hesitantly at me.

"Mm-hm."

"Jeff calls it my 'sixth sense.'" He used his fingers as air quotes.

"Uh-huh."

"When I touch people, I feel their emotions, their moods."

"O-kay." I humored him, a little confused.

"I'm serious. That's my problem. I feel people's emotions."

This isn't where I thought we were going. "Huh? What? Are you like some sort of psychic vampire?"

He laughed a deep baritone.

That laugh went all the way to my toes.

"No. I'm not a vampire, and I don't see dead people. Also, I can't read your thoughts, but I could control your emotions, in a way, by channeling mine."

I was perplexed, to say the least. With a raised eyebrow, I looked over at Jeff. *Was this the crux of Danny's mental illness, that he thought he could control people like a Vulcan mind meld? How was I supposed to react? Play along with Danny's illness?*

Jeff nodded. "It is true. Danny has a sixth sense. The main reason I'm seeing him is to help him learn how to control it by blocking himself from other people."

"I don't get it. Is this some sort of joke? Jeff, I really don't think this is funny." Irritation flashed. I wasn't sure what kind of game Jeff was playing, but I wasn't having any part of it.

Clearly Danny's illness is worse than I'd been led to believe. *What was Jeff thinking allowing Danny to live in this queer little world where he had super powers?* Our last lunch discussion flashed through my mind. Maybe Jeff was a bit of a nutter himself, and poor Danny had this terrible shrink playing around in his psyche. *Did he have some sort of schizophrenia or multiple personality?* The more I thought about it, the angrier I became, and I rose from my chair to leave.

"Cara, NO!" Danny reached for me. His hand stopped, millimeters from my left arm. "Please don't go. We aren't joking. Please stay … hear me out." He voice was urgent and pleading.

I looked at his hand hovering but not physically touching me. Then I searched his face. He seemed sincere and so … normal … his grass-green eyes held mine, begging me to stay. Damn, the man was handsome, and I couldn't force myself to walk out on that puppy dog look.

Gradually, I returned to my seat, and Danny, just as slowly, moved his hand back to the armrest. I took a minute to glimpse at Jeff. He wasn't moving toward or away from me but waiting in that quiet way of his for me to make up my mind. I breathed in and out for a few seconds. The night couldn't get any weirder, and dinner tantalized my senses, so I swallowed the rest of my wine in one gulp, leaned back in the comfy armchair and sent a smile toward Danny.

"Okey dokey, boys. I'm all ears. Why don't you start at the beginning and use small words, not psychobabble." This was aimed at Jeff. "Tell me exactly what's going on. First, how about some more wine?" I waved my empty glass in the air.

Jeff stood. "Sounds like a good idea. I'll get the wine." He swung into the kitchen and popped back out quickly with the open bottle. The golden wine splashed quietly into the glass, when it was full, he left the bottle on the coffee table. Jeff and Danny's drinks had barely been touched.

"Danny, why don't I take a stab at this?" Jeff looked for his approval. Danny nodded and returned his intent gaze to me.

"Cara, remember our last lunch? I asked a number of strange questions."

"Yes." *How could I forget?*

"I was asking in order to gauge your reaction to the mystical or supernatural and paranormal."

"Uh-huh." I nodded.

"Well, your answers showed me you have an open mind and are willing to accept things aren't always as they seem."

"O-kay."

"As I said earlier, Danny has what might be classified as a sixth sense. I don't know if it's a neurological difference or perhaps a genetic one. Whatever the case, it seems Danny can feel your emotions—anger, pain, joy and happiness. I've been working with him for almost two years to learn how to block the emotions of others while corralling his own. You see, Danny also has the ability to," he paused, snapped his fingers, "he has the ability to ... Danny help me out."

Danny never turned to look at Jeff but continued to watch me intently. "I can impose my emotions on others."

"How does that work?"

"When I touch them, sometimes my emotional energy flows outward."

"So, scientifically how does that work?"

"We don't really know," responded Jeff. "I've been working with Danny on a psychological level."

"You haven't run blood tests and MRIs?" I was surprised.

"I've had blood tests. They don't reveal anything unusual. And, I'm not willing to open myself up to the medical community to become a pincushion or guinea pig. I couldn't handle a bunch of doctors putting electrodes all over my body and touching me," Danny bit out.

"My work with Danny is private. I've promised him I wouldn't consult with other colleagues. We don't focus on the reasons so much as how he can overcome them."

"Wouldn't knowing the reasons make it easier to overcome them?" I asked, confused.

"Perhaps. But as Danny said, blood tests haven't shown any reason for his abilities. If we start visiting hospitals for MRIs and scans, we could open up a can of worms. Unfortunately, my research hasn't turned up any other cases with these same capabilities. It's a bizarre combination of abilities, and my research into the paranormal, such as ESP, hasn't revealed a similar case. When it comes to the supernatural, there are a lot of phonies out there trying to make a buck, and it's difficult to discern truth from fiction. There may be other people out there with a sixth sense similar to Danny's, but it's been tough trying to find the real deal. Danny and I determined this was the best way to work, even though it may take longer for a solution."

I turned to look at Danny who leaned his elbows on his knees and stared at his hands. I arrived at a crossroads. Either I would accept this story, which both Danny and Jeff seemed to genuinely believe, or I would have to deny the story, believing that within the cosmos of the world everything was black and white without areas of gray.

The reality was, I'd had premonitions, or what some might call "women's intuition," when bad things were going to happen. Thinking back almost ten years ago, I felt physically ill and full of dread one morning when I woke in my dorm room. That day my mother was in a wicked car accident. It put her in the hospital for a week. Another time I walked into a convenience store and broke out into a cold sweat accompanied with dizziness. I stumbled back to my car without purchasing anything only to find out the store was robbed at gunpoint later that night.

Moreover, I unequivocally believe life exists somewhere outside our galaxy. It just seems too arrogant to believe we are the only life form in this vast universe. So … did I or didn't I accept this person has an anomaly in his genetic makeup that made him more sensitive to emotions? I had always considered myself to be open-minded, but if I denied the possibility this was true, how open-minded was I really? I'd come to trust my instincts and today my instincts told me to jump on the roller coaster of life and ride this one out.

I sucked in a breath and made my decision. "Danny, what do you need from me?"

His gaze flew to mine with brows winged up in surprise. "I hadn't thought of it that way." He paused, "I guess I need your understanding."

"Plus, maybe, my acceptance?"

Danny's head slowly bobbed. "Yes. I suppose that too."

"Well, as strange as this all seems, I do have an open mind. I don't know if I can understand exactly how you feel per se, but I guess I can accept you have some sort of ability and I'll do whatever I can to help you."

"That's uncommonly generous."

"Do you need to try your 'blocking' capabilities with me? Should I be your guinea pig?" I smiled, trying to lighten the tension radiating off Danny.

"Not tonight. Maybe we'll try that some other time. Tonight I just want to have dinner and get to know my lovely landlord." Our gazes connected.

Were my knees weak due to the wine I was knocking back or due to pheromones? "Well...whatever you cooked smells delicious. Can I help in the kitchen?" Changing the subject right about now was probably a good idea.

"That would be great. Perhaps you can put the salad together."

"My specialty. Lead the way." I got to my feet and felt slightly off balance. My hand reached for the armrest to steady myself.

Danny stood and examined me for a moment, probably trying to decide if I was going to fall over. I tilted my head and allowed a questioning eyebrow to go up. His eyes mesmerized me, and a fluttery sensation warmed my belly.

He jerked, as if coming out of a groove. I guess he determined I wasn't going to topple over onto the coffee table. "Follow me."

Danny pulled lettuce, tomato, carrots and celery out of the

refrigerator and placed them next to a blue pottery bowl by the sink. I asked for water and drank the entire glass before picking up a knife to begin chopping and assembling.

"So, how did you get involved in the computer programming business?" Men always enjoyed talking about their work. Also, this would be an innocuous topic that might set us in the right direction toward having a relatively normal evening.

"I've been doing it since I was in high school. I went to Duke on an academic scholarship and graduated with a computer science degree. For one of my classes during my junior year, we had to design a game. Turned out I was good at it." He shrugged. "I sold my game to a company out in California. They design all sorts of computer gaming software, including software for handheld devices, apps for tablets and phones and also for Nintendo. When I graduated, they offered me a job. Instead of taking their job, I chose to start my own company, DJ Gamez, and be a contractor. Is that too much information?"

"Not at all. Don't you ever have to go to California and meet with people, sign contracts, or attend conferences?" I returned to chopping carrots.

"Nope. We do everything via e-mail, phone, or Skype. They know I'm a weird computer recluse and don't question it."

"Kinda like that movie, *The Net*, where Sandra Bullock did everything at home and no one knew what she looked like."

He pondered that for a moment. "Well, with Web cameras, we know what everyone looks like, and there's really no intrigue. I also do pro bono work on a few child development websites; they're targeted computer learning games for elementary and middle school age children."

Jeff stuck his head in the kitchen doorway. "Hi, kids. It looks like you two are getting along just fine. Danny, I'm going to head out. I'll see you Wednesday at ten."

My head swiveled around. "You're not staying for dinner?"

Jeff shook his head. "I decided since you didn't run screaming from the apartment, I should duck out after the cocktails. I think you'll be more comfortable at dinner talking one-on-one without the shrink hanging around."

"You're welcome to stay, Doc." Danny seemed to have a touch of panic to his voice.

"All the same, I think you two need to have a chance to get to know each other without a third wheel." Jeff winked reassuringly at Danny. "You don't need me to run interference. You're doing just fine on your own."

Danny gave me a skeptical look.

"He's right, you know. You're doing fine." I nodded.

"I'll see myself out." With a smile and a wave, Jeff headed downstairs noiselessly shutting the door behind him.

Danny sent me a look as if he didn't know what to say.

I searched my mind for a topic of conversation to dispel the sudden tension. "Thank heavens he left, eh? I mean, who wants a nosy shrink listening to our conversation, analyzing everything we say. Am I right?" I gave a sarcastic snort.

A relieved smirk crossed his features. "You're right. What was I thinking? Now I have you all to myself in my secret scientist lair." He gave a lecherous drawl and rubbed his hands together.

"Oh, do you turn into Mr. Hyde when no one's looking?" I was trying hard to be funny.

Unfortunately, for emphasis, I flicked the knife I used to cut the tomato, with half of said tomato attached to the end, resulting in said tomato flipping across the room to land with a smooshing smack in the dead center of Danny's chest. I watched in horror as the tomato slid down his white shirt, leaving a trail of red juice and seeds, and then splatted unceremoniously onto his left shoe. My eyes practically bugged out of my head as I stood, helpless to slow the tomato's progress. My face flamed up in mortification, and I smacked a hand over my speechless mouth.

Danny looked at the tomato listlessly sliding off his shoe. His eyes traveled up my body to my face. He threw back his head and let out a deep belly laugh. It was such an infectious sound I couldn't help but join him.

"I'm ... so ... sorry." I giggled, trying to catch my breath.

When he was finally done laughing, Danny took a few deep breaths and looked at me with a touch of awe. "I don't know when the last time was I laughed that hard. I don't think you could make that shot again if you tried."

"Probably not."

He broke up laughing again. "You should have seen your face." He laughed. "Your eyes were like big saucers." He made Os with his hands and laughed some more. "You turned as red as a beet. That was great. You sure know how to ease the tension." More laughter.

"Oh, Danny, I'm so sorry about your shirt. I'll take care of the cleaning, and if it doesn't come out, I'll replace it."

He waved me off. "Forget it. It's no big deal. I'll go change." He took a moment to wipe the tomato off his shoe and throw it in the trash. "Why don't you finish up the salad? I'll be back in a jiffy." He left the kitchen, his shoulders still shaking in merriment.

Danny would probably look pretty good without his shirt. Putting away smutty thoughts, I finished making the salad and put it on the table. I removed Jeff's place setting and put the wine and our glasses on the table. I was taking my seat when Danny returned.

"How's this?" He rotated around. He'd changed into a deep blue polo which set off his tan, making him even more handsome, if that was possible.

"It looks good to me. Listen, I feel really bad about your shirt. Are you sure I can't take care of that for you?"

"No way. It's not every day I have a beautiful woman throw tomatoes at me. Don't worry about it." He flicked his wrist. "I'm just glad you've agreed to stay for dinner."

"I wouldn't miss it. The smell has been tantalizing me since I arrived. What are we having?"

"I hope it meets your standards. I'm a bit nervous cooking for such an excellent chef. We're having chicken curry with raisins and lamb kebobs with tomatoes and peppers."

"Sounds great. Should we get started with the salad?" My stomach rumbled in anticipation.

"Be my guest."

The meal was a sensuous variety of tastes and textures. The chicken curry was spicy with a little bit of sweet from the raisins. The kebobs were savory. Lamb could easily be overcooked and become stringy, but Danny's was cooked with just a touch of pink on the inside. During the course of the meal, we finished the first bottle of wine and opened another. I was glad I didn't have to drive because I felt rather pleasant and mellow and my head started to get a delightful swimmy feeling.

After dinner Danny suggested we take our slices of fresh blackberry pie and coffee down to the backyard. I agreed, hoping the fresh air and coffee would clear my head a smidge. Wine brought down my inhibitions, and I might have laughed too loud and invaded Danny's space a bit too much. He didn't seem to mind, but I didn't want to make a fool of myself. After all, this was our first "date," and I was still his landlord. Better to keep things on the up-and-up.

Although, the more I was with him, the more attracted to him I became. His strong hands holding the delicate wineglass while he drank mesmerized me. His lips were full. What would it be like to kiss them?

What? Mental head slap. *Don't go there!* I shook my head to erase such thoughts. Curious to see more of the upstairs apartment, I asked to use the bathroom before going downstairs.

Danny pointed me in the right direction and said he would take the pie and coffee to the garden for us.

In the bathroom I splashed a bit of water on my face to cool things down and get a grip. Danny was too attractive for my own good. It wasn't just a physical attraction. He was intelligent and had a wonderful self-deprecating sense of humor. I expected this weird little fellow with no social graces and instead found this great guy who seemed so *normal*. Moreover, it didn't hurt he threw out lines telling me I was beautiful or lovely. Like any woman, I could be charmed by flattery.

"Don't go down that road. It isn't where you want to go. He's your tenant, and he's got issues. *Stop it*. Stop it," I hissed at myself in the mirror.

With renewed determination to keep Danny at an arm's length, I headed out to the backyard. He wasn't waiting on my back patio where I expected him to be, so I wound my way toward the gazebo. Sure enough, he'd laid out two plates of pie and two coffee cups. The flickering candle in a small lantern shed a warm glow of light.

"This is perfect." I sat across from him. Taking a forkful of pie, the delicate taste of sweet blackberries exploded on my tongue. "Your pie is mouthwatering. Mm."

"I wish I could accept the kudos for the pie, but I can't. I ordered it from the bakery on Main Street. Jeff picked it up for me." He gave a sheepish grin.

"I'll give you kudos for ordering such a yummy pie." I took a sip of coffee and looked across the small table.

Danny wrapped his fingers around his steaming cup.

Growing up as a child with this weird "sixth sense" must have been difficult. "Danny, can I ask you more about your special ability? Or would you prefer not to talk about it?"

He snorted. "Special ability. I'm not sure about that, but you're welcome to ask any questions. I'm sure you have many."

"When did you first notice it?"

"I began noticing strange things in high school." He paused. "I think it was onset by puberty. The first time happened when I was fifteen. I bumped into a group of girls and suddenly felt giggly and euphoric and … not quite myself. I found out later the cheerleader I bumped into had been telling her friends about being invited to the upcoming dance by the captain of the baseball team. It was strange the mood washed over me, and I couldn't figure out why I felt this 'in love' sensation."

"From what I recall, the transference didn't happen again until nine months later, then again about ten months after that. It wasn't until I was twenty my abilities began showing up on a regular basis. During my senior year in college, I started to withdraw from human contact. I avoided situations with large crowds, sat far away from people in class, and moved into an apartment by myself. I dated a few girls during my early college years, but as the occurrences started happening closer together, I wasn't comfortable dating."

"Wow, that must have been difficult for you," I whispered sympathetically.

"I think it was worse when I realized not only was I picking up other people's moods and feelings, but I transferred mine to them. I was concerned about transferring an angry or depressed mood." He picked up his pie.

"Why depressed or angry? How long do the moods last if you transfer them? Don't they stop after you walk away?"

"Unfortunately, no. My work with Jeff shows the temperaments can last for quite a while. I've given Doc the blues for about two hours. We think when I transfer my moods, the intensity and staying power of the mood depends upon the receptivity of each person and also how they were feeling before. If you are concerned or unhappy before I touch you, it will only increase if I'm unhappy." Danny considered the dessert fork resting in his hand and added in a quiet but gruff voice, "I'm worried about touching someone and making them so depressed they commit suicide."

I reached forward to place a comforting hand on his arm and stopped just in time. Instead, I placed it on his armrest and leaned toward him. "Danny, I'm so sorry. That's quite a burden to carry."

He regarded me and worked up a small smile. "It's gotten better since I've been working with Jeff. I've worked with him so much I can block him automatically without thinking about it."

"How do you do it? How do you block people?"

His brow furrowed and seemed to be searching for the words. "I think ... it's like ... mind over matter. I think about my mood and, in my mind's eye, I see myself touching someone normally or without transferring my feelings. Perhaps something in my brain goes up like armor. I don't really know. I think I'm bungling this explanation." Danny frowned. "It's getting easier for me to keep from transferring my feelings, but I still struggle with absorbing other people's moods."

"When we shook hands, what happened? It wasn't static electricity, was it?"

"Yeah, I thought you felt that." He sighed ruefully. "I dropped my guard and felt your emotions, but I don't think I transferred mine."

"What did you feel?"

"You were nervous … and also surprised." Danny gazed at me. "I understand being nervous about meeting the weirdo, but what was the surprise about? My eclectic computer décor?"

"Um, nooo, not exactly," I could feel my cheeks turn rosy with embarrassment. I had been surprised because he didn't look like Mr. Mole.

Danny's shadowed gaze scrutinized me, waiting for an answer.

"I was surprised by your looks. You weren't what I'd pictured."

"So, what were you imagining?"

"I plead the fifth."

Danny chortled. "That bad, huh?"

"I don't know what you mean."

Danny laughed harder. "C'mon. You're getting even redder. Did you think I was covered in warts? Looked like the Elephant Man? I'm dying here."

"Okay, okay. It's not that bad. I thought you were going to be this nerdy computer geek. Not some tall, fit, blond guy. I mean, you're a recluse, for heaven's sake. Where's your hunchback? I'd never met a recluse before and in the movies they were always crazy-eyed freaks."

Danny's laughter stopped immediately. "But I am a freak," he murmured.

I realized my mistake immediately, and my heart went out to him. "Danny, no. No and no and no. Stop that. We all have our issues. You're a good-looking man, and I know you're going to learn how to use this blocking technique. With my help, and Jeff's, it's going to work out. You'll be able to get back into society and be around people, just like the rest of us. Seriously, we're going to make this work. Look at tonight. When was the last time you had dinner with a friend?"

"You think I'm good-looking?" He quirked his eyebrow and a smile hovered.

"All right. Now you're just fishing."

"That's true. It's been a long time since I've had a date with a woman. Thank you for making it so easy."

My face heated with pleasure. I contemplated the coffee mug in my hand and softly replied, "You're welcome."

Reclining in the chair, I stretched out my legs and stared at the nighttime garden. We sat in companionable silence as the sounds of chirruping crickets and croaking frogs serenaded us. *How would I describe our evening to my friends? Did I even want to tell anyone?* Originally I planned to have a sit-down with Mandy and Jackie to fill them in on my little hermit. Only, he wasn't my "little hermit" and nothing was what I'd expected. I felt Danny's intense scrutiny as I ruminated on my conundrum. A tender smile tugged at my lips.

"What's going on up there? I can see smoke coming out of your ears."

"I'm wondering what to tell my friends, or if I should tell them anything at all. What do you think?"

"Good question. If you try to explain, they'll probably think you're crazy allowing me to live above you."

"You're right." I sighed with resignation. "Perhaps I'll keep our meeting to myself for now. At least until you're ready to get back into the public arena."

"Cara," Danny cautioned, "that could take a while. I'm not nearly ready for that yet."

"Yes, yes, I know. I'm going to help you, and it'll come eventually. Trust me. I have faith it's all going to work out."

"Then you have more faith than I do," he muttered grimly.

The glowing hands on my watch pointed to eleven ten. The night was getting late. "Don't worry. I have enough for the both of us. And on that note, I need to go in. I've got to get my beauty rest for work tomorrow. My boss, Greta, doesn't like it when her employees look like something the cat dragged in." I began to stack the plates and cups on the tray. "I'll just help you clean up first."

Danny put out a hand to stop me. "Don't worry about this. I'll take care of it. I didn't realize how late it had gotten. Thank you for such a lovely night. It's the first time … in a long time … I've felt normal. You made it seem so easy. It's been great talking with someone besides Jeff or my coworkers via webcam. I appreciate your understanding."

"The meal was delicious. Thank you for the invitation. Next time, I'll make dinner." I smiled.

"I look forward to it."

Chapter Nine

June

It was more than two weeks before Danny and I sat down for dinner again. Life at the library became incredibly busy due to the start of summer vacation. We created programs for students of all ages, which meant all day there were a variety of activities going on. In the mornings we catered to the preschool through kindergarten crowd with story time and crafts. Twice a week at noon, the elementary children brought in a sack lunch and ate while watching a Disney movie. For middle schoolers, we held afternoon pottery, art, and woodworking classes that ran for three or four days in a row. The high schoolers were invited to attend our mystery, romance and poetry book groups in the evenings, and once a month we held a teen flick night. You had to be in at least ninth grade and show your student I.D. The movie started at eight and the library sold water and popcorn. The movie tickets cost two dollars and had to be purchased in advance. Our first movie was a teen thriller released during the winter. They packed the house.

We hired college students to help run the summer programs, but by the end of the week, I was ready to drop. The summer help thrilled me. The college students were smart, excited and energetic. On the other hand, training the kids fell to me, which meant late nights of planning and creating detailed instructions for each program. Once things got rolling, I'd be able to allow the students freedom to run the classes on their own, but until we reached that comfort level, I had to keep an eye on things and provide direction.

It was ten on a Thursday night and I dragged myself to the front door, when out of the corner of my eye I sensed movement at the end of the porch. My stomach lurched and my heart began to race as adrenaline spiked. I gripped the keys in between my fingers and prepared to defend myself.

"You should put your porch light on a timer so you don't come home to a dark house." Danny's deep voice came out of the shadowy gloom; when he stepped forward a shaft of moonlight shone down on his blond hair.

"Hey, neighbor, long time no see." Relief filled my voice. My heart slowed only minimally, no longer pounding from fear.

"You haven't been around. I was beginning to wonder if you'd gone on vacation." Danny approached with a vase full of summer flowers. I caught a whiff of Irish Spring soap and something spicy. Not only did this man make my toes curl, he smelled scrumptious as well.

"I wish. Our summer student programs started up and that, along with our end-of-summer event, has kept me busy. How about you? How have you been?" I fumbled with the lock on my front door as Danny leaned toward me, filling my senses.

"Just fine, though I've missed seeing you around."

Me too. "Why don't you come in? Have you eaten? I haven't and I'm starving. I'm planning to forage in my fridge and see what comes out. You're welcome to join me." I dropped my bag and keys on the foyer console and headed into the kitchen.

Danny followed, depositing the flowers on the kitchen island. "You haven't eaten dinner yet?"

I looked at him from around my fridge door. "Nope. And I'm about to faint from hunger. It looks like I've got leftover Chinese." I grabbed a takeout carton and gave it the smell test.

Danny shook his head. "No thanks. I'm fine. I've had dinner. I'll just keep you company while you eat, if you don't mind."

"How about something to drink? Want a beer?"

"Sure. A beer would be great."

I handed him a bottle, and he lowered himself on a chair at the kitchen table.

I piled Pork Lo Mein and General Tso's Chicken onto a plate and popped it in the microwave to heat up. Then I grabbed a beer and took a deep drink. The microwave pinged; I pulled out my dinner with a hot pad and parked myself across from Danny.

"So, what's up? Why are you skulking around on my front porch late at night?" I shoveled noodles into my mouth.

He hesitated and began picking at the beer bottle label. "Actually, I was wondering if you were really serious about working with me on my blocking."

"Yes, absolutely. When?" I asked between bites.

"Whenever you're available." He looked up and my stomach did a little flip-flop as his silent eyes melted my bones.

"Let's see." I pondered my work schedule. "I get off at two on Saturday and I have all day Sunday off. Do you want me to make us dinner Saturday night and we can work then?"

"It seems like you're having a busy week as it is. Why don't I take care of dinner on Saturday?"

"Oh, but you made dinner last time. I think it's my turn."

Danny chuckled. "You've been feeding me for weeks. I think it's still my turn. Besides, you look like you could really use a break. You look exhausted."

Sighing, my shoulders slumped as I wilted. "You're right. I'm literally counting down the hours until Saturday afternoon. I'd love it if you took care of dinner on Saturday."

"Why don't I come down around six and we can work before dinner?"

"That'd be fine. Oh, and I forgot to thank you for the flowers. They're stunning, as usual."

Danny flashed a crooked grin. "You've been away so much I figured you'd need a replenishing."

"Yes, there's a sad dead bouquet in my bedroom. I need to clear it out but I just haven't had the time or energy. I haven't been out in the garden in a while either. So, thanks for taking the time to bring a little of the garden inside."

"Looks like I'm not the only one who hasn't been able to catch up with you," he pointed his beer bottle at my answering machine. A bright red four blinked at me.

"I know. My cell phone is the same way. I'll listen to them tomorrow morning." I sighed with resignation.

Danny unfolded his athletic body, his muscles contracting and flexing in graceful harmony. "I need to let you get your rest. I'll see you Saturday."

"Ok," I made an effort to stand but Danny waved me away.

"Don't get up. Finish your dinner. I'll see myself out." He unlocked the French door and gazed back at me with a smoldering look and whispered, "Sweet dreams, Cara." The gravel crunched under his feet as he headed to the rear staircase.

It took a moment before I began to breathe again and uncurl my toes.

"Whoooeee," I whispered with quiet reverence. "That man is hot." And ... I had absolutely no idea what to do with him. If he was a normal guy I'd met at a party or a bar, I'd return his flirtatious smiles and banter with innuendos of my own. *The problem in a nutshell: first and foremost, I'm his landlord and we have a legal agreement.* The lawyer in me said don't mix business with pleasure. *Second, he has issues…big ones, monumental ones; I mean, this whole sixth sense deal is novel for me.* I was committed to helping Danny with his "gift" and didn't want to screw up his ability to get back into the real world. *And third ... well ... one and two were reason enough.* However, all of the reasons didn't stop me from thinking about Danny's smiling eyes and sexy body as I drifted off to sleep. I definitely had sweet dreams that night.

The next morning I didn't have to be at work until ten, for which I was eternally grateful. When I woke, drooping heads of dead flowers met my gaze. The water rotted the stems and the smell of decay wafted through the room. I scrunched my nose in disgust as I took the pathetic bouquet downstairs to throw it out and clean the vase. I punched the red message button as I cleaned up the mess that had piled up in the kitchen over the past week.

The first call was from Mom. "Hi, Cara. Just checking to see how you're doing. I'll try your cell."

The second was a telemarketing computer voice. I soaped

up the flower vase as it played.

The third call was from my favorite FBI agent.

"Ms. Baker, this is Special Agent Bryant with the FBI." I was up to my elbows in soapy suds, and that's the reason I didn't immediately delete the message and instead allowed it to play out. "Listen, I know that our deal didn't end up the way you wanted, but I really need you to contact me. Something important has come up regarding the Colquitt case." He left his number.

"Bite me, Agent Bryant." Childishly, I rolled my eyes.

The machine beeped and the fourth message began, "This message is for Cara Baker. This is Special Agent Hutchins. I don't know if you remember me. I'm Agent Bryant's partner. I need to speak with you. Please contact me." He also left his secret FBI phone number.

What the heck is going on? Didn't they get the memo? Hello, I no longer work for the DA's office. Criminy. Can't they just leave me alone?

Stomping to the front hall, I pawed through my overstocked handbag in search of my cell phone, finally dumping the mess onto the floor. Wallet, Kleenex, lipstick, mirror, comb, lotion and my hot pink cell phone dropped out of the bottom. I scrolled through the incoming numbers. Sure enough, two blocked numbers with unknown names were listed. I supposed I should feel special. Not one, but two, FBI agents provided me with their super-secret numbers.

I sat back on my heels. My jaw clenched and it was a close call to keep from chucking my phone at the wall. I needed to cool off, and instead of giving into childishness that would cost me a new phone, I headed upstairs to take a shower. While I showered I pondered why two FBI agents were trying to contact me regarding the Colquitt case. My biggest case and eventually the reason I left the law. I didn't trust Agent Bryant because he was the reason my case never went to trial.

Well … that was unfair. I'm sure it was some suit further up the food chain that made the decision, but Bryant was the messenger and the only one I dealt with personally, so my anger and frustration were justifiably aimed at him.

I had a vague recollection of meeting Agent Hutchins, a tall, dark-skinned gentleman who wore the requisite black FBI suit. He remained in the background and allowed Agent Bryant to do all the talking. Hutchins showed up for the initial meeting, but I didn't recall seeing him after that. I didn't have anything against Agent Hutchins.

By the time I was dressed, I concluded I should return Special Agent Hutchins' call. Just to make sure I wasn't missing anything important. However, I decided to put it off until the weekend for two reasons. One, I needed to focus on work without what was sure to be, a distraction. Two, I figured it would irritate both Agent Hutchins and Agent Bryant to get a call back on the weekend. I couldn't pass up a chance to aggravate Special Agent Bryant. Having determined a course of action, I rolled out to face another busy day at work.

Chapter Ten

It was after three when I arrived home from the library on Saturday. I dropped everything in the front hall and went directly to the kitchen to fix myself a tall cold glass of iced tea. Taking my drink into the family room, I flopped down on the couch to unwind for a few minutes and allow the tension and kinks in my neck to ease. I kicked off my high-heeled sandals, propped my feet up then allowed my eyes to drift shut. I told myself it was only for a few seconds, and the FBI phone call could wait another minute or two.

When I awoke, the sun slanted through the windows. I looked around in disoriented confusion. The clock on the cable box read five sixteen. *Danny*! I jumped up, my vision swam and I sat back down. *Whoops, head rush.* As my head and eyes cleared, I realized I wasn't expected to meet Danny until six. I still had time to call the FBI and freshen up for dinner.

I stared at the cordless phone for a few minutes and tried to determine what I'd say.

"Hi, Agent Hutchins. What can I do for you?" No, too helpful. I wasn't the FBI's doormat.

"Hi, Agent Hutchins. I got your message and thought I should let you know I no longer work for the DA's office." No, too much information. They were the FBI. They probably already knew I wasn't a lawyer anymore. Hell, they probably knew the color underwear I bought from Belk's last week.

"Hi, Agent Hutchins. This is Cara Baker returning your call." Yes, that was better, businesslike and not too forthcoming. I dialed the phone number and waited while it rang. It was my lucky day. Voice mail picked up and I was able to leave my succinct message guilt free. *I've done my due diligence. The ball is in their court.* Now I was ready for a nice dinner with my very handsome neighbor.

At precisely six, Danny rapped on my front door. He wore his usual khaki shorts and paired them with an emerald polo. The color accented his arresting green eyes, and his spicy fresh scent seeped into my senses. I gave an enthusiastic smile and invited him in.

He carried a grocery bag of, I assumed, our dinner.

"Do we need to put anything in the refrigerator or oven?" I led the way into the kitchen.

Reaching into the brown sack, he pulled out a bagged salad and handed it to me, "Go ahead and put this in the fridge."

"What else is in the bag?" I tried to peek inside.

He folded down the top and possessively held it against his chest. "No peeking. It's a surprise."

I rolled my eyes and made a grab for it. "I hate surprises. Just let me see."

Danny pulled the bag out of my reach. "You know what they say about curiosity and the cat, right?"

"Ugh, I don't like cats. Fine. I'll wait for my surprise." Crossing my arms, I sulked.

"You know you're cute when you pout."

"I'm not pouting."

"Sure you are and it's cute. You're lip kind of sticks out …"

I rolled my eyes again and uncrossed my arms. "Okay, professor, so where should we do this? Kitchen? Parlor? Family room?"

"Why don't we sit down in the family room and face each other on the couch?"

I led the way and plopped down on one end of my comfy, beige micro suede couch.

Danny followed, crossing in front of the coffee table, and sat at the other end. He turned to face me.

"What do I need to do? Should I touch you or do you need to touch me?"

"It will be easier if I make the initial contact. If you would, just hold out your hand."

Slowly, I reached out with my right hand, hesitated and then pulled back. "Before we start, maybe you should tell me what your frame of mind is. If it's possible for you to transfer your mood, I think I should know if you're feeling angry or upset or something ... Is that rude?"

Danny shook his head. "No, you're absolutely right. After all, you're offering to be my guinea pig. You should go into this with your eyes wide open." He paused and looked at me in consternation. "I'm not angry. I'd say my mood is excited, and a little apprehensive."

"Okay, I can handle that. To be honest, I'm kind of excited about this too. It's an adventure." I closed my eyes, took a deep breath and stuck out my hand. It was probably only ten seconds, but it seemed like forever as I sat, waiting for Danny's touch.

His breath picked up, his shirt rustled as he moved and finally a warm hand softly closed over mine.

My heart sped up. A sizzling heat flowed up my arm and headed south to my belly. *Holy cow, he's not blocking me. This is pretty cool.*

"Cara," Danny murmured, "you can open your eyes now."

I slowly opened one eye and squinted at our hands.

"It's working, I'm blocking you."

I gulped eyes wide. "You ... you are? You're sure you're blocking me?"

He smiled and nodded. "Yes."

"Are you sure? How do you know for sure?" My voice warbled in panic. If he wasn't blocking me, then I was getting hot and bothered all on my own.

"I know because I can feel it. You'd also be able to tell by looking at me."

"What do you mean? How can I tell by looking at you?"

The question seemed to make Danny uncomfortable. He broke contact, readjusted his position and looked away, staring over the back of the sofa.

I felt bereft when he took his hand away, yet I was still hot under the collar.

"The good doctor told me, when I'm not blocking, my eyes change."

"Really?" My attention diverted from the sexual attraction. "That's fascinating. Do they change color? Like to blue or brown? Or purple? Do your eyes become purple?" I enthusiastically bounced on the couch.

"No, they don't change color. I guess they become a brighter green." Danny didn't seem to share my enthusiasm.

"Cool! Maybe I'll get to see that sometime."

He regarded me with a puzzled expression. "Cara..." He paused. He seemed to be fighting a strong emotion. "You are an unusual woman."

The shrill ring of the phone broke the tension and allowed me to cool down. I reached over and snatched the handset off the coffee table, looking at the caller ID. It was unknown. Of course, the FBI, with terrible timing, was returning my call. "It's no one important. They can leave a message."

After two more rings, voice mail picked up. I turned back to Danny when we heard the muffled singsong of my cell, coming from the front hall, where it was buried in my purse.

Danny's eyebrow went up, "Are you sure you don't need to get that?"

Grimacing, I nodded. "I'm sure. They'll leave a message."

The ringing stopped. Danny's head tilted to the side and he wore a concerned look. "Is it something you want to talk about?"

"Definitely not. Besides we're here to focus on you. So, we should try again." I held out my hand imperiously.

Danny waited with patience.

My neck began to burn but I remained mute. Explaining calls from the FBI wasn't a road I'd willingly go down. I dropped my hand and placed it in my lap as the silence continued.

"Why don't you try initiating the contact?" Danny leaned toward me with an open palm and an expectant look.

This time I kept my eyes open and watched warily as I placed my palm in his large one. His fingers gradually curled around mine.

Heat and a gentle tickle ran down the back of my spine. There was no change in Danny's eye color, but his pupils dilated. "How easy is it to block me? Are you working hard?"

"It's not too bad. I still have to think about it, unlike when I work with Jeff, but it's not a physical effort for me. It's more of a mental one."

"How do you do it while we're talking? Don't you find it distracting?"

"Excellent question." He paused. "I suppose, through my work with Jeff, I've trained myself to do the two things at once." He paused again. "In the beginning I had to have absolute silence so I could concentrate on blocking him out, but as we continued to work, it began to be something I did in the background, like chewing gum. You can still walk and talk while chomping on a stick without actually thinking about making your jaw muscles move up and down. Right? Does that make any sense?"

It did make sense in a roundabout sort of way. "Yes, I suppose so."

The doorbell rang. I dropped Danny's hand like a hot potato and jumped up. "What is with people?" I scowled. The thought flew through my mind there was a possibility Special Agent Bryant would bypass the phones and come knocking on my door. His timing couldn't have been worse.

"That's probably dinner," Danny said in a neutral voice.

"Dinner?" I looked at him, baffled.

"Yes, I'll just take care of the delivery guy, shall I?"

While Danny went to the front door to pay for the delivery, I tried to pull myself together.

Good Lord, what's wrong with me? The FBI boys aren't going to haul themselves all the way down to South Carolina to talk to me. Get a grip.

Danny strolled into the kitchen carrying a large white box with Pisano's Pizza Parlor stamped upon the top. I'd passed Pisano's a few times but hadn't taken the time to eat there.

Danny opened the box with a flourish, and I was hit with the tantalizing smell of warm bread, garlic, melted cheese, spicy meats and tomatoes. The pizza was topped with olives, green peppers and onions on one half. The other half was a meat lover's dream with pepperoni, ham and sausage.

"The pizza looks fabulous. I've never eaten at Pisano's."

"Then you're in for a real treat. I didn't know what you'd like so I split the difference." Danny opened the refrigerator and pulled out the salad. "Do you have a bowl for this?"

I reached into a cupboard and handed him a large white serving bowl. "Corkscrew?" He pulled a bottle of red wine out of the grocery bag.

I fished around in a drawer and came up with a silver corkscrew and then reached into an overhead cabinet for plates and glasses. While Danny wrestled with the bottle of Chianti, I tossed the salad and set the table.

"Thank you for taking care of dinner. I haven't had pizza in ages." We sat across from each other.

"You're welcome. *Slainte!*" Danny toasted and dug into a meaty slice.

We both ate silently, enjoying the fattening pleasures of a gooey slice of pizza. The full-bodied Chianti slid smoothly down my throat.

"So, who did you think was at the door?" Danny inquired nonchalantly.

I froze mid-bite, caught off guard. Shrugging, I feigned aloofness. "No one specific."

Danny took an unhurried bite of pizza, slowly chewed and swallowed. "Cara, please don't lie to me. I'm not stupid. Even without feeling your emotions, I can tell something's bothering you. It has something to do with those phone calls. Is someone harassing you?"

I cringed. He was right. I shouldn't lie to him. It'd been a long time since I'd allowed anyone into my private life. I was making new friends in Denton, but they didn't know anything about my former life in Pittsburgh. I'd gone out of my way to keep conversations focused on my life here. Because I worked at the library, everyone assumed that was what I did back in Pennsylvania. Only Greta knew I'd been a lawyer. When she hired me and asked why I wanted to become a librarian, I gave her a sanitized version of my life-changing needs. Yet, here was Danny, sharing the most secret and personal part of his life with me. I should reciprocate, but I just couldn't. Call it denial. Call it cowardice. I wasn't going to taint my new life by digging back into the unhappiness of my old one. I'd compartmentalized it that way—new and old. I was determined to stick with new. New made me happy. Old angered me. Old was filled with guilt and pain and regrets.

Danny watched me with a placid expression during my internal struggle.

"No one's harassing me." I exhaled.

"But something is wrong."

I didn't deny it. "Here the two of us are—you're the one seeing the shrink and I'm the one acting like a lunatic."

"Look, you don't have to talk to me, but I just watched a number of emotions play over your face, and it seems like you've got your own demons. If you don't want to talk to me, you should talk to someone. Maybe one of your girlfriends can help." He gazed at me with concern, his brow furrowed and mouth turned down.

"I appreciate that. Don't worry." I forced a smile. "It'll all work out. It's just that ... I need to have what is due to be an unpleasant conversation with someone from my past. And I want to do it on my time."

Danny studied me and then reached across to grip my hand. "I care about what happens to you, Cara. Remember that. If you ever need anything, I'll be here for you."

"Thanks." His concern touched me. "Hey, you're blocking me."

"So I am." Danny grinned.

We finished our dinner in comfortable silence. My mind wandered from one topic to another, as thought processes often did. There were still details that needed to be ironed out before the end of summer and checklists ran through my head. All of the food vendors were booked; a week before the event I'd need to follow up. We were renting tables, chairs, glassware, silverware and linens for the night, and I needed to book a meeting with our contact, Sylvia, at Charleston Events. The library received some large ticket items for the auction, such as trips, jewelry and Beau's sporting goods. With the hope of bringing in more money, Greta decided we'd have a live auction later in the evening. George offered to be the auctioneer. I needed to see about getting him a microphone and a podium. Maybe I could rent them from Charleston Events as well.

I must have been staring off into space for quite a while, because I came back with a jolt.

Danny snapped his fingers in front of my face, "Earth to Cara."

I refocused on him.

"What were you thinking about? You were a million miles away."

"I don't know if I've told you, but we're having an auction to raise money for the Denton Regional Library at the end of the summer. Black-tie affair with all the trimmings. I'm in charge of the food."

"Yes, I heard about it from Jeff. Thanks for reminding me." Danny dug into his back pocket and produced a wrinkled white envelope; he placed it on the table between us. "Here you go."

"What's this? Are you buying tickets for the auction? Will you come?" I seized the envelope with excitement.

"No. I'm not ready for that. Too many people." He shook his head.

I deflated slightly. Of course, the auction was going to be a crush of bodies, making it likely people would be bumping up against one another. There was no way Danny could get through the night without shaking hands with people. I'm sure he wasn't ready to block large crowds.

"It's a donation."

"Thanks. Are you donating some of your games?" Looking down, I ripped open the envelope and pulled out a check. I was struck speechless. When I found my voice, I croaked, "Holy cow, Danny! This is for five thousand dollars! This is a Gold Level Sponsor. Is it from your company?"

He shrugged. "Whatever you think is best. Using my company name would make it a little more anonymous."

I scrutinized him, unsure of his true wishes. His face remained purposefully nonchalant. "Do you want the anonymity of your company's name? If it's a personal donation, we'll print your name in a number of different places, from signs to the program. I'll do whatever you want."

"I'm not looking for glory, and I've been living with anonymity in the community for a long time." He hesitated. "I think I'd like you to use the company name."

I rolled the information around in my head. A five thousand-dollar donation out of the blue was sure to cause questions. "What if Greta asks about the company? Can I tell her?"

"If you feel it's necessary. Tell her what you think is best."

I thought I'd like to shout from the rooftop my upstairs neighbor was not only a gorgeous hunk of a man who made me think dirty thoughts, he was also remarkably giving and kind.

However, considering Danny's reluctance to move around in public, it would probably be best to provide him anonymity. "Thank you. This is very generous. I just wish you could be there."

He sighed with regret. "Me too."

Chapter Eleven

Sunday morning I awoke with renewed energy and a determination to tackle painting one of the guest rooms. I'd decided to paint it a medium blue with gray undertones and planned to decorate with yellow and red accents. I'd used an antique quilt, inherited from my grandmother, as inspiration. Currently, the only furniture in the room was the double bed, a nightstand and a redwood rocking chair. It didn't take me long to move these pieces into the center and lay down my painting tarp. The next step was one I dreaded with a capital D. Taping. It took me as long to tape as it did to paint. Unfortunately, I wasn't one of those professionals who painted so cleanly they didn't need tape. I was a messy painter. Don't get me wrong … when the walls were finished, they'd look outstanding. However, I would have paint in my hair and on my arms, face and pants, and generally at some point, I'd actually step in the paint, leaving little blue footprints behind. Therefore, taping was an unwanted necessity. I'd also learned to tie back my hair with a scarf, in order to reduce time during the post-painting shower. To break the monotony, I put on my headphones and cranked the music.

My mind wandered as I worked the roller up and down the walls in a rhythmic motion. Agent Hutchins had been the one to return my call last night while Danny and I ate dinner. He'd left messages on my cell and home numbers, requesting I return his call as soon as possible, or in FBI speak ASAP. I decided to procrastinate and contact him later. After all, there was no need to ruin my day off. I worked steadily through the morning, painting two coats and was about to reach the "'stand back and admire" stage when there was a knock. I stood at the top of the stairs about to head down, when I realized the knocking wasn't coming from the front door.

Danny's muffled voice came from behind the door connecting my hallway to the shared alcove and his stairwell. "Cara, hello, are you home?" Knock, knock.

"Coming!" Unlocking the door, I swung it open. Danny leaned against the doorjamb, dressed in navy shorts, a white polo and sneakers. His hair was still damp, either from sweat or from a recent shower.

I took a whiff and smelled the clean fresh aroma of Irish Spring (my new favorite scent). The hair was damp for the latter reason. "What's up?"

His jade eyes raked my paint-stained appearance. A sly smirk formed and his eyebrows rose. "I'm here to shanghai you for the afternoon and, judging by your appearance, none too soon. What on earth have you been doing? An art project? Is it something kinky? You look like you've been rolling in paint." He tugged playfully at my ponytail.

He was right. I let out a sigh with my bottom lip, blowing the bangs out of my eyes. "I'll have you know, I just finished painting the guest room."

"I hope it came out looking better than you."

"Hey! I resent that remark. Why don't you take a look?" I scowled and with my best Vanna White impression, gestured toward the room.

Sticking his hands in his pockets, Danny ambled down the hall and let out a low whistle as he stepped into the room.

I tapped my foot impatiently and waited for his verdict.

"Did you mean to get paint all over the closet doors like that?"

"What!" I ran into the room, practically knocking him out of the way. "Where?"

He let out a guffaw. "Gotcha."

"That is so not funny. You about gave me a heart attack." I gave him a playful shove, making sure to avoid contact with his skin.

"This looks good. Have you been working on it all

morning?" He toured the room and stopped next to the windows.

"Yes. I'd just finished when you knocked."

"Then this is perfect timing. Go get changed. We're going out." Danny made shooing motions with his hands.

"Going out?" I laughed. "Where are we going?"

"It's a surprise. I'm driving you out to one of my favorite spots."

"That's funny. You're driving." I snorted sarcastically. "What are you driving, the lawn mower?"

"My car, of course."

That shut me up. I blinked. "You have a car?"

"Yup."

"How come I've never seen it? You don't park it in the carport."

"There's an alley behind the fence." He pointed. "Across the alley is a garage I use"

"A garage? Seriously?"

"Seriously."

"Huh. I didn't know this house came with a garage."

"It doesn't. The garage officially belongs to the neighbor behind you, Bobby Lee Custis. I rent the garage from him. It's on the far backside of his lot and he doesn't have a need for it. Now stop arguing and go get changed."

"Okay. Time out." I made a T with my hands. "First, I need to strip the tape, tidy up and then shower before stepping a foot outside of this house. I mean, look at me." I spread my arms wide to reiterate my paint-covered appearance.

He crossed his arms with a heavy sigh. "You don't make it easy for a guy to kidnap you for an afternoon."

I laughed and shook my head.

"Okay, we'll compromise. You go shower, and I'll strip the tape."

"Oh, but you don't..."

"Cara. Do you seriously think I'm not competent enough to strip tape?"

"No, but…"

"That's right. No buts. Go. Get. In. The. Shower." He clapped his hands for emphasis. Giving up, I shrugged and headed down the hall toward my bedroom.

"And if you're not ready in twenty minutes, I'm coming in to get you." Danny hollered the ultimatum out the door.

I squealed and hotfooted it to my room. I wasn't sure if he was serious, but I wasn't ready to find out. Just to be safe, I locked the door.

It was closer to thirty minutes before Danny knocked on my bedroom door. "All right, Baker! I've stripped your tape, tidied up and given you an extra ten minutes. If you're not out in fifteen seconds, I'm busting down this door."

"Don't get your pants in a wad, Johnson! I'm coming." I whipped open my bedroom door in the midst of pulling my hair into a damp ponytail, since Mr. Impatient wouldn't give me enough time to completely dry it. My feet were bare, and I wore navy shorts and a white T-shirt.

"What should I wear on my feet? Sandals? Flip-flops? Tennis shoes? Are we going to be walking?" I questioned with cheeky impertinence.

"Cute, Cara." Danny gestured to our matching outfits. "Sneakers will be fine."

In the shower, I'd realized I wore a huge grin and felt exhilarated by our back-and-forth banter. Excitement and anticipation flowed through my body, and there was a pronounced spring in my step. I seized my handbag and followed Danny through his stairwell landing and down the back staircase. He locked up behind us.

"Is your front door locked?"

I nodded.

We traversed the backyard and exited through the gate. Across the alley, and twenty feet to my right, stood a small yellow brick garage. Its black door faced the alley.

"Stay here. The garage is too tight for you to get in. I'll pull the car out."

Danny unlocked the garage door and headed into the

darkness. After a minute, there was a deep rumble as the engine caught, and Danny slowly backed out a low-slung sports car. Yet one more thing I was unprepared for. My jaw hung open as the car growled to a stop next to me. The vehicle was deep blue with luscious curves built for wind resistance, wide high-performance tires and bubble-covered headlights.

The door opened; Danny leaned across the center console. "C'mon, get in."

I gingerly sat down. The plush leather bucket seat hugged me close, and the door closed with a quiet thump. The engine rumbled as Danny expertly shifted into gear and rolled down the street. The dashboard lit up, full of gadgets, buttons and screens; it reminded me of a rocket ship. The car was a two-seater convertible, but Danny had left the top up. With wide eyes, I watched his profile. He exuded a sense of smugness, and a playful curve drew up the side of his mouth.

He jumped at my voice, as I accused loudly in the small space, "What the hell is this? This isn't a car! This…this is a luxury driving experience! This is something you only see in the movies. They don't even make commercials for this type of car."

Danny glanced my way. "Is there something wrong with the car?"

"There's nothing wrong with this car. This … this … is a car men dream about buying when they hit the jackpot." I slit my eyes at him. "Did *you* win the lottery?"

"Nope, not a lottery winner."

"What is this, anyway? I know it's not a Ferrari, because that's *my* dream car. Is it a Lamborghini?" I asked pointing to the trident-shaped logo on the steering wheel.

"It's a Maserati."

"Italian?"

"Yes."

I let that sink in for a few beats. "Who are you? Are you related to some wealthy family? You know the type. When they speak your name, they say, 'oh, yes, the Boston Johnsons' in snooty accents."

"Nope. Not related to a rich family. I'm related to Beverly and Sam Johnson, retired and currently living in Jacksonville, Florida. My dad was a CPA and my mom was an elementary school teacher." He took a breath. "Look, I'm single. I don't spend money going out. I don't have debt. My expenses are low. My business is doing well, and I like to drive fast. So, I afford myself this luxury."

"Humph!" I crossed my arms and shifted in my seat.

Silence reigned. Once again, I was rethinking my preconceived notions about Danny. This was a very cool car, and I kind of wished Danny would let me drive. It made a quiet, smooth hum as Danny sped along the highway heading east. The leather bucket seats were supple and smooth against my skin, and even though the car was compact, there was ample legroom. Danny's long legs seemed to fit comfortably as he drove about fifteen miles over the speed limit.

"So, what model of Maserati is this? It looks like a race car. I love the color." I ran my hand along the chrome and blue dashboard.

"Thank you. The car was custom built to my specs. The color is called Blu Mediterraneo. This particular model, the MC Stradale, is their racing vehicle. It has a four point seven liter V-eight engine and three electronic driving modes—auto, sport and race." He said with pride. "You can purchase a special racing package and the car will come outfitted with four-point harness seat belts, a fire extinguisher, a roll cage and a Maserati racing uniform with a suit, gloves and helmet. Because it's their racing vehicle, this model doesn't usually come with a convertible top. I had it custom made. It may be the only one in existence."

My eyes glazed over during the vehicular lecture and I cut to the chase, "How fast does it go?"

"Very fast."

"How fast have you gone?"

Danny gave me a wry glance. "Faster than I should have."

"Are we going to go fast today?"

"Not today."

"You're no fun."

Danny shook his head at my feigned pout.

"Have you ever taken it out on a race track?"

"No. I'd like to, but with the singular changes I've made by installing the convertible top, I doubt a race track would allow it. Without a roll cage, racing may be too hazardous."

I breathed deeply, inhaling the faint scent of the leather seats. "Daniel Johnson, you are full of surprises."

"Is that good or bad?" He looked at me from the corner of his eyes.

"Good. Today it's definitely good." I relaxed and determined to enjoy the ride in this magnificent vehicle.

Once we could see the water, Danny slowed and turned north on a two-lane road that alternately hugged the coastline and wove through small seaside towns. About an hour later, he wound us through a state wildlife refuge, taking a low bridge over swamplands. Eventually, he parked on the side of the road near a barely discernible wooded path.

"Here we are." A blast of muggy heat hit us as we got out. Danny locked the car and started walking through the forest along a tree-lined path.

"Is the car going to be all right here?" I skeptically glanced around.

He looked back. "Cara, it's a car. It doesn't need a babysitter. It'll be fine."

"If you say so." I shrugged. "If this were my car, I'd never leave it parked just anywhere. You know, anything can happen."

"I was that way at first but, after a few months, you get used to it. Now, come on. There's something I want you to see."

I followed Danny into the woods, and after a few minutes of walking, I could hear the whisper of the ocean. The path came to an abrupt end. A rocky outcropping with scrubby underbrush overlooked the water. A salty offshore breeze blew across my body, making the summer heat and humidity bearable. I stepped to the edge of the boulders, where the granite cliff dropped away thirty feet or more. The tide was high and the ocean beat against the rocks, its timeless song a never-ending constant as the waves rolled in and out. To the left, sylvan woods grew directly up to the cliff line, with small breaks of brush and sandy beach grasslands. On the right, the shore curved in toward the water, where a coved marina nestled in a small seaside town.

Raising a hand to shade my eyes, I gazed off into the distance and watched a ship move slowly along the horizon. "How often do you come here?"

"I try to get out here at least once a month, sometimes more. I've been busy developing a new game and haven't been out since March. Right before you moved in, as a matter of fact." He stuck his hands in his pockets and kicked at a stone. "I find the ocean takes me to a … Zen-like place."

The narrow path we'd hiked was overgrown with scrub and vegetation and displayed little use. "Does anyone else ever come here?"

"I've never seen anyone else, which is why I like it." Danny shrugged, his stance erect and stiff, watching my reaction.

The rugged beauty of the remote spot enveloped me. I plopped down on a rock, crossed my legs and closed my eyes. The breeze blew the wispy hairs around my face. The ocean waves sounded peaceful and calm as they rolled over the rocks below and, in the distance, a seagull called. Danny's body warmed me as he took a seat on the adjacent rock.

Chapter Twelve

We remained on our perch, alternately talking and lapsing into silence to stare at the water as the day passed. The shadows grew long. I talked about work, my decorative plans for the house, and my parents' trek across the country in their Winnebago.

Danny told me about the game he was developing and growing up in Arlington, Virginia. He spoke briefly about his sister and parents.

It was peaceful and serene. It was comfortable. It felt right. This was the reason I left Pittsburgh. I longed to harness this perfection of tranquility, to bottle it up so I could take it out when the stresses of life bore down.

Unfortunately, as much as we would like to stop time, real-life needs intruded. In this case, my right leg and bum fell asleep. I stood to stretch and work the feeling back into my numb limbs. Joints cracked and my stomach grumbled.

Danny stood up laughing. "I need to feed you. Do you like crabs?"

"Sure."

"I know a good place."

His warm hand wrapped around mine as we wandered back to the car. I was exceedingly aware of his palm snug against mine. It made my belly flutter and my heart race like a jackrabbit. He must be blocking me and I was glad he couldn't feel my overreaction to his simple act. We arrived back at the car, which, to my relief, looked none the worse for wear. Danny opened the passenger door for me and then paused and blocked my entrance. Holding the fancy key at eye-level, he swung it back and forth.

"Do you want to drive?"

My breath caught, but I stopped myself from grabbing it out of his hand. "I don't know if I should."

"Scared?"

"I'm just not sure I should drive such a costly vehicle."

"You know how to drive stick right?"

"Yes. Of course."

"Then what's the problem?"

"Danny," I said as if addressing a small child. "This is a very expensive car."

"C'mon, Cara, you know you want to. You're practically drooling. Don't worry. You won't wreck it."

"What if I do?"

"You won't."

I chewed my bottom lip and waffled.

He flashed a smile at me and threw down, "Are you chicken?"

I rolled my eyes. "I'm not chicken."

"Yes, you are." He flapped his arms. "Chicken. Bak, bak, bak." To my astonishment, Danny danced around imitating a deranged winged animal. "Bak, *baak. Chick-en!*"

I snatched the keys from his hand. "Gimme those." I bit my cheek to keep from laughing, while stalking around to the driver's side.

I had to adjust the seat forward so I could reach the pedals and reposition the mirrors.

Danny put the top down and the car rumbled to life under my hands. Even in first gear I could feel the muscle of the powerful V-8 engine vibrating beneath me. It felt erotic and sexy, driving with the wind caressing my hair. It disappointed me to discover the crab shack, Danny directed me to, lay only fifteen minutes away, tucked behind a small-town marina on the river. I impressed myself and Danny by parallel parking on the first try. After putting the top back up, I was sorely tempted to hold onto the Maserati keys. *It's such a sweet ride.* In the end, I returned them to Danny, dropping them in his open palm.

"See, I told you, you weren't going to wreck. Did you enjoy driving?"

"Absolutely. Now I'm wondering what line of business I can get into that would afford me a car like this." My fingers drifted across the hood. "Perhaps, bank robbery?"

"That's one way."

"See!" I gave Danny's arm a light punch. "You're a bad influence, encouraging me into a life of crime."

"No way. I just let you drive my car. I said nothing about crime. You can't pin that on me." He shook his head.

We'd arrived at what I could only say was a true shack. It was a place I would never, in my life, voluntarily walk into on my own. The restaurant was built on pilings and jutted out over the water, its wood siding gray and weatherworn. It looked decrepit, and I was a little afraid it would collapse and fall into the river. The door hung drunkenly on its hinges and creaked as Danny opened it for me. The smell of steamed seafood hit me, along with the tangy under scent of lemons. When I hesitated to enter, Danny placed his hand on the small of my back to guide me in. My eyes adjusted to the gloom and found a sign in front of me with arrows: to the left for takeout customers, the right arrow said "Seat Yourself."

Six square tables, all empty, were covered with butcher paper. The tables sat four, with scarred wooden chairs surrounding them. I chose a table by a relatively clean window that overlooked the water. Danny sat next to me with his back to the window and faced the interior of the establishment. The restaurant had dark wood paneling. Lantern sconces hung throughout the room. The décor consisted of netting strung along the walls with primary-colored plastic lobsters and starfish caught up in it. A captain's wheel with additional lighting hung from the ceiling, while two fans lethargically circulated the air.

I leaned toward Danny and whispered. "Is the food okay here?"

He responded at full volume. "Best crab around. How many should we order? Two dozen? Three?"

"Uh, two sounds fine with me." Concerned with the sanitation of the food, I didn't want to encourage Danny to order too much.

A reedy, aging waitress dressed in short shorts and a too-tight Captain Buck's Crab Shack T-shirt came over and introduced herself as Carla. She took our order and disappeared back into the nether-regions of the kitchen to get our drinks. Twenty minutes later she brought out an overflowing tray of steamy blue claw crabs and proceeded to dump them directly onto the papered table. The hushpuppies and cornbread arrived in a red plastic basket, melted butter in plastic bowls, and Carla doled out crab crackers, mallets, picks, and tiny forks.

"Do you folks need anything else?" She rasped in her gravelly smoker's voice. Danny eyed me. His eyebrow raised in a silent question.

I shook my head. "Nope. Looks like it's all here."

"Let me know if you need anything."

By this time another couple had arrived and sat down at the table farthest away from us. Carla headed over to take their order.

Again, I leaned toward Danny. "Do you think that couple knows something we don't? Or did they take the table closest to the door in order to make a quick escape when this joint falls in the water?"

Danny gave a hearty laugh. "You worry too much. Try the crab." He held out a buttery portion.

So, I did and was pleasantly surprised. The crabs were succulent and flavorful, and the cornbread was moist with a touch of sweetness. Over the next hour, Danny and I cracked, sucked, picked and peeled two dozen crabs. I ate half a dozen, while Danny packed away the rest. There were only two tables filled, but the takeout counter ran a steady business.

I sat back to digest the filling dinner. "Danny, why will you come out in public here, but not at home in Denton?"

"It took me a long time to come in here," he mused, glancing around. "I watched it for months before I came in. I know when this place isn't very busy. I watch the people who arrive. I never walk in or out through the door when there are other people in the vicinity. I sit with my back to the wall and out of the walking paths to reduce the chance of someone touching me."

I remained silent.

"I know it makes me sound like a spy or something, but you have to realize whenever I go out in public, every move I make is aimed at the least amount of contact. If I could fade into the walls, I would," he said in a matter-of-fact tone.

I didn't know how to answer. His confession made me realize how he isolated himself so he wouldn't hurt anyone, and conversely so no one was allowed into his psyche.

"I wish there was something I could say or do that would change your situation. I can research the area restaurants and do what you did here."

Danny struggled to produce a wan smile. "Thank you, Cara, but I couldn't ask you to do that. You're doing enough as it is. Not many women would offer to be my guinea pig."

Danny proffered the Maserati keys, but by the time we left Buck's, the sun had set and I declined. The ride home remained quiet. I think we were both pondering the day. It had been perfect. As much as I'd enjoyed my dates with Jeff, they didn't compare to the comfort and underlying excitement Danny and I shared together. I felt as though every experience was heightened just being in his presence. He made me laugh with his wicked, dry sense of humor, sending zingers out when I least expected. I made him laugh. He found me quirky.

Even so, I sensed he was waiting for something. I believed he waited for one of two things, either for me to freak out and run screaming, or his greater fear, for his blocking to stop working when he touched me. I wasn't worried about his blocking. He hadn't shown anger or depression in front of me. Actually, I sort of hoped he'd screw up and transfer some of his emotions. Then I'd know if he was as crazy attracted to me as I was to him.

We arrived home close to eleven. Danny stopped outside the garage to allow me to get out and drove in while I waved a sad good-bye to the Maserati. After locking up the garage, we meandered through the backyard in an effort to spin out the evening. Eventually, we ended up on the dark back patio. The moonlight shone down through the trees, reflecting off the glass doors. My senses were heightened. Our breathing and the thrum of my heartbeat was loud in my ears. I turned. Danny was so close; his body heat radiated. Hunger bounced between the two of us.

Danny's intense gaze held mine and then dropped lower to my mouth. I might not be able to feel his emotions, but I could tell where his mind was headed. My lips parted in anticipation.

His mouth was soft and insistent, lighting the slow burning embers of passion I'd struggled with all afternoon. My arms snaked around his neck as I plastered myself against his solid, warm muscular chest. His hand gripped my shirt at the small of my back, pulling me close, as his other hand gently cupped my cheek. He nipped along my jawline. My legs turned rubbery and I hung on for dear life as his lips moved to nibble my ear. My nipples hardened to pebbles and a rush of warmth filled my feminine core. I felt the change when he returned to attack my mouth. Suddenly, a blazing frenzy of desire shot through my body like a lightning bolt; the electricity flowed all the way to my fingertips, making them tingle. I moaned and took short panting breaths. Wrapping one of my legs around Danny's waist, I pushed my yearning mound against his hardness and thought I'd orgasm right then and there.

Danny seized my upper arms and shoved me away. He broke contact and stepped farther back, creating a vast gulf between us. The passion still burned through me, but where his body had been quickly cooled. I whimpered, thrown off balance by his unexpected departure. My wobbly legs betrayed me by giving out and I plopped down on the ground.

I was glad I had been warned. Danny's eyes glowed, an eerie bright, almost iridescent green. They were so bright I could see them in the dark. My breathing rasped heavily in my ears, and I realized that somewhere along the way, Danny had stopped blocking me, but with the desire coursing through my body, I was having trouble wrapping my head around the ramifications. His chest heaved and his breaths came out in ragged gasps. He, too, sat down, staggering slightly to one of the deck chairs, putting at least six feet of distance between us.

I placed my head between my legs to slow my panting.

"I can't begin to tell you how sorry I am," his rough voice grated out.

My eyes popped up.

He ran his hands through his hair. Frustration emanated off him. "I should never have touched you," he vehemently whispered.

I cleared my throat. "Danny, we're both consenting adults with no attachments."

"Cara, you do realize I stopped blocking you, don't you? I couldn't block you. I lost control." He hung his head in shame.

"Yes, I understand that—"

"I should be shot. I should never have talked Jeff into introducing us."

"Danny, it's okay. You're being too hard on yourself."

"Am I? Am I *really*? Cara … I've been coveting you since the first day I saw you standing next to that beat-up Honda staring at the house with longing. You don't understand how I wanted you to look at me with that same longing. Then you sat here at this table," he banged his hand on the wrought iron, "talking with the realtors about the tenant agreement. You were so reasonable while the blonde went on and on and you defended my living here. I called Jeff as soon as you left and told him to release any information he wanted. To reassure you so you'd buy this house and I could be closer to you." He paused, staring into the dark house, his voice low and husky. "I watched you leave every morning and waited for your return. I watched you wander through the gardens picking flowers, wishing I could come down and walk with you. Tell you about the garden. Touch you." He got up to pace. "Getting notes and food from you became the highlight of my days. I agonized over what to write. I bought the Waterford vase for you, because I wanted to give you something beautiful, because you are beautiful and deserve beautiful things." His tortured gaze returned to mine. "Do you know why I finally had Jeff introduce us?"

I shook my head, mute.

"You came out one evening in a racy summer dress, showing your long legs, wearing sexy sandals with your hair pulled back, and I knew you had a hot date. You hopped in the Mini and sped off with a wave. I was green with jealousy. I couldn't stand the thought of some stranger touching you, hearing you laugh, enjoying your splendor. That's when I knew. I had to throw my hat in the ring. I called Jeff that night and asked him to set it up immediately." He dropped his head into his hands. "I was there just around the side of the carport waiting until you returned to make sure you didn't bring your date home with you. I don't know what I would have done if you had," he said in a wretched voice.

Danny was talking about the night Mandy and I went to Charleston to eat at The Chowder House. He thought I'd had a hot date. I could have laughed, but the air was filled with a fierce tension, and I didn't want Danny to think I was laughing at him.

"It's wrong. I should have left well enough alone."

"Why is it wrong?"

"Look at me." He indicated his face. "I'm a freak."

"Don't say that! Don't call yourself that."

"I am. This … this … curse will never go away."

"Danny, stop!" I held up my hand in an effort to make him halt the verbal abuse. "Listen to me." I stood and began to pace. "I've had the most wonderful day. I've laughed until my sides hurt. I've experienced tranquility, and comfort, and the grandeur of nature." I counted off on my fingers. "I ate a delicious crab dinner in a crappy run-down shack that I thought might collapse on us. I've been allowed to drive one of the most expensive sports cars on the road. I've had an amazing day. And to top it off, I've just experienced the most erotic encounter I've ever had in my life." I pointed at him, "All of it with *you*."

"But my abilities can be dangerous."

"Pish."

"Pish?"

"Pish and tosh."

"I beg your pardon."

"Daniel ... what's your middle name?"

"James."

"Daniel James Johnson, hasn't anyone told you that life is dangerous. Driving a car is dangerous. Riding a bike is dangerous. Living is dangerous. That's part of what makes it exciting." I threw my arms wide. "I don't believe for one minute that you could physically hurt me. Yes, you are special. Your abilities make things ..." I struggled for the right word, "challenging."

"Challenging?"

"Yes, challenging. So, we just have to work harder. I have to work harder to help you." I thumped my chest.

"It's not that simple."

"Damn it!" I stomped my foot. "It *is* that simple."

"Did you just stomp your foot?" Danny grinned with a hint of amusement.

"Yes." I did it again for emphasis. "I will not allow you to hole yourself up in your apartment just when you're starting to get out and live again." My voice quieted. "Danny, I get you're scared because you lost control and stopped blocking me. Hell, I lost control. We have chemistry ... passion ... lust. Call it what you like. I haven't had that in ... a while. You can't quit on me now."

"You make it sound like I'm letting you down."

"If you quit now ... you will be letting me down."

He didn't respond.

"Danny, don't let this go. There's something here, between us." My hand pressed against my heart. "I can feel it, and I know you do too."

He sighed, "But what if ..."

"No!" I made a slashing motion. "No *what ifs*. Just let it be. Please, for both our sakes."

"Okay. Against my better judgment, you win. For now."

Sinking down on a chair opposite Danny, I sighed. "You

won't regret it."

"I'm more worried that you will."

I gave him a sunny smile, "Never."

Chapter Thirteen

It was Monday morning, and I had the day off. As I lay staring at the ceiling, I tried to decide how to spend my day. I figured Danny and I needed some distance, to let things gel. If I rushed him he might push me away.

Instead, I resigned myself to returning the FBI phone calls. I couldn't put it off any longer. Both Bryant and Hutchins had left phone messages again yesterday, and their persistence made me nervous. Rolling out of bed, I shuffled downstairs to start the coffee, my liquid courage. I drank half a cup and dialed. Hutchins didn't answer. I braced myself and dialed Special Agent Bryant.

"Bryant."

"It's Cara Baker."

"Listen, I have some news. The U.S. Marshals have lost contact with Tony Rizolli." I paused to digest this.

"Cara?"

"You must be joking! How the hell did that happen?"

"His tracking anklet was cut, and he disappeared."

"Do they think he's been whacked?"

"They're not sure."

"Why are you calling me? You do realize I no longer work for the DA's office."

"Yes, we know that."

Exasperated I asked, "Then why are you calling to tell me this? Not much I can do."

"I'm concerned about your safety. Tony bore a lot of hostility toward you."

"The FBI's concerned, or you're concerned?"

"I'm concerned." He stated matter-of-factly.

"What does the FBI think?"

"The FBI thinks there's a leak in the Marshals' office and Rizolli's six feet under."

"Why does Tony have so much animosity toward me? He walked into a shiny new life provided by the American taxpayers."

"The money."

I took a moment, rubbing a hand across my eyes. "What does he know?"

"We're not sure. I think one of the pencil pushers at the Marshals' office told him about the Cayman accounts during relocation. There was very little legitimate money he could take into the program. He wasn't happy about it."

I sucked in a breath. "Agent Bryant...."

"Call me Tom."

"Tom, what exactly are *you* worried about?"

"If Rizolli isn't sleeping with the fishes, he's a loose cannon. I don't trust him. You may be in danger."

"And?"

"And you need to watch your back. Call me or Hutchins if you see anything suspicious. I mean anything out of the ordinary. If you see a strange car in the neighborhood, get the plates and call me."

"I'll take that under advisement, Agent Bryant. What about Denise?"

"She's covered. I've called in some favors."

"Fine. Please let me know if anything new develops."

"Be in touch. And, Cara ... I'm sorry."

"Tell it to Denise Colquitt." On that note, I hung up.

Chapter Fourteen

July

"I'll have a vodka martini, lemon twist, no olive." Sorting myself out, I sat on the barstool next to Jackie, who wore a beautiful yellow designer dress and sipped a glass of chardonnay. "Sorry I'm late. Have you been waiting long?"

Jackie shook her head. "No, darlin', only got here a few minutes ago."

I pointed at the second glass of wine on the bar in front of her and cocked my head. "It's the Friday night Happy Hour special, drinks are two for one."

"Excellent."

"So, what's up?"

"I've had a hell of a week and am in need of a drink…or six. My friend Mandy, from the library, is going to be joining us."

"This is Steve. He'll be our bartender for the evening." Jackie smiled and gave a finger wave to the cute waiter who reminded me of a young Tom Hanks.

Steve placed two blue martini glasses in front of me and glanced over my shoulder.

"I'll have a Michelob Light." Mandy winked at Steve and slid into the stool on the other side of me. "Hiya, girlfriend."

I introduced Mandy and Jackie then sucked down half a martini in a single gulp. "I may be drinking heavily tonight, ladies."

"I hear ya, girl," sighed Mandy.

"Just make sure I get home by midnight. I've got to be at work by eleven tomorrow." I directed the request at Jackie.

"O-kay. What's the story?"

"You see, it's all because Greta is out this week."

Mandy nodded as Steve passed two Michelob Lights across the bar.

"Who's Greta?"

"Greta is our fearless leader and the regional director of the library. She's on vacation, which is exactly why everything went to hell in a handbasket this week, because I'm in charge.

I went on to explain. "It all started on Tuesday morning. When I arrived at nine, I thought it was kind of sticky and warm in the building. So, the first thing I did was check the thermostat. It was indeed warmer than it should be. I called maintenance, and they told me someone will be out between noon and four. It wasn't too hot, so I decided to open the library at our normal time. The temperature that day zoomed up over a hundred degrees so by one thirty, the library was sweltering. I became concerned about the computers getting overheated and made an executive decision to close the library and send everyone home for the day." I paused to finish off my first martini. Pushing the empty glass away, I pulled the second martini into place.

"Unfortunately, I had to wait in the sweltering heat for the maintenance guy to show up. I sweated like a pig and ruined a beautiful silk blouse in the process. Finally, about twenty after four I got a call from the maintenance office telling me the guy's truck broke down and he wouldn't be able to get out to fix the air until Wednesday morning. We were up first on the list and can I be there at eight to let the guy in." I sipped my martini.

"Sure, I say. No problem. I'll be there at eight. So, eight on Wednesday, I'm at the library. No maintenance guy. Eight fifteen, no guy. Eight thirty, no guy. I'm sitting outside in the humidity because it's actually cooler outside than inside. However, I was smart." I tapped my noggin. "I wore shorts and a T-shirt. I'd left my work clothes in the car in case I needed them later. At eight thirty I called maintenance. 'Where's the guy?'

"'He's not there yet?' asked the maintenance lady."

"'Nope,' I told her."

I shook my head. "Donna, the maintenance lady, says she'll find out what's going on and call me back. Five minutes later, Donna calls back to tell me that the guy is on his way. He should be there in fifteen minutes." Another martini sip. "Just after nine the guy shows up. When he steps out of his car and walks up to me, I figured out exactly why he's an hour late. He stinks like a brewery, is looking a little green around the gills and there is what I believe to be vomit stuck to the collar of his shirt."

Jackie gasped, wrinkling her nose.

I nodded. "Apparently, he tied one on last night. He overslept and now he's hung over. Normally, I wouldn't care, except today he's kept me waiting for an hour. I'm hot. I'm sticky, and his stench is turning my stomach."

Mandy nodded in vigorous agreement. "Oh yeah, he was nasty. That boy needed a shower."

"That is atrocious. I hope you reported him," Jackie said, appalled.

I brandished my pointer finger. "The first thing I did was tell him to go to the bathroom and pull himself together. I gave him five minutes then told him he'd better get working on the air. In the meantime, while he was in the bathroom, I started calling the staff to tell them not to come in and to call me back at two. I figured I'd have a report by then. Mandy was already on her way so she stopped by Dunkin' Donuts to get me a donut and hangover boy a cup of coffee. After the guy comes out of the bathroom looking nominally better, he starts doing his job. An hour or so later he comes back to tell me the thingamajig in the air valve whosiwhatsit is on the fritz and needs to be replaced. 'So what does that mean?' I ask. He says he's got to go to the warehouse and bring a new one. 'How long will that take?' He says…" I used finger quotes. "'About an hour.'"

I readjusted my skirt. "Considering this guy's track record so far, I give him my cell number and tell him to call me when he's back at the library, at which point Mandy and I proceed to

Lulu's Diner on Main Street to get out of the heat." I took another drink. "While we're there, Donna calls to see how it's going. I tell her about the hangover and that a part is broken and he's gone to the warehouse to get the new part." Making a hand telephone, I held my thumb to my ear and pinkie at my mouth. "Donna says, 'What warehouse?'"

My eyebrows shot to my forehead and I shrugged with my other palm up. "I don't know…the maintenance guy warehouse?"

Both Jackie and Mandy cracked up. "So, she says, 'I'll call you back.'"

"You were so funny. When you hung up, you looked at your phone like it was an alien." Mandy laughed.

"I felt like I was being punked." I looked around the bar. "Are there some pretzels or nuts here?"

Jackie motioned to Steve, who trotted down to our end. "What can I get for you ladies?"

"Perhaps some menus. I believe we'll be orderin'. In the meantime, do you have some pretzels or somethin' we can snack on?" Jackie asked.

"I'll have another martini, please, and a water." I waved my empty glass. "Make it two waters," added Mandy

Steve handed out menus, silverware rolled in linen napkins, and waters and placed a basket of bar snacks directly in front of me. Apparently, it looked like I was most in need of snacks.

"So, what happened next?" Jackie prompted.

I rolled my eyes. "Donna called back about twenty minutes later. She told me Earl, the senior air-conditioning man, would be out soon, and he'd call when he was on the way to the library. Sure enough, a little while later a very deep-voiced Earl called and said he was at the library. Leaving Mandy to the comforts of the air conditioned diner, I trudged back to the library."

"Hey, I had to wait for the food we'd ordered," she said defensively.

"Very true, my friend." Jackie nodded sagely.

"Earl turned out to be a tall laid-back black man with gray-green eyes. You don't often see that." I gazed off. "Anyway, the best part is he's sober, smells clean, and seems relatively competent, so I tell him my lunch is waiting at the diner and to give me a call when he figures out the problem. He's agreeable to that and heads in to do his job."

"Wait a minute," interrupted Jackie. "What happened to the other guy?" Steve arrived to take our orders and passed out more drinks.

When he left, I turned back to Jackie and shrugged. "Not sure at this point. When I asked Earl, he just shook his head. I didn't push for answers."

"His name is Dave. I like to call him Dave the Dumbass," Mandy piped in.

"Me too!" Jackie cried in agreement, swinging her glass for emphasis.

"Mandy and I ate lunch and we were playing cards when Earl walked into the diner. He strolls on over to our table and tells us, 'It's all fixed.'"

"It's all fixed? Whaddyamean? The other guy said it needed a new flux capacitor."

"Earl looked rueful and shook his head. Nope. It did need a new part, but he had it on the truck. He says, 'it'll take a while to get the place cooled down since the day is so hot, but by tomorrow morning it should be fine and the library should be able to open.'"

"I swear the two of us gaped at him like big-mouthed bass." Mandy giggled.

"Sure enough, when we got back to the library, cold air was coming out of the vents. The temperature had reached well over ninety degrees, and I knew we'd have to stay closed until Thursday. So we left the 'Closed' sign on the door, and I went home to upload a message to the website and contact the staff."

"Well, that's just awful! Dave the Dumbass didn't know what he was doin'." Jackie smacked her hand on the bar.

"That's only half the story," Mandy said.

I nodded, my head starting to feel a little buzzy.

"Oh, my word! There's more?" Jackie turned her attention

on Mandy.

"Oh yeah," Mandy nodded. "There's more."

"You tell Jackie this next part. It really dealt with you anyway." I was pleased to pass the storytelling on to Mandy so I could drink some water and eat the bar munchies. Otherwise, I was afraid I'd be completely plastered before dinner arrived.

In her Alabama drawl, Mandy continued the story. "Thursday we get in early to fire up the computers and get thangs organized. I've got a computer class at ten, so I'm copyin' my handouts as the computers warm up. Then I realize half a dozen of the machines aren't warmin' up. So, I start troubleshootin' the problem. You know, checkin' the cords and power buttons.

After a while I realize they just ain't workin' and ask Cara to call maintenance … again. I think they felt sorry for us because that Donna girl immediately sent out Brandon. Guess what he finds?"

Steve the Tom-Hanks-look-a-like bartender arrived with our food. I unwrapped my silverware and dug into a grilled Portobello mushroom sandwich. "Mm … this is the best sandwich ever."

Jackie waved a forked piece of grilled chicken in my face. "Hush, I want to hear what Brandon the maintenance guy found."

Mandy took a few bites of her blackened tuna. "Ok, so on the back side of the computer lab wall is the air exchange unit, and apparently Dave the Dumbass was in there. And he spilled his coffee down the wall, into the electrical socket, which then shorted out half the dang computer lab." Mandy illustrated the coffee spill effect with her hands. "Luckily, Brandon was able to take care of it, but he had to shut down power to the entire lab and the reference section in order to work on the electrical boxes. So, I had to reschedule my computer class." Motioning to cute Steve, Mandy ordered another round of drinks.

Jackie shook her head in disbelief. "This Dave fellah is unbelievable. I hope they fired his ass."

"They sure did." Mandy rolled her eyes and we exchanged a

look.

"What? What am I missin'?" asked Jackie.

With a mouth full of dinner, Mandy waved her hand in my direction. I took that as an invitation to carry on the story.

"Today we have our program 'Lunch and a Movie.' That's where elementary school kids come in with a sack lunch and watch a Disney movie. So, I've got a packed house of little kids and about twenty minutes into the movie, Jennifer, one of our volunteers, taps me on the shoulder and whispers, 'We have a situation.'"

Mandy burst into laughter. "Poor Jennifer, she's such a timid little thang. She looked like a deer in headlights."

"What's the situation? What's the situation?" Jackie asked in a panicky voice.

Placing a hand over my eyes, I shook my head. "Dave the Dumbass is outside in a tizzy. He's pacing back and forth in front of the library, waving his arms and yelling like a homeless lunatic. He's totally freaking people out. Plus, in another half hour or so, the elementary kids are going to be leaving and I didn't want them to see this."

"Omigod. What did you do?" Jackie leaned into my face.

Emphatically, I smacked my hand on the bar. "I'd had enough of this incompetent fool. He screwed up the A/C job and shorted out the computer lab. Now he's scaring people trying to get into the library. I called the cops. Mandy gave me her stun gun. Then George and I went out to confront him."

Jackie's eyes bounced back and forth between Mandy and me. "You carry a stun gun?"

Mandy dragged the little black weapon out of her handbag and buzzing it, she gave an evil smile. "Don't leave home without it."

"When we approached, the liquor was emanating off of him. So, very firmly, I told him he's causing a scene and needs to move on. First, he gets belligerent, asking me who I thought I was. Then George steps in to do the father figure thing, calling him son he goes, 'Son, it's time to go home,'" I say in a deep George-like voice. "Well, he swings around, points at me and, at the top of his voice, yells, 'this bitch got me fired!' Then George, all calm and soothing, tells him he's been drinking too much and needs to go home to sleep it off. He can't behave like this in front of the library, a public building. At which point Dave turns on George. 'Don't you call me son, old man! I ain't your son!' He's waving his arms around wildly." I waved my arms imitating Dave. "He clocks George on the side of the head. POW!" I clapped my hands, and Jackie jumped. "George goes down."

"Holy cow!" Jackie said with shocked wide eyes.

"More like holy shit," Mandy responded.

"Holy crap is right. I don't think he really meant to hit George but that was the last straw. I zapped him, zzzzzt, and down went Dave the Dumbass." I took a drink. "Then I turned to help George."

"Was George okay?" Jackie asked with concern.

"Yeah. Once I'd decommissioned Dave, a bunch of people ran out to help George. He was a bit shook up and had a goose egg on his temple, but with some ice and aspirin, he was able to drive himself home."

Jackie's mouth hung open. "What happened to Dave?"

"The cops showed up and hauled his sorry ass to the clink. He stunk from the booze, and I musta zapped him hard because he wet himself. When the police asked why I used a stun gun on Dave, one of the patrons whipped out his phone and showed a video of the entire episode he'd taken."

At this point, Jackie was giving a loopy giggle and Mandy was bent halfway over laughing. She sat up and wiped away some tears. "It was great. You were my hero. Jonah, the fellah who took the video, is gonna put it on YouTube." Mandy hooted and gave me a punch in the shoulder. She knocked me askew, subsequently spilling half the martini in my hand. "Oops, sorry. Steve! We have spillage. We need another drink over here...and a napkin." She hollered down the bar.

Steve arrived with a rag to clean the mess and removed our dinner plates.

When our hysterics finally calmed, I said, "The police told George he could press charges. He felt sorry for the guy and declined."

My storytelling was over, and the last remnants of my energy were sapped. I felt like a deflating balloon. The martinis kicked in, and I fell quiet, contemplating the bottom of my cobalt-blue martini glass while Mandy and Jackie talked over me. I thought about the phone conversation Danny and I had on Wednesday evening. Enough time had lapsed since Sunday, and I'd decided to call him to tell him about the air-conditioning fiasco, which gave him a good laugh. Initially, the conversation was stilted, but after a few minutes, we became comfortable. We made plans to get together on Sunday to work on his blocking. I thought back to this past Sunday, which now seemed an eternity ago. Buck's run-down shack, with the waitress worn down by a hard job and too many cigarettes, served some of the best steamed crabs I'd ever had the pleasure to consume. And afterward...I kissed Danny and it was amazing. The thought popped into my head along with a self-satisfied smile.

Suddenly, the chatter going on around me silenced. "What? What did you say?" Jackie peered at me.

My eyes grew wide like saucers. "Wait, what? I didn't say anything."

"You just said you kissed Danny and it was awesome," Mandy answered.

"Amazing. She said amazing," Jackie contradicted.

I smacked a hand over my mouth. *Crap! Did I say that out loud?*

Chapter Fifteen

"Are you talking about Daniel Johnson, your tenant?" Jackie pointed an accusing finger at me.

With a hand still attached to my mouth, I shook my head in denial.

Mandy's eyes opened wide and her mouth made a large O. "You did! You did! You kissed your tenant. You sly dog. When did you meet? What does he look like? Is he cute?" She machine-gunned questions at me.

I continued to shake my head in denial.

Jackie leaned into me. "Cara Baker, tell the truth…have you met your tenant?"

Against my will, my head bounced up and down.

Mandy shrieked while Jackie sucked wind. "And did you kiss?" Jackie pressed.

Slowly my head nodded.

Another shriek from Mandy and more wind sucking from Jackie.

"Spill. I want to hear everything.'" Mandy clapped her hands.

All the booze made me loquacious, and I dribbled out the tale of meeting Danny. Luckily, there must have been a censor in the back of my mind that kept me from blabbing all of his secrets through the alcohol-induced purge. I think I told the girls he had germ issues and that was why he didn't like going out in public. There was no way I was going to tell them the truth about his abilities.

Jackie listened with a pinched mouth and a concerned air. She'd hit the roof if I told her about his sixth sense.

Mandy, on the other hand, found the entire episode exciting and listened with an adventurous spirit.

Both ladies were riveted by my tale of meeting Danny and our Sunday afternoon drive up the coast. When I got to the part about the Maserati, Mandy almost bounced off her chair.

"Omigod! Omigod! I've seen that car around town a few times. That's an awesome car. I can't believe you actually got to drive it. What was it like?" She squealed clapping her hands.

"It was very sssmooth." I ran my hand along the bar. "I felt very cool driving it."

"So, your tenant, he's good-looking, right?"

I leaned in toward Mandy and drunkenly whispered, "Hesh H-O-T, hot! And the kiss knocked my socksh off."

Mandy giggled in response.

Jackie just shook her head in disapproval. I needed to defend him. "He donated five thousand dollars for the Silent Auction."

"He did?" Mandy asked.

"Oops, lishen, that information is kind of on the down low. Keep it to yourselves, okay? Danny doesn't want a lot of press." I grimaced at my mistake.

Jackie seemed mildly impressed. "Just be careful. That's all I ask."

I knew Jackie was sincere and genuinely worried about my safety. I placed a reassuring hand on hers. "I am being careful, Jackie. Don't think I don't appreshate your conshern. I do, I really do." My head bobbed. "You're a good friend to worry about me. Trust me. Danny isn't a threat, and I think I really like him."

She squeezed my hand in response.

Mandy continued to ask innocuous questions about Danny, and, at some point, an alarm bell went off in my head. I was no longer in control of the verbal vomit. Luckily, Steve walked by at that moment. "Check please."

Mandy looked at her watch. "Oh, is it time to go already?"

"I think I need a cab." I looked for Steve's return so I could ask him to call me a taxi.

"Well, look at these beautiful ladies."

We turned.

Beau sidled up to the bar. He put his arm around Jackie, and she tilted her head back for a kiss. "Hello, Cara, and who is this other lovely young lady you have with you tonight?"

Jackie introduced Mandy.

Steve arrived with the check and Beau passed him a black credit card.

"Hi there. Wait, some of thas mine-n-'Mmmandy's," I slurred, holding my hand out to see the check.

Steve looked between Beau and me undecided what to do.

Beau waved Steve away. "My treat, ladies. A little birdie told me y'all might need a lift home." Beau looked significantly at me.

Jackie nodded. I nodded. Mandy shook her head, wobbled off her stool then straightened up and nodded.

"Barnes Taxi at your service, ladies."

"How did you know we needed a ride?" I tried to understand through the alcohol-induced haze why Beau had showed up just when we required him.

"I texted him about twenty minutes ago. I think the two-for-one got us in trouble. Thanks for coming, hon. Girls, we ready to go?"

"Bathroom first." I slid off the stool.

"Me too." Mandy followed with Jackie behind her. We left Beau to finish up with the check.

Departing the bar was a blur. The next thing I knew we were idling in front of my house. I sat in back on the passenger side and Jackie turned, facing me. "Cara? Wake up, 'Sleepin' Beauty.' You're home, darlin.' You need to get out of the car."

"Sshhure, I knew that." I rubbed my eyes.

Beau chuckled from the driver's seat.

"Hey, I gotta be at work by 'leven tomorrow. Someone give me a wake-up call."

"I gotch yur back, girl," Mandy replied.

I struggled to find the handle so I could open the car door.

Jackie turned to Beau. "Honey, I think she might need a hand."

"No, I'm fine. I've got it." I opened the door and promptly fell out onto the grass. Mandy leaned across the seat to peer out at me. "Hey, you 'kay?"

"Cara, are you all right? Beau, go help her." I heard Jackie call from inside the car.

Feeling like a fool, I jumped up. "Ish all good. I'm dine and fandy. No problemo." I pushed the Jaguar's door closed, thanked everyone for a fun time and the ride home and turned and ran slap into Beau, who'd come around the car to help. He escorted me to the door.

As soon as we stepped up to the front porch, we were flooded by light. I halted, gripping Beau's arm, and whispered, in that not-so-quiet way drunks do. "Someone's in my housh, and they turned on the light."

A confused Beau looked at me, then at the light. "Cara, darlin,' I think it's on a motion sensor. See right there, that red light?" He pointed.

I squinted at the light. Sheesh, it was bright. "Oh yeah, Danny musta done that for me. He shaid I needed it for shafety. Why's it so bright?" I held my fingers up to filter the light.

"It looks like he's installed a floodlight for you."

"Isn't he a doll? He kished me, and it was hhhott." I leaned on Beau's arm. For some reason, I couldn't get my key to work.

"Why don't you allow me?" With a smirk, Beau held his hand out for the keys.

The door popped open when another deep voice intoned from behind. "Cara, are you okay? What's going on?"

Swinging round, I stumbled. "Danny! You fixshed my light. Aren't you a doll?"

Danny's arms were crossed and his eyebrows were all scrunched up. He did not look happy.

"Whas wrong?" I squinted at him, confused.

Beau stepped forward with his hand held out. "Hi, I'm Beau

Barnes. The ladies had a bit too much to drink. My wife, Jackie, called me to drive them all home."

He indicated the car where Jackie watched from the front seat, and Mandy leaned out the window. "Is that him? Oooohhh. Cara's right, he's a cutie patootie," Mandy whispered loudly to Jackie. Apparently, we go deaf when we drink and can't seem to control the volume of our undertones. My face flamed up and I didn't hear Jackie's response.

Danny visibly relaxed and shook hands. "Good to meet you. I'm Danny, Cara's upstairs neighbor. Thanks for driving her home."

"No problem." Beau turned toward me. "Will you be all right now?"

"Shmashing! Thanks for the ride, Beau. Oh, and for dinner too. You're the bessstest girlfrien'ss husband a girl could have." I patted his shoulder and waved to the ladies in the car. "Night, night." The screen door slapped behind me as I carefully walked to the bathroom.

Behind me Danny and Beau talked in muted tones. "She's pretty bombed. She might need some help."

"I'm on it. I'll make sure she's okay."

I missed the rest of the conversation. When I arrived at the half bath, I shut and locked the door then proceeded to revisit dinner and a few martinis.

After the last of the heaving, Danny banged on the door. "Cara, are you all right? Unlock the door. Cara! Let me in."

I rinsed my mouth, splashed water on my face and blotted it dry with the hand towel. In my alcohol-induced fog, I knew I didn't want to see Danny with barf breath, so I dug out a Tic Tac from the bottom of my purse before opening the door.

Danny's eyes looked frantic and he grabbed my upper arms. "Are you all right?"

"Dine and fandy." I shook my head. "I mean fine and dandy. I feel much better now. I think I should get some ashpirin and drink shome water." Danny released me and I lurched toward the kitchen. "Thanks for fixshing my light. You're the bestest upssairs neighbor ever!" I pawed through the drawer where I kept bandages and over the counter medicines when suddenly the world tilted.

Danny scooped me up and plopped me down on the couch. "I'll get you the water and aspirin. You stay here."

I winked and tried to make my fingers do the O.K. sign, but they didn't seem to be working properly.

Danny came back with a glass and two pills, which I downed.

Then I laid my head back against the pillows and kicked off my shoes. "I think I'm just going to rest here a minute." I closed my eyes.

****

A shrill ringing beside my head awoke me. I knocked a book and other sundry things off my bedside table until I finally found the handset and answered in an effort to make the hideous clanging stop.

"What?" I groaned.

"Yo, girl," a scratchy-voiced Mandy replied. "It's ten. You have to be at work by eleven and lookin' good. Greta's back from vacation today."

"Ugh. Martinis are the devil's invention."

"I hear ya. I have a class at one, so I'll see ya later."

I hung up and looked around. My teeth were fuzzy, my mouth was cottony, and it tasted like cat crap. It felt like someone dropped a bowling ball on my head, and my eyes were on fire. That's when I realized I was fully clothed in my own bed. I wasn't sure how I got there. In true Scarlett O'Hara style, I decided it wasn't important and would think about that tomorrow. Levering myself up, I walked feebly to the bathroom and turned the shower to hot.

Twenty minutes later I felt slightly better. My hair was styled, but my eyes were a wreck. They were puffy and bloodshot. Putting on my favorite pink robe, I headed down to the kitchen for some vegetable magic. The smell of coffee assaulted my nostrils and stomach as I entered. It took supreme willpower not to retch at the odor.

Danny stood in front of the sink, cozily pouring himself a cup of joe. "Morning, sunshine."

"Ouf," was all I could muster.

"Would you like a cup of coffee?" he asked solicitously.

I shook my head and made an icky face. "No thanks. Tea is what I drink when I'm hung over. Tea with lots of sugar." I unearthed a cucumber from the vegetable drawer, sliced off two pieces and headed upstairs to finish getting ready.

When I returned to the kitchen, Danny was cooking eggs and hash browns. A cup of tea steeped on the counter. He pointed with the spatula. "There's your tea, and the eggs should be ready in a few minutes. Wow! That cucumber really works. Your eyes look clear. How's the head?"

"Like I told Mandy on the phone, martinis are the devil's invention." I popped two Advil with my tea and sat at the table.

"Is that who called? I wondered." Danny loaded up the plates and brought them to the table.

I should have been surprised he was here cooking breakfast in my kitchen, but I was just too hung over to question anything this morning.

I took a few bites then focused on him. "So what happened last night?"

"What do you remember?"

"I remember falling out of Beau's car and then not much else."

"You fell out of the car?" He chortled in disbelief.

"Yeah, pretty much. I'm sure I embarrassed myself last night, so I'd better hear what you saw." I grimaced.

"Well, I heard a commotion and came down to find a strange guy opening your front door for you." He looked rueful. "I have to say, I was kind of pissed." He shoveled in a few eggs. "Then Beau introduced himself and explained the situation. We spoke for a few minutes while you locked yourself in the bathroom to throw up. You know, you scared the daylights out of me when you didn't answer and wouldn't open the door. I thought I was going to have to break it down. Then you pretty much passed out on the couch. I carried you upstairs. I was worried you'd be sick again and slept most of the night on the chair in your room. Later, I moved to the bed in your guest room."

I didn't know what to say. When we parted last week, I wasn't sure where our relationship stood. However, last night he took care of me, going so far as to carry me upstairs and sleep in my guest room. This morning he made me breakfast. He was playing the part of a very tolerant roommate, or really sweet boyfriend. In either case, he'd gone above and beyond, while I'd clearly made a fool of myself.

"Thanks, Danny. I'm sorry I was such a pain in the butt. I don't normally get that hammered. It's just drinks were two-for-one last night..." It was a lame excuse.

"It's all right. I don't mind. We've all had similar nights, when you need to blow off some steam. Beau said something about you and Mandy having a bad week at the library."

I rolled my eyes. "Something like that."

"I liked him."

"Who? Beau?"

"Yes. Maybe we should have dinner with Jackie and Beau sometime."

Stunned, I stared at Danny. "You mean like a double date?"

"Yes, I suppose that's what I mean."

"Like at a restaurant?"

"Actually, I was thinking here at the house. I could grill something."

"Are you ready for that?"

"Let me think about it some more ... maybe." He shrugged.

I was so staggered by the suggestion all I could do was gawk.

He looked at his watch. "What time do you need to be at work?"

I came out of my stupor. "Eleven. Why? What time is it?"

"Ten 'til."

"I have to go. We'll talk about this later." I scrambled around getting my keys, sunglasses and handbag. "I'll call you tonight." Opening my front door, I saw that the carport was empty. "Where's my car? ... It's still at the bar. *Shit.*"

"C'mon. I'll drive you." He grabbed my hand and we ran out the rear door through the garden and out the back gate. Danny opened the garage while I paced the alley. The Maserati rumbled to life and pulled alongside. I climbed in. It didn't take more than five minutes to get to the library, so I exited the car right at eleven.

I paused, leaned over and kissed Danny's cheek. "Thank you for everything. I know 'thanks' is inadequate for all you've done. I'll call you later and we'll talk."

****

Sunday evening Danny and I sat in the gazebo, having finished a steak dinner. I grilled to make up for the embarrassing Friday night fiasco. During the meal, I related the Thursday and Friday events that led up to the drunken bender. When I got to the part about Jonah putting the incident on YouTube, Danny became as excited as a puppy dog and insisted on seeing it. He ran upstairs to fetch his laptop and, sure enough, after a few minutes of searching, he found it.

Jonah's perspective from the parking lot put the three of us in profile to the camera. Dave got all riled up, flinging his arms about, screaming, calling us names. Jonah zoomed in to get a close-up of Dave's inflamed features and buggy eyes, reminiscent of Arnold Schwarzenegger in Total Recall. After George hit the ground, Dave gaped in confused astonishment as if he couldn't comprehend what had just happened. Then, while his attention was diverted, I took control of the situation. I stalked up to him with a determined look on my face. In the video you heard the zap of the stun gun as I hit him on the neck. He dropped like a stone. Danny found this portion hysterical and insisted on backing up to run it three more times. With a whoop of glee, he high-fived me. It was humorous. However, as an active participant, the incident was still too fresh in my mind to laugh over. Instead, I gave a weak smile.

Danny closed the computer and scrutinized me. "Were you afraid?"

"Yes."

"You handled yourself well. In this video you looked as cool as a cucumber."

"Everything happened so fast. Initially, I thought Dave would be on his way when we spoke to him reasonably. But, while we were out there, he started to aim his anger at me, and I realized he was out of control. I felt the fear creep in." I shuddered, thinking about the hatred and animosity Dave hurled at me.

Danny searched my face. "How did you combat the fear?"

"I knew I had a roomful of kids that needed to be protected from Dave's violence, so I clamped down on the fear. Back in Pittsburgh, I took a few self-defense and mixed martial arts classes. When I realized Dave was truly unreasonable, I began searching my mind for the moves I was taught and that helped me calm down. Once he hit George, the anger took over. Dave's lucky I didn't kick the crap out of him after he went down. I was tempted." I said ruefully.

"I found the video enjoyable."

I shook my head.

"You had every right to get plastered after a week like that. After being pushed to the limit, you needed to blow off some steam."

"Hmmm…listen, about that," I hedged. "I might have told the girls about meeting you."

"I kind of figured, by some of the comments they made Friday night." He paused. "How did you explain my issues?"

"Yeah …" I stalled. "Well, it's a little bit of a blur … but … uh … I might have told them you had germ issues and that's why you didn't like to be touched." I flinched, waiting to be lambasted.

Danny sighed with acceptance. "Well, I suppose it's better than the truth."

"Look, I'm really, really, really sorry. I wasn't going to tell them anything about you. It slipped out." I tried to look contrite. "I blame the martinis."

"It's okay, Cara. I get it. Our date at the beach was on your mind. It would be abnormal not to mention me in passing. If my situation was normal, I would have met Jackie when she showed you the house. What did they say?"

I hesitated. "Mandy was really excited. She thinks it's a big adventure and you're this man of mystery, like a spy or something."

"And your friend Jackie?"

"Well…Jackie is a tough nut. She's a bit of a mother hen toward me, so …"

"So Jackie doesn't approve."

"It's more like she worries I'll get hurt or something."

"She's right, you know."

I waved his comment away as if it was a bothersome gnat. "You and Jackie worry too much."

That night Danny escorted me up my staircase to our shared landing. He leaned in and gave me a quick peck on the cheek, but I wasn't about to let it go at that. I grabbed the front of his shirt to pull him down to my level. Standing on my tiptoes, I moved in and planted a slow sensuous kiss. I sucked on his bottom lip and he moaned. His arms slid around me, as he became an active participant, and his soft tongue swept along the inner recesses of my mouth. Breaking the kiss, he pulled me to his chest and I buried my face in his collarbone. Both of us panted.

"You're going to be the death of me," he rasped.

A Cheshire cat grin spread across my face. I leaned back and looked into his eyes. They were his usual grass green darkened with passion, but without the telltale glow of last week. "I just wanted to show you we could do this."

He rested his forehead against mine. "You were lucky you know. I wasn't even focused on blocking you that time."

"Then you're getting better at it. It's becoming a natural reflex."

"You're playing with fire."

"Yes. It's making me hot," I whispered in his ear and flicked my tongue across the lobe.

He groaned and air whistled through his teeth. "Cara," he ground out.

Deciding to end the torture for the evening, I surrendered, stepping back with my hands upraised. "Okay, okay. You win. We'll take this slow. I only wanted you to realize spending more time together and, with a little practice, maybe we could explore this ... desire we feel."

I received a hard stare.

"By the way, I forgot to thank you for fixing my outdoor lights with the motion sensor."

"You thanked me already."

"I did?" I frowned scrunching my eyebrows.

"Yes, but considering your next move was to get sick in the bathroom, I'm not surprised you've forgotten."

"Oh, well, thanks again. I really appreciate it. How did you hook it up? Is all the wiring outside?"

Danny looked uncomfortable, shifting his weight back and forth. "Cara." He ran a hand across his face. "I have a key to this door." He tapped the door leading into my hallway.

"Oh, really?" I crossed my arms and glared. "Where did you get it and when did you think you were going to tell me about that?" My voice hit a shrill note high enough to crack glass.

Danny let out a sheepish sigh. "Jerome gave it to me. As he got older, he seemed to take comfort in having me upstairs and thought if there was an emergency, he could count on my help." He defended, rubbing the back of his neck. "I figured you'd have changed the locks when you moved in, so I never said anything. The day I bought the motion sensor, I planned to wait until you were home to put it up. Then ... well ... I didn't have anything else to do, and you didn't come home ... and I decided to try the key to see if it still worked." His face was red.

"I see." My anger deflated immediately, and I allowed my arms to drop.

"Look, I know I should have told you or given it back when you moved in ..." He trailed off with a guilty look.

"It's all right, Danny. As it stands, I, too, take comfort knowing you're upstairs in case of an emergency. I'm glad you've got my back. It makes me feel safe."

This made him smile. "I've always got your back."

Chapter Sixteen

August

My summer romance with Danny carried on, working itself into a happy but slightly frustrating groove. We ate meals together a few times a week, and most Sundays we spent some or all of the day together. Danny loved to take drives, and he allowed me to drive the Maserati, up and down the coast roads, finding beautiful unpopulated spots of nature. Sometimes when I had a weekday off, we packed a lunch, put the top down on the Maserati, and headed to a quiet beach for some fun in the sun. I loved to see Danny in nothing but swim trunks. His washboard abs and remarkable muscles were like watching the magnificence of body in motion. Although he begged me to get a bikini, I laughingly refused and stuck with my reliable, if relatively demure, one-piece suits. We flirted unmercifully with each other, and many evenings ended with make-out sessions that practically burned down the house, leaving us hot, bothered and unsatisfied. Danny was afraid of losing control, and I was afraid of losing Danny. There was an unspoken rule how far we allowed things to progress. I loved the romance and intimate courtship, but I was no longer a teenager guarding my virginity. If we didn't move the physical relationship forward, I was going to burst.

On the other hand, Danny slowly moved out of his hermit shell. With a smidgeon of prodding on my part, we decided to move forward and invited Jackie and Beau over for dinner. The dinner went smooth as butter. Beau and Danny got along as well as males do. They talked sports, grilling and golf. Likewise, after she spent time with him, Jackie couldn't help but succumb to Danny's charms. Moreover, her attitude toward our situation lightened considerably following our evening together.

After such a successful dinner with Jackie and Beau, I decided to invite Mandy and Eric over for a movie night. We had a blast watching a DVD of the latest screwball comedy, while we drank Cokes and munched popcorn. We laughed so hard our sides hurt. Mandy was so pumped to meet Danny her approval was an automatic given. What surprised me was the camaraderie that sprung up between Danny and Eric. Apparently, Danny had built the gazebo and arbors in the garden, and once Eric found out, he was full of questions. Eric wanted to build a deck on the back of his house and, after our movie night, came by the house one afternoon to talk shop. Afterward, he started calling and texting questions. Eventually, their deck-building conversations turned into friendship.

The next time Mandy and I had a girls' night out, Eric invited Danny over to drink beer and watch "manly" movies. Mandy and I assumed they included lots of BGEG—also known as blood, guts, explosions, and guns. Much to my surprise, Danny accepted the invitation and apparently had a prodigious good time. Due to my overindulgence with the martinis, I was off the sauce and offered to be the designated driver. I conveyed Danny over to Eric's and picked him up at the conclusion of the night. As we left, he and Eric cracked inside jokes that went right over my head, and, to my astonishment, they high-fived all the way out the door. Danny later explained he had an easier time blocking males, and he only drank one beer to make sure there were no slip-ups. It was a pleasure to observe Danny making friends and coming out of his self-imposed exile.

The summer weeks passed quickly, and before I knew it, the silent auction was upon us. I'd spent the prior week confirming all of the food and working with the party rental company. Normally, in the summertime the library closed at five on Fridays, but this Friday we closed an hour early. Additionally, in order to set up for the auction, we closed all day on Saturday.

The sold-out invitations said six thirty, but four staff members, including George and Greta, would be dressed and ready to open the doors by six to greet everyone. Since I needed to be available to help the food vendors set up, I planned to leave just before six to get dressed and return by seven.

Most of us arrived at the library by ten on Saturday morning to get things rolling. Staff members organized donations into gift baskets and numbered all the lots, and Greta had designed and printed a catalog of auction items. I spent the day working with the rental company, rearranging library furniture and books and putting tables in the auction room. We also set up two bars and food stations around the library. There were a dozen high-top tables scattered about, and we covered half a dozen of the library's tables and chairs with tablecloths and chair covers for patrons who wished to take a load off. The rental company also provided the glasses, dishes and silverware.

Mandy had taken it upon herself to order personalized napkins with the date and event name. The linens were a royal blue and matched the color scheme Greta had chosen for the invitations. To provide additional ambiance, we placed faux plants with twinkle lights in strategic locations around the room. A local florist donated flower arrangements for all the tables. Bridget Crandall, the owner of the local bakery, designed a beautiful four-tiered cake that looked like books in exchange for a pair of tickets to the event.

By five, my food vendors began to arrive. Their meals filled the library with mouthwatering scents. Lucky for me, the staff members from the various restaurants seemed to be fairly competent, and, after I directed them to their assigned locations, they were able to organize themselves and work directly with the rental company for any additional needs. At six the harpist arrived to provide music in the auction room. Eric's quintet also arrived and set up to play in the main area.

At six fifteen Greta, dressed in a black satin floor-length gown and shawl, shooed me out. "Cara, you need to get changed. You've done a fabulous job. George and I can handle things from here."

I glanced over her shoulder. George adjusted his bow tie while conversing with Linda Lincoln. "I just want to check one more thing over at the Tandoori station."

"It's fine. Go home. You don't want to miss the auction, do you?"

"Okay, okay. I'll be back soon." I gave in after checking my watch.

Hopping into the Mini, I zipped home. Danny waited on my front porch swing and waved as I drove into the carport.

"Hi, hon. Tonight's the auction and I've got to get changed."

"I know. I brought my camera to get a few snapshots of you in your finery." He held a fancy black digital camera from its string.

"Thanks. I didn't even think about getting photos. Could I borrow your camera for tonight? We might want shots for future brochures and promotions."

"Sure thing." Danny followed me into the house and went to wait in the family room, while I sped upstairs to get my shower.

Forty minutes later, I hollered to Danny, "Okay, here I come," and sashayed down the stairs. Danny stood at the bottom of the landing, mouth agape. The forgotten camera hung by his side.

"Hey, don't you want to take some pictures?" I smiled with cheeky impertinence.

Danny awoke from his reverie, whipped up the camera and started snapping away. "You look amazing."

I'd chosen a bold floor-length cherry-red silk gown that hugged my curves. The top was held up with thin spaghetti straps and formed a gentle V of draped material in front. The backside had an even deeper V ending near the base of my spine and had silver beaded ties that gently crisscrossed halfway up. Tall, strappy silver sandals adorned my feet, and I carried a matching silver handbag. Dangly rhinestone earrings swung from my lobes to complete the ensemble. Since I had so little time to get dressed, my hair was swept into a sophisticated

French twist. Could I pull off this daring outfit?

"I hope it's not too much. Is it trashy?" I voiced my anxiety.

"You're gorgeous, babe. It's elegant. Not trashy. You're making me rethink my attendance."

"Really?" My eyes lit up.

Sighing, he shook his head. "No, not really. Sorry."

I nodded and patted him on the shoulder. "That's okay. I understand." Walking past him, I moved toward the kitchen.

Danny took his first gander at the back of the dress and let out a low whistle. "Jesus, Cara, you just about gave me a heart attack. That dress should come with a warning sign."

I whipped around to face him, my eyes clouded in dismay. "That's what I mean. It's cut too low, isn't it? I look like a tramp, right? I'm gonna go change. I have a black cocktail dress that will work just fine."

Danny clutched my arm as I started past him. "No way. You look fantastic. You have to wear that dress."

"I don't know." I chewed my lip.

Placing a finger beneath my chin, Danny gently kissed my jaw line and worked his way up to my mouth. His kisses made me completely forget my angst. "You're stunning. The dress looks beautiful on you. Go and have a fabulous time. Call me if you need a ride home."

I opened my mouth to protest, but he cut me off. "No matter how late. I'll come get you." Danny eyed me up and down and seemed to reconsider. "Maybe I should drive you over now."

Laughing, I gave him a playful shove. "I'll be fine. I'm not going to get tanked up. This is business. Besides, I know better. If I start drinking, I'll come home with all sorts of junk I don't need and paid too much for."

Chapter Seventeen

It was past seven when I arrived at the library and parked in the last space of the rear staff lot. The front lot was full and people had started to park on the street and in the neighboring lots of a dry cleaner, jeweler and nail salon. I was able to slip in the rear door and mingle with the patrons already in attendance, thus avoiding a big front-door entrance. Eric winked and gave a thumbs-up. His pretty-boy good looks in his bow tie and cummerbund reminded me of an ad for *GQ*.

In my absence, the library had turned into a bustling hive of activity. A majority of the attendees held drinks, and all of the high-top tables were occupied as folks devoured the fare. A steady murmur of conversation flowed around me as I progressed through the throng to check on the food stations. Feeling a tap on my shoulder, I paused.

"Your dress is fab-u-lous! Where on earth did you find it?" Jackie handed me a glass of champagne. She was attired in a simple but elegant black floor-length sheath dress, with a gorgeous triple strand of pearls and a matching earring set.

"You don't think it's too much, do you?"

"Darlin', my husband wanted to know who the hottie in the red dress was." She gave a tinkling laugh.

Looking over her shoulder, I sent a finger wave to Beau, whose ears flamed a vibrant crimson matching the vest that peeped out from beneath his tuxedo jacket.

"Hi, Cara. Great dress." He smiled sheepishly in my direction.

I grinned back. "Thanks, Beau. Good to see you. You two look marvelous. I'm so glad you came." I gave Jackie a quick hug. "I found this dress at a little boutique called Claire's in Charleston. You'd love it." I brushed self-consciously at an invisible piece of lint. "Have you eaten yet?"

"Beau's hit all the stations. I stuck with the seafood from The Chowder House. It was delicious."

"Yeah, Anton's a dream in the kitchen. The Tandoori cuisine is tasty as well. You should try it." I glanced around, checking the food stations and the general flow, as we talked. "Are you going to bid on anything?"

Jackie flipped through the catalog to browse the choices. "Actually, there are a few packages I'm interested in. Beau what do you think about this 'Night Out on the Town'?" She pointed to the catalog.

Beau looked down. "Which one?"

"Right here. It has a fifty-dollar gift certificate for The Chowder House, a suite at The Governor's House, a Bed and Breakfast in Charleston, and two tickets to the theater. It says the value of the package is five hundred."

Beau shrugged. "Whatever you want, sweetie. That sounds fine to me." He wandered off to explore the Chinese food station.

"Have you registered for the auction yet?"

Jackie shook her head.

"The registration desk is to the right of the auction room. You don't need to register for the silent auction items, but you'll need to get a paddle if you're going to be bidding at the live auction."

"What about you? Are employees allowed to bid?"

I laughed. "I don't think Greta cares who bids as long as the check doesn't bounce."

Mandy trotted up wearing a short, strapless, glittering gold dress with matching gilded peep-toe platform pumps. The shoes were so high it was like watching a circus feat to see her navigate the crowd. With the elevated shoes and big fluffy hair, Mandy almost reached my chin. As usual, her cobalt eyes shone and she smiled, full of bubbly excitement. "Isn't this great? You look fantastic in that red dress, Cara. You totally have the curves to carry it off. Half the men in this room are checking you out. Has Danny seen it yet?"

My ears heated and I nodded. "Yes, he almost swallowed his tongue when he saw the back."

"If I wasn't so sure of Eric's attachment to me, and your interest in Danny, I might be jealous."

I reacted with a hoot. "Mandy, you must be living on a different planet if you think I can compete with you, but thanks for the compliment. Jackie and I were just talking about the auction." I indicated the catalog she was still thumbing through. "Are you planning to bid?"

Mandy nodded. "There's a Bath and Body Works basket I'm looking at. I'm also thinking about bidding on the ladies golf set. Eric likes to golf."

"Have you ever golfed?" Jackie asked.

Mandy shook her head. "Nope, but Eric has offered to teach me."

Jackie and I exchanged a look. "I'll just bet he did."

Mandy gave a knowing grin. "Private lessons."

She swayed over to the bar, while Jackie moved off to register and get her paddle. I spent time browsing the silent auction items.

There was a Day Spa Package I bid on, as well as a basket full of grilling items. The regular auction included an antique poison ring and a large oil painting I planned to bid on, but I didn't hold out too much hope of acquiring them. I contemplated the room. The jewels draped on some of the ladies indicated there were several big spenders in the house. A few hot items saw a lot of action, and I bid on them just to increase the prices. As I browsed the tables, two different gentlemen offered to buy me a drink, and a man old enough to be my father asked if I was interested in accompanying him on one of the cruise packages. I politely declined all offers.

While looking over the live auction items, an insurance salesman the size of my Mini trapped me and tried to sell me a great deal on a combination Life, Home and Auto package. Jeffrey Nolan stepped up and saved me from having to answer.

He approached with a smile, his hand out. "Hello, Cara. It's good to see you. You look lovely."

It'd been weeks since I'd seen Jeff. I think the two of us subconsciously avoided each other, Jeff out of deference to Danny, and me out of guilt, having completely lost interest in him.

I shook his hand and indicated the overloaded tables. "Planning on bidding?"

"Nothing in the silent auction, but I plan to bid on the mountain bike and kayak."

"That's great. Good luck." I quickly ran out of small talk.

"Cara, can I speak to you for a minute?" He indicated an empty side hall.

"Sure." I led the way. "What's up?"

"I don't know what you're doing for Danny, but I've been working with him for four years and haven't seen nearly so much improvement as I've seen in the past eight weeks. You've been a good influence on him. He's getting out more and meeting new people through you. He's shown marked improvement on his blocking technique. And, for the first time in years, I see true happiness."

I smiled, taking pride in Danny's improvements. "I'm glad to know he's getting better. He's become very special to me."

"I think he feels the same way about you. His face lights up when he talks about you."

Considering my past with Jeff, I scrambled to return an appropriate answer.

Jeff let me off the hook. "You may be interested to hear he's reduced our sessions to once a week."

Danny and I rarely spoke about his sessions with Jeff, and I was surprised. "Is that okay with you?"

He shrugged. "I would've liked to see him continue for twice a week a little longer." He paused. "I'm going to be honest … I fear what may happen should things go wrong between the two of you."

"What should go wrong?"

Jeff raised an eyebrow. "Let's not play games. The two of you are getting in deep, and I'm concerned for both of you. Danny hasn't perfected his blocking, and I've been the recipient of his bad moods. Moreover, what happens to him when you decide to end the relationship? With both of you living in the house, things could get sticky, and I worry Danny could regress."

I sucked in a breath and dived in. "Jeff, since we're not mincing words, let me say this. I appreciate your concern on my behalf however, you needn't be apprehensive. I'm a big girl and I can take care of myself. As for the relationship, why do you say 'when' it ends? Perhaps we should say 'if.' And, as for Danny, who's to say *he* won't eventually end it?"

"Cara, when a smart man finds a woman who makes him feel like you make Danny feel, he doesn't let go."

"I don't know." I shook my head. "There are days I believe I'm much more entrenched in the relationship than he is. I think because he's been doing it for so many years, Danny's better at hiding his feelings." I paused for a moment. Jeff was right. If things between Danny and me went south, he could regress back into his hermit hole, a disaster I wished to avoid at all costs.

"Look, Jeff, I don't know how to set your mind at ease. I'm well aware there are no guarantees in life, so let me just say I don't think a relationship with Danny will ever end. It may change, but I'll do everything, and I mean everything, in my power to make sure he continues his foray into society. Okay?"

"I guess that's the best I can ask. I didn't want to cause a pall on tonight's festivities, but I felt the need to bring my concerns to your attention. We haven't seen much of each other, and I decided to take advantage when the opportunity presented itself."

"I understand."

"And, Cara…"

"Mm?"

"I'm happy for you and Danny. I thought you ought to know I'm dating a woman from Charleston."

I sighed with relief. "That's fantastic, Jeff. Is she here tonight?"

"As a matter of fact she is. If you don't mind, I'd like to introduce you."

"I'd like that." I grinned.

Jeff's date, Gloria, was a lovely brunette in her forties, who wore a deep blue, sequined calf-length gown. She was a CPA and ran her own firm in Charleston. She had a no-nonsense attitude, but when she looked at Jeff, her expression softened. As I walked away, I held high hopes for the two of them.

At eight the silent auction came to a close, and by eight-thirty all of the bidding sheets were removed. Greta stepped up to the podium and thanked the attendees, the donors, the mayor, Linda Lincoln and the library staff. She took a moment to express her gratitude to John Hanley of Hanley's GMC dealership for matching every dollar raised up to ten thousand.

"Before moving on to the live auction, I want to take a moment to especially thank Cara Baker for all her hard work and her ingenious idea to hold this event to begin with. Cara, where are you?" Greta's gaze searched the audience, landed on me and my not so subtle frock, and pointed. My face went up in flames, matching my dress, and I sent a wave in her direction. The audience clapped and a number of people surrounding me smiled. More gentlemen offered to shake hands. The dress was making me popular.

"Now if everyone will take their seats, Mayor Tucker Wynn would like to say a few words and then we'll begin the live auction." Greta gracefully stepped away from the podium while the crowd shuffled to find seats.

My eyes roved the room looking for a place to sit. Per my recommendation, waiters circled the room with glasses of champagne and wine while the announcements were made. By the time George started the live auction, at least seventy percent of the room would be holding an alcoholic beverage. My glance found Greta who looked directly at me; she seized a glass from a passing waiter and raised it in salute. I winked in return, sharing the joke. We knew the more freely the alcohol flowed, the larger the checks. As I wandered down the aisle, Jackie yoo-hooed and waved at me. Excusing myself, I stepped over other patrons already seated and maneuvered my way to the empty chair next to Jackie. Mandy and Eric migrated our way and were able get seats directly behind us.

Once the crowd settled to a dull roar, Mayor Wynn stepped up to pontificate on the importance of giving back to the community and reading in education. We were hopeful he wouldn't live up to his moniker. However, hope sprang eternal. Since this year was an upcoming election, Mayor "Windy," as he was known to the townspeople, decided to utilize his captive audience and provided us with his family values stump speech.

After twenty minutes, Greta took the bull by the horns and began applauding. The audience took the cue and joined in and wouldn't stop until the mayor finally stepped aside. It reminded me of the Oscars when the orchestra starts the music over the winner's ongoing speech, building to a crescendo as a beautifully gowned woman hustles the victor off stage.

George approached the podium and clapped the mayor on the shoulder. "Thank you, Mayor Wynn. Now it's time to announce the winners of the silent auction."

Unfortunately, I missed out on the grilling set but was delighted I'd won the Day Spa package. Jackie won her Charleston weekend package, but Mandy missed out on her Bath and Body Works basket.

The first items up for the live auction were jewelry and home décor pieces. I didn't win either of the two items I bid on. However, half an hour into the auction, I could tell from the general atmosphere in the room the alcohol had kicked in. A few of the patrons got into hot bidding wars over an antique silver tea set and one of the most dreadful oil paintings I'd ever seen. It was painted by a local Charleston artist. I speculated the bleached blonde who eventually won the painting would wake up in the morning with a bad hangover and buyer's remorse.

Jackie, Beau, and I had a hard time keeping a straight face during the oil painting auction, because Mandy and Eric were being naughty, cracking jokes over its awfulness.

Mandy leaned forward and whispered, "That woman's boobs look like they were blown up with a bicycle pump. She should sue her surgeon for over inflation. Bless her heart."

Beau started a faux cough to cover our giggles. One thing I'd learned while living in the South, it was acceptable to toss out any insult about a person as long as it was followed by the phrase, "bless her heart."

George turned out to be an excellent auctioneer. He kept the auction moving along at a fair pace and cajoled patrons into increasing their bids without them even realizing it. Beau's sporting good items were the last to be auctioned and wrapped up the night. Mandy didn't get the golf clubs, but Jackie offered to lend her a set. She suggested Mandy refrain from making the investment until she tried the sport.

During the live auction, the rental company and wait staff broke down the food stations. They left a single bar open inside the auction room. By the time the sale ended, it was about ten thirty. The remaining guests either cashed out or stood around comparing their winnings. More than an hour later, Greta locked the front door behind the last straggler. The rental company was almost finished packing up their items, and the hired accountant crunched numbers on Greta's office computer. George, Mandy, Eric, and I gathered around a table taking a load off, while sipping from half a dozen open bottles of wine and champagne left by the bartenders.

Greta joined us and helped herself to a glass of Pinot Noir. "Well, folks, I'd say the fund-raiser was an unmitigated success. A job well done." She turned to me. "Cara, you'll be happy to know the accountant gave me the preliminary numbers, and it looks like we're close to netting almost thirty-two thousand from the auction alone."

Our jaws dropped.

"That means you and Mandy will have more than enough money for remodeling, and we'll be able to erect an extensive tot lot in the courtyard."

George held up his glass. "To Cara." The table chorused his toast.

"To success," I responded.

"Hey, whose red Mini is parked out back?" One of the rental company staff members approached our booze-covered table of decadence.

I craned my neck around to face her. "That would be me. Why?"

"You've got a flat tire."

"Really?"

"Flat as a pancake."

George leaned over. "I can help you change that."

"Thanks, but that's not necessary." I patted his hand. "I'll give Danny a ring and ask him to pick me up. Tomorrow morning I'll call the auto club to come out and change it."

Eric shook his head. "Don't call Danny. We'll give you a ride home."

Twenty minutes later I let myself into the house and waved at Mandy and Eric as I closed the door. The front windows of the house were dark and I was glad I hadn't called Danny to drive me home. I didn't want to wake him. Slipping off my shoes, I walked into the kitchen, flipped on the lights and took a bottle of water from the fridge.

It was a lovely night. The humidity had cleared out earlier in the day and it had cooled down to the low seventies. Barefoot, I stepped out on the back patio and took a moment to enjoy the nighttime peace. The scent of late summer blooms filled the air. With the auction behind me, the stress lifted from my shoulders like the removal of a boulder.

The wine mellowed my mood, which would account for the reason I didn't jump out of my skin when a catcall pierced the calm night. I looked up and saw Danny's silhouette as he stood on the Juliette balcony, his forearms leaned against the black metal railing.

The little balcony reminded me of Shakespeare's tragic play about star-crossed lovers. Mounting a patio chair I called, "Romeo, Romeo, where for art thou, Romeo. It is the sun and I am your Juliet."

I shook my head with a grimace. "No, that's not right. Aha,

it is the east and you are the sun." Drama-class style I flung up a hand, stepped back on my dress and promptly lost my balance. My arms wind-milled, water arced through the air like a fountain and I fell back onto my rump in the gravel. It took me a moment to orient myself. I tested all my limbs and seemed to be okay. My bottle, a dozen feet away, rolled gently on the ground in a half circle, the water slowly glugging out.

Gradually, I got up and assured Danny. "I'm okay. I'm okay. It's all good." I looked up to see if he was laughing at me and found an empty balcony. "Danny?"

Moments later the gravel crunched as Danny hurried toward me from the side gate entrance. "Cara, jeez, are you okay?"

"Dan-nee, you came down, my knight in shining armor." I flung my arms around his neck and fell into his chest.

He staggered under my unexpected weight. "Are you drunk?"

Pushing myself back, I gave him a wounded look. "I am not drunk." I replied full of self-righteousness, then pinched my thumb and forefinger almost closed. "I may be a little bit tipsy."

"Did you drive home?" he asked with disapproval.

"Nope." I shook my head.

He rubbed a hand down his face and frowned. "Babe, please tell me you didn't walk home in the dead of night in that dress. It's not safe, and I told you I'd come pick you up."

"No, I didn't walk home. Eric and Mandy gave me a lift."

"Oh. Okay. That's good."

"I'm glad it meets with your approval. Now, if you don't mind, I'm hungry. I'm going to make myself something to eat." Turning, I lifted the front of my dress so I wouldn't trip and regally waltzed into the kitchen.

Danny followed. "You're bleeding."

"What?" I looked over my shoulder.

He frowned. "Your left arm is bleeding. You must have scraped it when you fell down."

Sure enough the underside of my forearm had a long scratch that ran from the elbow down to the wrist.

Danny took over. "Here, let me tend to that." Turning on the tap, he placed my arm beneath the running water. "Where do you keep your bandages?"

I pointed to the medicine drawer, and he pulled out hydrogen peroxide, antibiotic ointment, gauze and tape. Then he ripped off a paper towel from the roll and wrapped it around my dripping limb.

"Here. Hold this." He indicated the towel.

Gentle warm hands splayed against my waist and lifted me up onto the granite counter. He took the paper towel away and doctored the wound. My breath turned shallow as he focused intently on the job. Blowing lightly on my skin, he sent shivers down my back. I couldn't believe being patched up by Danny was turning into an erotic episode. On the other hand, for the past few weeks my senses had continually remained at heightened points of desire. Watching him walk turned me on. Right then, as Danny taped the last bit of gauze in place, I determined the next step in our relationship needed to happen soon. Tonight, if I had my way. First, a few things needed to be clarified.

"There. All finished." Proud of the handiwork, he grinned at me.

"You really are my white knight, aren't you?"

"I thought you said I was your knight in shining armor."

"Either way. Listen, I've got the munchies. I didn't have time to eat and I'm in the mood for grilled cheese. How about you?" I pushed myself off the counter.

Danny eyed me for a minute. "Tell you what. Since I'd rather not patch up burn marks, why don't I man the stove and you can put the sandwiches together."

I punched him lightly on the arm. "You're on. No stove. The Panini Maker is in the pantry. I'll get out the bread and cheese."

When the sandwiches were made, without bodily harm coming to anyone, we sat across from each other and I gave Danny a run-down of the event. "It looks as though the preliminary numbers came to over thirty-two thousand. Add that to the ten thousand matched by Hanley's GMC, and we'll have more than forty thousand to upgrade the library. I can't wait." I rubbed my hands together.

"Glad to hear the event went better than you planned." Danny took a swig of beer.

"Yup, and a gentleman offered to take me on a week-long cruise to the Virgin Islands."

Coughing and choking over his beer, Danny wheezed out, "You what?"

"You heard me. A very nice gentleman offered to take me on a cruise."

He watched me speculatively. "What did you say?"

"I told him I didn't think my boyfriend would appreciate that." I studied his face for a reaction, but the only emotion I detected was relief.

"Oh. Well, good." Danny sat back and relaxed. "You don't have a problem with that?"

"A problem with what?"

Blowing out a sigh, I swam into deeper waters. "Danny, I called you my boyfriend."

"Umm-hmm." He waited patiently for the punch line.

"Are you my boyfriend?"

"Well, I certainly hope so, Cara. We've been 'dating,'" he used finger quotes, "for a while, and I don't let just anyone drive the Maserati."

"We've been dating for quite a while, correct?"

Puzzled by my cross-examination he nodded.

I stood with a sultry smile. "Good. Then I think it's time to take things to the next level." Slowly removing the straps from my shoulders, the silk dress slid down my body, catching for a moment on my hips then made its way down to form a rosy puddle at my feet.

Eyes wide, Danny sat frozen, except for the hiss blowing through his teeth.

I stood clad in nothing but a small red lacy thong. Since it seemed Danny wasn't taking the hint to come ravish me, I crooked a finger at him, turned and with a sultry, hip-swaying pace, headed for the stairs. When I reached the bottom step, I finally heard music to my ears, the kitchen chair crashed to the ground and heavy footsteps hurried to follow me. I waited for him to catch up.

His mouth ravaged mine while his hands swept up and down my back, burning my already overheated skin.

Danny's gruff, passion-filled voice tickled my ear. "This is probably the stupidest thing I've done in a while but, woman, you've pushed me beyond endurance, and I can't hold out any longer."

I let out a triumphant throaty laugh. He put words into action and tossed me over his shoulder to carry me up the stairs. When we reached my bedroom, he gently laid me down on the bed. Kissing every part of my neck and shoulders, he finally worked his way down to my breasts and hard rosy nipples. I arched toward his mouth, groaning with pleasure. My shaking hands tugged the shirt from his pants and roamed lazily along his back. His muscles jumped at the initial contact.

Releasing my nipple, his breath cooled my skin. "God, you're gorgeous. I've wanted to tear that dress off you since you waltzed down the stairs five hours ago." His mouth worked its way down to my stomach, tickling the sensitive skin.

I pulled the shirt over his head and ran my hands through his thick silky hair. His tongue darted around my belly button and headed south. I was panting with desire when his teeth gripped the itsy-bitsy thong. He dragged it down my legs and tossed it aside. With his forefinger, he gently tickled the arch of my foot and began those slow melting kisses up my calf and the back of my knee. Halfway up my thigh he stopped, tormenting me, and started over again at the ankle of the opposite leg. This time he made it to the inside of my thigh and then stopped.

"You're driving me insane. You know that, right?"

With a deep sexy chuckle, his tongue flicked out, teasing my clitoris and making me arch halfway off the bed with a moan. Levering up on my elbow, I reached for his belt buckle. "Now, now, now. I need you right now."

"Are you on birth control?" Danny stood up, shucked off his shoes and released his pants.

Slightly breathless, I pointed. "Bedside table. Box of condoms."

I couldn't wait for him to find it, so I rolled over and crawled across the bed to rifle through the top drawer. When I turned back, Danny's beautifully muscled body crawled toward me, his throbbing erection enormous. Holy cow! I double-checked the box. "I hope these are big enough to fit you."

"Babe," he grumbled. "Just put it on."

I pushed his shoulders back and reversed our positions. Straddling him, I leaned over. My breasts lightly swished against his furry chest. Slowly, I impaled myself upon his pulsating shaft.

That's when Danny lost control. His eyes began to glow and a wave of passionate heat and electricity poured into my body, increasing my sensitivity. It rocked straight to my feminine core. Danny rolled me onto my back, thrusting hard. My climax slammed quickly into me, sending me over the edge with a scream just as bright white light flashed. Danny collapsed on top of me, panting heavily into the crook of my neck. He stayed for only a few seconds to catch his breath and then rolled off, breaking all contact.

My fingers prickled. My eyes drifted open.

A soft glow emanated off Danny's skin. He sat on the edge of the bed with his back to me and ran his hands through his hair, still trying to catch his breath.

"Danny?" I reached out.

He flinched away from my touch. "Danny, look at me."

He shook his head.

"Daniel Johnson," I said with soft patience. "I've seen the eyes before. Please, look at me."

He turned with a tortured look, his green eyes bright and still glowing.

"That was incredible."

Danny raised a skeptical brow.

"When can we do it again?" I asked with a mischievous smile. With a little more coaxing, I convinced him to cuddle up next to me, and we gave the phrase "afterglow" a new meaning.

We made love two more times into the wee hours of the morning, both times slow and simmering without the lights and fireworks. Both times left me humming but not the mind-blowing electrical kick of the first time when Danny lost control. It took me hours to come down off the testosterone high Danny's lapse had infused into me. I think it gave me a small understanding of the male gender's utter obsession with sex.

Chapter Eighteen

I awoke to a late morning sun peeking around my red curtains. Stretching, I felt for Danny's presence. He was gone. I sat up and glanced around. My clock read eleven eighteen.

"Danny?"

No answer. I rolled out of bed and shuffled to the bathroom, walking a little stiffly, but enjoying the soreness that only comes from a good night of loving. When I came out, tying my robe into place, Danny swaggered into the room with two mugs of coffee, his jeans riding low, the top button undone. He looked delicious. I sniffed. He smelled delicious like coffee and Irish Spring. His hair was damp and a lock fell over his forehead.

"Morning. How are you feeling?" He handed me a mug.

I gave him a knowing smile. "A little sore but good. Very, very good." Gingerly, I sat on my chaise lounge and swung up my feet. "Oh, I think my feet hurt the worst. Those sandals are beautiful but killer."

Danny placed his mug on the bedside table and sat at the end of the chaise. Pulling my feet onto his lap, he started to work magic on my poor battered arches.

I melted at his touch.

"So what's on the agenda for today?"

"After I get dressed, I need to call the auto club and have them fix my flat." I took a deep drink of fine Columbian Dark Roast. Danny had excellent taste in coffee.

"You have a flat tire? When did this happen?"

"Last night during the auction. That's why I didn't drive home."

"I hope you didn't drive home because you'd been drinking."

"That too." I glanced sheepishly beneath my lashes.

He shook his head. "How bad is it? Can the tire be repaired?"

"Dunno. I haven't actually looked. One of the caterers told me about it and I figured I'd just deal with it today."

"I'll take you over after breakfast."

"I'm afraid there's not much for breakfast. I'm out of milk, eggs, bacon, oatmeal, pretty much everything. We even finished the cheese and bread last night. I might have some dry cereal in the pantry we can munch on."

"I've got eggs. How does an omelet sound?"

"Like heaven." I'd forgotten there was a whole other kitchen in the house. "Do you know how to make omelets?"

He gave an affronted look. "Of course I know how to make omelets. You forget I've been a hermit for the past ten years. I'm exceedingly self-sufficient in the kitchen." He gave a last squeeze to my foot and stood. "Why don't you get your shower while I put breakfast together?"

"Sounds like a plan. I'll be up in twenty."

****

The Mini listed at a backward angle. This was due to the fact both the rear tires were flat. Not just flat, sliced open like vicious wounds. I stared unbelievingly as Danny phoned the police to report the vandalism. Bending down, I reached out to touch the damaged tire.

"Don't touch anything. There might be fingerprints." Danny snapped out.

I gave him a mocking look. "Okay, Perry Mason. I don't think the police will dust for prints. This isn't a homicide crime scene. It's just vandalism."

"It's a tire homicide."

The comment brought a smile. However, my mind was

rolling the beginning of a particularly nasty thought around in my brain. I didn't like where the thought was headed, because it meant I'd be calling Special Agent Bryant. It was possible Bryant might feel this particular incident could be considered, "out of the ordinary."

After Danny hung up with the police, he phoned a local garage to ask about a tow truck. Since two tires were slashed, I wouldn't be able to put on a spare and be on my way as expected. I needed to have the car towed to a station and both tires replaced. Slowly circling the Mini, my eyes roved the vehicle. I searched for further damage. Nothing. All soft-top convertibles are vulnerable to an angry knife, but there was no additional destruction beyond the ruined tires. If this was an intimidation tactic from Tony Rizolli, I would have expected to see the top obliterated, perhaps the interior slashed and the paint ruined. The two tires left me scratching my head. Who did this and why? I couldn't think of anyone in Denton in whom I could have inspired such hostility.

I turned away from Danny and my car and dialed Special Agent Bryant. His voice mail picked up.

"Agent Bryant, this is Cara Baker. I'm not sure if this means anything, but two of my car tires were slashed last night. Please give me a call to let me know where the Rizolli issue stands." I spoke in muted tones.

The local police arrived in the form of a young officer who introduced himself as Deputy Lyncham. He shook my hand and, with a lazy drawl, asked, "Well, ma'am, what seems to be the problem?"

I pointed to the tires and let the vandalism speak for itself. Danny watched from the far side of his car.

The deputy wandered over, squatting to get a better look. He pulled a pen from his pocket and stuck it in one of the holes. "It looks like someone took exception to your tires. When did this happen?" His shaded eyes peered at me.

"Last night. I arrived just after seven for the auction. Around midnight one of the catering staff told me I had a flat. She intimated it was only one tire. I decided to wait until today to take care of it. I didn't see the damage until now."

Lyncham examined the building and small parking lot. "Not much light out here. Easy to slash and run. We've been experiencing some vandalism in the area."

"What kind of vandalism?"

"Broken windows at the school, graffiti, someone set a trash can on fire in the town square and petty theft. We think it may be local teens. I understand there was some sort of affair held here last night."

"Yes." I went on to explain the generalities of the event.

He shook his head. "Well, ma'am, let's fill out this report for your insurance company. If we catch one of the teens who did this, he's bound to sing like a canary. They always do. I'll take your information and contact you if we find the culprits."

Over the next hour we filled out paperwork, talked to my insurance company and dealt with the tow truck. I debated calling Agent Bryant back to tell him the situation was likely local teen vandalism but changed my mind for two reasons. First, I wanted an update on the Rizolli situation. I'd feel much better knowing either Tony's body was found floating in a river or the U.S. Marshals had located him. Second, my cell phone ran out of juice, and I didn't have a charger with me.

Danny dropped me off at the garage where the tires would be replaced, and we made plans to get together for dinner. Once my car was fixed, I made a trip to the Pig to restock my pantry and pick up something for our meal.

After unpacking my groceries, I thumbed through the mail collecting on my kitchen counter. My hand paused at a manila envelope. No return address. Postmarked from Pittsburgh. One fluid slice of the letter opener and two newspaper articles fell out, and with them the cozy, tranquil, happy life I'd been creating in small-town America came crashing down. My ears buzzed. I blindly reached for a kitchen chair before my legs gave out.

The first clipping was an obituary, the second a brief article and photo describing the too-short life led by a lovely, generous soul named Denise Colquitt. The article brushed over the horrific rape and subsequent medical and mental problems Dee struggled to overcome. It went on to describe her heroic personality and the foundation she started for victims of violent crimes. Denise was survived by her mother, Annette, and her sister, Natalie. A brief mention was made of a father she barely knew who left and eventually divorced Annette when Denise was only five and Natalie a toddler. The article stated her tragic death was the result of a toxic combination of medications she was taking, much like the death of the actor Heath Ledger. Dee died on Tuesday. The article was dated Wednesday, it mentioned the memorial service was to take place Saturday afternoon at the Catholic Church her family attended, and the funeral was set for Monday.

Tomorrow. Late afternoon. The rest of the article became too blurry to read as tears coursed down my cheeks. The newspaper fell from my shaking hands; it took a gentle descent to the floor, landing silently underneath the table. Out of sight but never out of mind.

The phone rang and I automatically picked it up. "Cara?"
"Yes."
"It's Agent Bryant."
"Sonuvabitch." My voice cracked.
A gusty sigh came across the line. "I guess you've heard about Denise?"
"Did you send this?" The hurt and anger burned in my voice. "Send what?"
"Nothing. Never mind. What the hell happened? I thought you had someone watching her," I accused, allowing the anger to overcome my tears.
"Someone was checking up on her. It was a lethal combination of her meds. She was taking something for insomnia, and it didn't jive with another one of her drugs."
"You sure that's all it was."
"That's what the coroner's report said."
I thought for a beat. "You know Rizolli was the reason she was on those medications to begin with."
Another gusty sigh, "Yes, Cara, I know."

"Has anyone found him?"

"Not yet. That's why I'm calling. What's going on down there?"

I explained the slashed tires on my car and how the police thought it was local teens.

"Have there been any other incidents?" Bryant's voice was clipped and professional, but the underlying concern came through.

"None."

"All right. Listen, I'm really sorry about Denise, and I'll be in touch if Rizolli pops up on the radar." He paused. "In the meantime, stay alert. Continue to keep your eyes peeled for anything unusual."

I felt a prickle run along my spine. Something wasn't right. "What aren't you telling me?"

He was silent.

"Bryant?"

"There's chatter that Barconi's put a hit out on Rizolli and he's brought in a professional to take care of it. A hit man who goes by the code name Eagle."

"If Barconi's brought in a professional, then you think Rizolli's still alive?"

"That's what I think, yes."

"What does the Bureau think, or the Marshals?"

"Officially, the Bureau doesn't believe it, and the Marshals have egg on their face for losing him to begin with, so they aren't talking at all. Personally, I don't think Barconi's smart enough to send up a red herring like Eagle. It's an awful lot of money to spend on someone if you already know they're dead."

Denise's face popped into my mind. "You sure Denise's death was an accident?"

He paused. "As sure as I can be with the information I've been provided."

"What the hell does that mean?"

"It's what I can give you, and since you're not with the DA's office, I shouldn't even be telling you this much."

His attack left me speechless.

A windy sigh blew across the line. "Sorry ... I made an ass of myself at a meeting this week trying to convince my boss' boss Rizolli's still alive and planning something. I've been sidelined. It's going to take me a little while to get all of the information about her death."

I didn't know how to respond. His honesty surprised me, and I appreciated the lengths he was willing to go to in order to find Rizolli. Getting chewed out by one's boss was never a pleasant experience. It was becoming clear Bryant might be on to something. Moreover, he was the only FBI agent willing to speak to me, as well as being concerned about my safety.

"Are you going to the funeral?" Bryant broke the silence.

I let out a bark of laughter and responded with dripping sarcasm. "Yeah, I'm sure the family would just looove to see me there." Yet, as sure as the sun rose, I knew I'd be at Denise's funeral. I needed to be there for my peace of mind. I needed to be there to say good-bye.

"None of this is your fault, Cara. Your boss didn't give you a choice. The FBI didn't give you a choice ... *I* didn't give you a choice."

"Excuses. There are always choices. I made a promise to that girl, and I broke it. I broke her trust."

"One of these days you're going to have to let it go."

It was my turn to let out a sad sigh. "I wish I could."

"I'll be in touch if I hear anything about Rizolli." Bryant hung up.

In the end, the bastard who ruined Denise's life was the indirect reason for her death, and I could do nothing to stop it. People, locations, conversations reeled through my memory like an old-fashioned movie stopping at the first time Denise Colquitt's name came across my desk.

Chapter Nineteen

October, Two Years Ago

The gray stuffy conference room smelled of perfume and stale coffee as we crowded around the scarred central table, chitchatting and drinking our fresh lattes while we waited for our boss, Jonathan Joseph Stephenson, Jr., better known as J.J. to his staff, Pittsburgh District Attorney, to grace us with his presence. Seven prosecutors, two paralegals, one investigator, and a sprinkling of administrative staff. At the head of the table sat a pile of overflowing file boxes. All of us received an e-mail Sunday evening requesting our attendance for a staff meeting promptly at nine. Though the chamber was standing room only, we represented a small group of over one hundred lawyers working in the district attorney's office. As luck would have it, I arrived early enough to snag one of the eight cushy seats that surrounded the boardroom table. To my right sat John Graham, assistant district attorney with fourteen years of experience under his belt, also my colleague and mentor. John could best be described as average. Brown hair, blue eyes, average height, and average looks. There was nothing average about the way John practiced law. When he was in the courtroom, his average demeanor turned passionate and compelling. Juries ate him up. John held the highest conviction rate among all the ADAs. He showed me pictures of his adorable daughter, Allison, dressed as a princess at her recent fourth birthday party.

Conversations tapered off when J.J. entered. He wore a black silk suit, a blue shirt with white collar and cuffs and a red tie, which set off his dark, Italian looks. As most DAs are, J.J.

was a political animal. He got elected to his current position by using old-boy connections and unions. However, he was well respected by the staff because his background carried five years in the public defender's office, as well as over a dozen years practicing as a defense attorney for a high-profile firm.

"Morning, folks." The room quieted. "We're here bright and early today because Lynn Merriweather, department head and senior prosecutor in the sex crimes department, was put on bed rest by her doctor this weekend."

Concerned mumbles spread through the room. Lynn was forty-one and pregnant with her first baby. Doctors considered her high-risk, and she wasn't due for three more months.

"Is she okay?" asked one of the female paralegals.

"She and the baby are okay, but she'll be bed-ridden until she delivers. She can do some paperwork from home. However, in addition to bed rest being prescribed, her blood pressure is too high and she needs to reduce her stress levels. Therefore, she will be taking a leave of absence until after the baby is born. With that in mind, you're here this morning to split up her caseload."

Groans greeted the news. There wasn't a prosecutor in the room who wasn't already dealing with a full plate, and J.J. was about to load us down even more.

"I know, folks. I know. Two of our paralegals, Christina Guzman and Alan Burgess, and Lynn's assistant, Rita Jeffers," J.J. indicated each person, "are familiar with the paperwork and will be available to assist you. Additionally, I'm well aware I've pulled some of you from other departments. Sex Crimes is low on personnel, since we're still trying to fill open ADA positions. So, I need some of you to step up."

That was me. Pulled in from another division. Ready to step up.

"Lynn's baby issues couldn't have come at a worse time, but whaddareyagonna do? She has two cases coming up for trial this week. My office will be taking over one of them and requesting a continuance for the other." He checked his watch, "You all know Claudia?"

We nodded as a petite silver-haired woman stepped forward from behind Alan. Claudia was J.J.'s extremely efficient executive assistant. She ran J.J.'s office like a Swiss watch. Most of us were both envious and a little fearful of Claudia. I don't think much went on in the office Claudia didn't know about.

"Claudia will work with you to divvy up Lynn's cases." J.J. tapped one of the overflowing boxes. "Request continuances if you need to. Some of the judges may be sympathetic, but no guarantees. I'm due in court. Shoot me an e-mail if there are any questions. And play nice." He winked and headed out the door.

An hour later, I had a dozen new files in front of me when Claudia pulled out the last case. "The State vs. Anthony Rizolli."

The room went silent.

John leaned forward, placing his elbows on the table. "Anthony Rizolli, as in Tony 'Thumbs' Rizolli? Jersey Mafia? Carlo Barconi's Crime Family?"

Claudia looked at John with a jaundiced eye but didn't respond. Alan Burgess finally broke the silence. "Yes, that would be the one."

All eyes swiveled to Alan, who reclined against the wall, arms crossed. "Why aren't the Feds prosecuting?" John directed his question at Alan.

"It's a rape and assault with a deadly weapon case. Cops charged him with attempted murder, but Lynn had to knock it down to assault. It happened in Manchester outside a neighborhood bar. Not pretty, but we have a witness and the victim survived. She'll testify. It has nothing to do with his Mafia ties."

"Witness still alive?" John asked.

"So far. Judge considered him a flight risk, so Rizolli's being held without bail."

One of the admins in the back piped up, "Why do they call him 'Thumbs'?"

Alan and John stared at each other in silent communication. John motioned with his hand and Alan's answer was delivered in a deadpan monotone. "Supposedly if you stand in Rizolli's way, you get your thumbs ripped off with a wrench before taking your dirt nap."

One of the newer prosecutors gasped. Unfortunately, the longer you remained in this job the more immune you became to the horrors one human could inflict upon another. After a while you became numb to the carnage. The thumbs thing was fairly appalling but not the worst I'd heard or seen by a long shot.

During the interaction between John and Alan, I read the victim's vitals—Denise Colquitt, age twenty-one, light brown hair, blue eyes, 5'6", waitress at McCormack's Irish Pub, high school diploma and some college credits. The top crime scene photo showed a blood-splattered sidewalk. I was having difficulty remaining numb to the atrocities listed in the police report.

"I'll take it," someone said. Every eye turned to stare at me. Apparently, I was having an out of body experience. Apparently, I was the someone.

Claudia took off her glasses. "Seems a little out of your league, Baker."

She wasn't wrong. My usual cases involved drugs, burglaries, prostitution, and larceny. Ninety percent of my suits never saw the inside of a courtroom. Most plea-bargained to lesser charges. That was my specialty, making deals. I was tops in that department. I made deals outside courtrooms in the gray marble halls of the Allegheny Courthouse or at Sammy's, the local dive bar steps from our office where ADAs, cops, courthouse workers, and sometimes defense attorneys hung out. Actually, quite a bit of work was accomplished at Sammy's. Judges loved me because I cleared their dockets. The cases that did go to court only lasted half a day, maybe a day at the most. High-profile murders, rapes, manslaughters, and assaults went to more seasoned prosecutors and other departments, which was why it was on Lynn's plate. Generally, my cases didn't bleed.

John, who'd recently moved into the Sex Crimes Division, gave me a speculative look. "You ready for this Baker? J.J. won't allow a deal."

I nodded. "I can do this. No deals."

With eyebrows cautiously raised, Claudia handed over the files. "Graham, you're second chair, and Alan, you work with her on this case. Because of the Mafia ties, it may become a public circus. Therefore, it's important we don't screw this one up. I think it's important to have a female lead. Baker, use Callan if you need investigative work. I'll let J.J. know. He may end up arguing parts of the case if this becomes televised and if the FBI doesn't take over first."

The meeting broke up, and I asked Alan to come to my office to debrief. Everything I needed to know would be in the case file, from the police report, forensics, hospital reports to the arraignment and preliminary hearing. Alan Burgess had been with the DA's office for a dozen years and I wanted to get his viewpoint on the case.

"Tell me Denise Colquitt's story."

"Colquitt has been waitressing for three years at McCormack's. It's a working-class bar with lots of regulars that stop by on their way home from work. She's enrolled at the local community college, taking classes to get an associate's degree in finance. She was on duty the night Rizolli strolled in."

"What was Rizolli doing in Pittsburgh?"

Alan shrugged. "He has an aunt on his mother's side who lives here. He was visiting her."

"Mafia connections?"

"None that we know of. The visit seems on the up and up. We can't find any connections between the aunt and Barconi's operation."

"Was he known to frequent the bar?"

"Not that we've found. No one recalls seeing him there. We checked his credit cards for the past six months. McCormack's never showed up."

"Okay. Back to the night of the crime."

"Rizolli arrived around nine and drank three beers in an hour. About ten he started hitting on Colquitt. Patrons say she fended him off most of the night. He got heavy-handed, grabbing her and pulling her onto his lap. Charlie Tanniger, one of the bouncers, intervened and told him to leave her alone. He backed off."

"So he stopped bothering her."

"Yes, but one of the patrons said he continued to watch her every move."

"Then what happened?"

"Rizolli closed the bar. He was one of the last to leave."

"How much did he drink in total?"

"Five beers from nine to last call at one thirty."

"Okay. Then what?"

"Colquitt is on clean-up duty that night. The waitresses rotate, which means they generally stay up to an hour past closing time. Denise is in the bar along with the owner, Michael Finnigan, who was closing out the registers, a bartender, Dave McLaughlin, who's cleaning the bar, and Charlie the bouncer. Colquitt leaves around two forty-five through the back alley door and Rizolli is lying in wait for her. He punches her in the head and face three times, knocking her to the ground. Then he covers her mouth and proceeds to cut her."

Alan seized the file and pulled out four 8 x 10 glossies taken at the hospital. Denise had wounds on her breasts, on her abdomen and along the right side of her face from brow bone to her chin. Some were deep wounds, others shallower slices. The left side of her face was bruised and her left eye was swollen shut.

Alan used a monotone voice as a way to distance himself from the dreadfulness in the file. "Then he cut off her jeans and raped her."

The photos were hideous and I couldn't fathom how someone survived such a brutal attack. "How did she survive?"

"We don't think she was supposed to, but Charlie the bouncer left through the alley door and saw Rizolli attacking her. He yelled and ran toward them. Rizolli took off, but Charlie had gotten a good look and a partial license plate, which the police were able to connect to Rizolli. He called nine-one-one and kept her alive."

"So, Charlie's our witness."

"Yes."

"Did he drink anything that night?"

"Nope. Bouncers aren't allowed to drink alcohol while working. The bartenders are allowed to give them free sodas throughout the night. The police were smart enough to test him at the scene. That's not the best part."

"Tell me the best part."

"The best part is Rizolli dropped the knife he used to cut Colquitt. We think it fell while he was pulling up his pants on the run."

"Tell me it has his fingerprints."

"Bloody fingerprints from Colquitt's blood and his DNA were found in the hospital's rape kit."

"So, we have a weapon, fingerprints, DNA and a witness. What's Rizolli doing? Is his lawyer trying to make a deal?"

"He pled not guilty. He wants a trial by jury."

"You're joking!"

Alan shook his head.

"Mafia send one of their high-priced lawyers down to defend him?"

"Initially, yes. We think Carlo wanted him to plea bargain and do his prison time. Get this, Rizolli fired the first five-hundred-dollar-an-hour lawyer Barconi sent. Now he's got a local Pittsburgh lawyer."

"Who?"

"Ronald Jamieson."

I shook my head "Never heard of him. What firm is he with?"

"No firm. He's on his own."

"What kind of game is Rizolli playing?"

"No idea. Barconi's got the Feds breathing down his neck and just wants this Rizolli business to go away. Word on the street is Barconi's not very happy about the rape. He thinks Rizolli's been disrespectful."

"If Rizolli doesn't play ball, do you think Barconi will put a hit out on him?"

Alan shrugged. "Maybe, but Rizolli's fairly high up in the

organization and is related to Barconi through marriage. Barconi would be taking a risk with all the heat the Feds are putting on him."

"Where's the girl now?"

"She lives with her mother and sister in McKee's Rocks."

"What about Charlie the Bouncer? Is he being protected? If Barconi's in on this, he'll try to intimidate Charlie to keep him from testifying."

"Charlie has a permit to carry a concealed weapon. He's been warned, and we offered protection, but he wouldn't take it. Said he's got bills to pay and can't go into hiding waiting around for the trial." Alan shrugged again.

"Where are the Feds on this? I'd imagine they want some action on this case to take down someone so high up in the Barconi food chain."

"We haven't heard a peep from the Feds."

Shocked by this information I stared. "Nothing?"

"Nada. Zip. Zilch."

"I don't get it. Where's the punch line?

"I don't know, but Lynn was just as disturbed by their silence as you are."

"When's the trial date?" I searched the file.

"Lynn pushed to fast-track it so it's only three months from today with Judge Harcord."

This news pleased me. Judge "Hard Court," as she was known by defense attorneys, tended to show preference to prosecutors and gave them more leeway during examination and cross. She played hardball with defense teams, sticking to strict rulings, and was known for her contempt fines. Rumor had it, Harcord's daughter was sexually abused by her second husband, who cleaned out their joint bank account and mysteriously disappeared three years ago. Since then a majority of the sex crimes seemed to make their way into her court. Mentally, I rubbed my hands in anticipation. Prosecuting my first big case in her courtroom was going to be a snap.

"Thanks, Alan. That's all for now."

Chapter Twenty

August

My eyes were swollen and red, and my face was blotchy from all the crying when Danny knocked on the upstairs door. I wiped the tears away and, with shaky hands, opened the door a crack, blocking it with my body.

"I'm sorry, Danny. I can't have dinner with you tonight." I avoided his eyes.

"Babe, what's wrong?" The light on the landing was bright enough to show my ravaged face.

I scrubbed my eyes. "I screwed up. I was supposed to put the bad guys away. I was supposed to help the victims. Now someone's dead because I didn't do my job. I made a promise and I broke it."

"Cara, what are you talking about? You're not making any sense. Just let me come in and I'll help you work this out." Danny tried to reach me, but I stepped back from his touch.

Misinterpreting my reticence, his hand dropped.

"Danny, I'm not the person you think I am. I'm not good enough for you. I'm not good for anybody. I'm a terrible person who doesn't keep her promises." The guilt ate away at my gut. "I don't deserve happiness," I whispered and closed the door, locking the dead bolt.

The knocking began immediately. "Honey, I don't understand. Open the door. I'm sure things aren't as bad as you think. Let me help you. Cara, you're scaring me."

Silence.

"I want to help you." The quiet words came through the

door.

Shaking my head, I plodded down the hall and climbed into bed burying myself under the covers in an effort to block out the knocking. Unfortunately, there was little I could do to block the memories as they spun through my head.

****

October, two years ago

My first meeting with Denise Colquitt took place in one of the small conference rooms scattered throughout the building. The room was painted a dull putty color and had a cold sterile hospital-like feeling to it. The district attorney offices were in an ancient building, updated piecemeal when money was available and when corrupt politicians didn't chew up available cash. We sat in the faux black leather and silver metal chairs surrounding a glass-topped boardroom table, donated by a law firm that had recently redecorated, with Denise, her mother, Annette, John, Simon Callan and me. Callan, our investigator, was just under six feet with reddish brown hair and nondescript hazel eyes. His manner made people want to confide in him, yet he also had the ability to blend into the woodwork when necessary. He was an excellent investigator, and I was blessed to be working with him. J.J. made sure to put our best assets on this case. Nobody wanted Rizolli to walk away on a technicality.

The introductions and explanations regarding Lynn's absence on the case had been made as Denise stoically nodded. We were eleven weeks out from the brutal attack. Denise's stitches had been removed, but the scar across her face was still an angry red. What we couldn't see was the bald patch in the back of her head where neurosurgeons went in to stop a small brain bleed that occurred when Denise's head was slammed on the hard asphalt during the assault. She would forever be on medication to stop the seizures caused by the damage. Crutches lay alongside Denise's chair. Her left knee remained wrapped and braced after the first surgery to fix the torn ligaments sustained while fighting off her attacker. John had brought in an extra chair to allow her to keep the injured leg elevated during our meeting. Denise wore a long brown skirt to accommodate the knee and a black turtleneck to hide the other scars on her arms and torso.

However, it wasn't the scars that disturbed me. It was the haunted look in her dark-shadowed eyes and her thin figure. It was a look of fear, from someone who'd always see the world differently, knowing she was a victim and that any stranger could inflict the most unspeakable atrocities. It was the look of someone who'd lost trust in her fellow man. Denise's pain renewed my determination to see justice done by locking Rizolli up for a long time. I was hopeful one day the fear and horror would leave Denise Colquitt's eyes.

My years in the DA's office had made me jaded and skeptical of human nature. In many ways it was a relief to be fighting for a true victim. The numerous drug, prostitution, and larceny cases I usually prosecuted drew a fine line between victims and criminals. From one day to the next, you never knew if you'd find yourself prosecuting a defendant who'd been sitting at the table next to you the prior week. Denise wasn't a criminal. I saw her purely as a victim and the reason for the existence of the system.

I could see why Rizolli was attracted to Denise. Her eyes were a pretty shade of blue, and she had thick, long chocolate brown hair that fell to just below her shoulders. She looked to be a cross between Italian and eastern European descent. Today her hair was down and she used it to shield the facial scar. The clothes she wore hung loose and limp. I estimated Denise had lost fifteen to twenty pounds since the incident and hadn't replaced her wardrobe with smaller sizes. Sadly, the weight loss made her face angular and too thin, losing the girl-next-door appeal that likely drew Rizolli. Annette had similar features to her daughter. She stood approximately two inches taller and sported the same brown hair but had dark brown eyes. However, Annette's thick tresses were cut into a short bob, suiting her age, and she weighed about thirty-five more pounds than Denise. Our research told us Annette was a single mom who supported her two girls by working at a daycare center and for a house-cleaning company on the weekends.

"Denise, I have some difficult questions to ask you. I want you to think before answering, and I need you to be truthful."

Denise nodded.

I turned and addressed Annette. "Mrs. Colquitt, you may find my questions invasive or disturbing, considering this is your daughter, but it's very important that from now on, no matter what you hear, you remain supportive of Denise. Do you understand?"

"I always support my daughter, Ms. Baker. Nothing she says will change that." Annette spoke in a firm but quiet voice while reaching out to squeeze Denise's hand.

"Thank you, and call me Cara."

Annette nodded.

I returned my full attention to Denise. "On the night of March third, did you have anything to drink?"

"No. Mike, the owner, doesn't let us drink on the job."

"Do you drink?"

"Sure. When I go out with friends, I have a few beers."

"How often do you go out and drink?"

Denise shrugged. "Maybe four or five times a month."

"Do you ever drink at McCormack's?"

She shook her head. "No. My friends know I don't like to party where I work. We generally stick to the bars downtown near Pitt U or Carnegie Mellon."

"Why don't you like to drink at McCormack's?"

"I just don't think it would be professional. I gotta work with those people. I don't want them to see me messed up."

"Fair enough. Prior to the night of March third, had you ever seen Tony Rizolli at the bar?"

"No."

"Okay, Denise, I need you to think before answering the next questions. Did you show any sort of interest—flirt with, touch, wink—toward Rizolli that night."

Annette jumped in. "Just what are you trying to imply, young woman?"

I knew this would be a touchy subject. "I'm not implying anything, but both of you need to realize the defense will likely ask the same question in court. I'm preparing you to be ready." Turning back to Denise, I waited for an answer.

She closed her eyes, pinching her nose with a thumb and forefinger. "You know, I've run that night in my head a hundred times, wondering if I did something that made him do this."

We waited for few moments.

Denise shook her head. "When I walked up to his table, I smiled and was friendly, but I never touched him or flirted."

"Why don't you tell me what you remember happening during the time he was in the bar?"

"He sat at one of my tables around nine. I was serving the table next to him, so as soon as I finished handing round the drinks, I turned to his table. I told him my name and asked him what he wanted to drink. He said he wanted a Killian's on tap and requested a menu. I had one in my pocket and placed it on the table in front of him. Then I went to get his drink."

"Do you tell all the customers your name?" Callan interrupted.

"Sure. Mike, that's the owner, says we get better tips if we tell them our name. I actually have some regulars that always sit in my station."

I nodded, making a note of the fact. "Then what happened?"

"He chugged the first beer right in front of me and asked for another."

"I think I said something like he must be thirsty. Then he said, 'You know it, sweet cheeks.' Like some sort of come on."

"Did you respond?"

"No. The table next to him signaled for me, so I turned away to help the other table. It took a few minutes before I got back to him with the second beer. Then he ordered a plate of hot wings."

"Did he say anything else?"

"Yeah, he winked and said to hurry back with his wings. I remember the wings came out pretty quick so, within ten minutes, I delivered them to his table and said something like, here you go."

"What time was that?"

"About nine-thirty I'd guess."

"When did he order his third glass of beer?"

"When I delivered the wings. He still had about an inch of beer in his glass, so I asked if he needed a refill. When I delivered his third glass, he smacked my bottom and called me darlin'." She shuddered, "He said, 'You sure are a pretty one, darlin'. I like women who take care of me.'"

"What did you do?"

"I walked away and mentioned it to Charlie. I don't like strangers touching me. Then later on I passed him and he grabbed my wrist to order another beer. I said fine but please let me go. The wrist grabbing kinda bothered me, so I had Joe, one of the other waiters, deliver the beer."

"Tell me about the lap incident."

"About half an hour after the arm grabbing, he must've been coming back from the bathroom because I was removing the empties from his table when he snuck up behind me, grabbed me around the waist and pulled me onto his lap and asked what I was doing when I got off work. I pushed my way out of his lap. I pointed toward Charlie and told him that was my boyfriend and he'd be driving me home."

"Is Charlie your boyfriend?"

Denise shook her head. "No, but I knew he'd play along and get this guy off my back. Charlie saw me point to him, so he came over and asked what the problem was. I told him what happened and also mentioned Charlie's role as my boyfriend. Charlie was great. He just nodded his head and told me to get back to work. I walked away and didn't go near the creep again. Charlie delivered his last two drinks."

"Do you know what Charlie said to Rizolli?"

"Not exactly, but I assume Charlie told him to back off or he'd boot him out."

"Okay. We're going to change the subject for a few minutes. Did you have a boyfriend as of March third?"

She shook her head. "No. We broke up in January."

"What's his name and how long had you been dating?" I flipped the page of my yellow legal pad.

"Brian McCluskey, about five years, since high school."

I scribbled down the information, and then I looked directly at Denise. "Were you two sexually active?"

She eyed her mom and then slowly nodded. Annette squeezed her daughter's hand. "Why did you break up?"

"He was going back to college in Florida, and the long distance thing was just too difficult."

"At any time during your relationship did you cheat on him?"

Her reply was quick and vehement. "No!"

"Since you've broken up with him, have you had sex with anyone else?"

"No." A quick headshake.

"Never gone home with a customer and had a one-night stand? It's important you answer truthfully."

Denise looked down at her hands. "No. I haven't had sex since Brian and I broke up."

"Excuse me, Ms. Baker, what's the point of this line of questioning?" demanded Annette Colquitt.

I turned to Annette. "It's possible the defense may try to paint your daughter as promiscuous, which could sway a jury. Therefore, it's vitally important I know the answers to these questions."

Annette sat back only slightly mollified. Denise continued to keep her eyes cast down as she fidgeted with a pen.

"Okay. Why don't we take a break for a few minutes. Alan, can you show Mrs. Colquitt where she can get something to drink?"

Annette looked at her daughter. "You want a soda or coffee, sweetie?"

"Soda is fine," she replied quietly.

John and Simon also left the room. Denise continued to fidget. I waited for her to look up.

"Denise," I hesitated, unwilling to tell her what was coming, "the next thing we need to discuss is going to be the hardest part. I'm going to ask you to tell me in your own words what you remember about the attack. This is the worst part of my job—making you relive it. Unfortunately, you'll have to do it again when we get to court if you testify."

Her blue eyes widened. Anguish hid in their depths as she gave a barely discernible nod.

"Today we can do this however you want. It'll be different in open court. There will be a judge, jury, lawyers … you get the point. If you want, today I can clear the room and it can be just you and me, or you can have your mom for support. I'd prefer to have the other lawyer, Mr. Graham, but if you're not comfortable with that, he doesn't have to be here."

Denise continued her wide-eyed stare.

"I'm going to go out and get a cup of coffee while you think about it. Okay?" I gave a supportive smile.

She nodded.

Chapter Twenty-One

August

The alarm clock read four in the morning. I'd set it for this ungodly hour around eleven last night, after I packed a bag and sent an e-mail to Greta informing her I'd need a few personal days for the funeral of a friend in Pittsburgh. After a quick shower, I dressed in a pair of comfy shorts and a T-shirt. The drive to Pittsburgh would take about ten hours and I planned to change into appropriate funeral attire at a rest stop along the way. Unfortunately, I'd already missed the Saturday memorial service, but the graveside service was set for four this afternoon and I was determined to see her laid to rest.

Softly I shut the trunk and doors as I loaded the Mini trying to make as little noise as possible. The reason for my stealth—to avoid waking Danny and engaging in a possible confrontation. My past was catching up to me, and today I took the coward's way out. Earlier this morning I slid a note underneath his door apologizing for last night's hysterics.

After coasting down the drive, I started the car and motored to the highway headed north.

****

October, two years ago

When I returned to the boardroom with a cup of coffee and a plate full of pastries, Denise sat still and alone, tuned out, staring into space. I called her name three times before she came out of her trancelike state and offered her a Danish. She accepted the blueberry puff but left it sitting on the plate in front of her, untouched.

"I'd like to tell you the story ... only you," she said softly but with firm resolve.

"Are you sure you don't want your mom in here with you?"

Her head moved side to side. "No. I don't want her to hear it until she has to. I know she'll be there in court when the time comes."

Placing my hand on hers, I waited until she looked up at me. "Denise, this isn't about your mom and if you need her support to get through this, she should be here."

"I think it'll be easier telling a stranger."

I nodded with understanding. Sometimes it was hardest to tell the truth to the people we loved because of the emotional attachments. "I'll ask Mr. Graham to take your mom to another room while we do this. We need to get some information from her anyway, and he can start working on that. When your mom comes back, I'll leave you alone with her for a bit while I speak with my colleague."

John's office was one floor up and midway between the elevator and J.J.'s suite of offices that took up the back quarter of the floor. The blinds were open and I saw, through the glass wall, John sat behind his oak desk while Simon sat in one of the ratty wooden guest chairs. I sat in the ugly chair next to Simon.

"It looks like she's only going to talk to me about the attack today."

John nodded sagely. "She doesn't want her mom with her?"

I shook my head.

"That's fine. I'll bring Annette into my office to review what happened at the hospital, the injuries sustained, and what the doctors are saying the long-term repercussions will be."

"Record it. If Denise decides to file a civil suit to sue for damages, her attorney may find your conversation useful." I turned to Simon. "Are the cameras in the room set to go?"

He gave me a nod. "Yes. I'll be down the hall recording everything."

"Good."

Fifteen minutes later our machinations played out. John successfully removed Annette to his office, and I sat across from Denise, heading into what I knew was going to be the most difficult part of her day, and mine.

"Denise, whenever you're ready you may begin."

After a few minutes of silence, she looked up and stared at above my head. "When I opened the back door, I remember I was laughing at something funny Mike said. Now I don't remember what it was. The door slammed shut behind me and automatically locked. Even if it hadn't locked, I'm not sure I would have been able to get back in. When he hit me the first time, it hurt but I was mostly shocked by the unexpectedness of it. I didn't know I could experience so much pain after the third hit." She shifted her focus to me, her eyes staring flatly with dilated pupils. "Until he held me down and started cutting me slowly." She pointed to the scar on her face. "He did this one first, nice and slow as I screamed into his hand he had mashed down on my mouth. Then he started slashing other parts with quick little flicks. I remember him saying 'who do you think you are, bitch? Nobody says no to Tony Rizolli and gets away with it. Do you think you're better than me? You're just some bar tramp. Where's your big bad boyfriend now, huh? He's next when I'm done with you.'"

My stomach churned as the story unfolded, and the yogurt I'd had for breakfast sat like a gurgling lump threatening to come back up. As hard as I clamped down on my emotions, making every effort to distance myself from Denise's description, there was simply no way to keep the revulsion at bay. While the story tumbled out, realization dawned—this was the first time Denise had recounted the entire attack and I was the recipient of the emotional orgy. Denise's distant intonation at the beginning fell away as the anguish, hurt, fear, and hate crept into the gruesome storytelling. The only reprieve from her horror was the fact she'd either passed out from the pain or her mind protected itself and she was blocked the memories of the actual rape. When she finally wound down, the room remained silent except for her hiccupping sobs and the creak of the chair as Denise rocked back and forth. Tears burned the back of my eyes and left a lump so heavy in my throat I had a tough time breathing past it. The box of tissues sat between us as Denise grabbed handfuls at a time to wipe her eyes and nose, littering the floor with the tear-soaked rags.

I sat frozen in place, fearing any movement would bring my emotions tumbling forth. Finally, I focused on the coffee cup to my left and grabbed it like a drowning man, chugging huge gulps in hopes of dislodging the lump. It didn't work. The droplets fell from their tiny precipices and began to snake down my face. Surreptitiously, I wiped my nose and eyes and turned away from Denise as her weeping began to quiet. There were a million ideas running through my head, and I was out of my depth. As a lawyer, I was trained to have an answer for everything, but for once in my life, I didn't know what to say. If this hideous act happened to me, I would have told the paramedics to leave me in the street and let me die. Denise was a stronger woman than I, and it fueled my determination to nail this monster to the wall.

After a while the waterworks ended. Denise blew her nose one more time, looked up at me and then swiftly away in embarrassment. Zeroing in on the untouched Danish, she plucked at the pastry, thoughtlessly pulling it apart with her too thin fingers, but she never took a bite.

"Denise..." I treaded softly.

Her eyes glanced off mine and returned to the table.

"You have nothing, nothing to be embarrassed about. You did not deserve this. No one deserves this," I said vehemently.

Her head came up and, for the first time, her tear-drenched eyes flickered.

I grabbed her hand. "I promise you ... *promise* you. We will get this bastard thrown in jail for a long, long time where he can never hurt you or anyone else ever again."

The intensity of my voice must have startled her because she sat back with wide eyes.

"Do you think you can help me do that?"

Slowly her head bobbed.

My grip relaxed as I realized how tightly I'd been holding on to her, but Denise surprised me. She turned her hand in mine and squeezed hard.

Her eyes, no longer dull, sparked with anger. "Tell me what I need to do. I'll do whatever it takes."

I envisioned Rizolli swinging from a noose and allowed a smirk to cross my features. "We'll talk more later. You did well. You've done enough for today."

Chapter Twenty-Two

August

The late morning sun beat through my windshield as I stopped to get a cup of coffee. The blast of humidity was stifling when I stepped out of the Mini's air-conditioned comfort. I checked my cell phone and found two text messages and a voice message. All three were from Danny. The text messages were succinct.

The first one at 4:38. *Where the hell are you going?*

The second at 5:12. *CALL ME!!!!* It included a frowny-face emoji.

The phone message was left at 4:46, and I didn't bother to listen to it. I imagined it was similar to the text messages. In an effort to reassure Danny, I sent a text message to him.

Need to do something. Don't worry. Will return in a few days.

As I completed the text, my phone rang. The caller's number was blocked. "Hello."

"Cara? It's Tom Bryant."

"What's up, Agent Bryant?"

"We have a lead on Rizolli."

"Where?"

"We had an APB out on him, and a person matching his description was spotted three days ago at a Cracker Barrel off I-95 in Northern Virginia. Where are you?" His voice sounded anxious.

"I'm on Interstate 77 on my way up to the funeral."

"Good. This sighting has put me back in play. I'll be in touch."

****

November, two years ago

After the emotional purging of our first meeting, Denise slowly came back to life. Getting Rizolli locked away became her main purpose for living; her anger seemed to drive her need for revenge. We met on a regular basis in preparation for trial. Denise called me with the smallest detail she remembered from that night or during the recovery following. Frequently, she came to the office to check up on things, and sometimes she watched as I interviewed and prepped witnesses who were in the bar the night Denise was beaten. Normally this would drive me, and any other busy prosecutor, absolutely bats. However, watching her marked improvement made me hold my tongue. I allowed her unannounced visits to continue. Over time she gained some weight and her eyes began to look slightly less haunted.

Annette spoke to Graham about the possibility of filing a civil suit following a positive outcome of the criminal trial. Off the record, we encouraged her to pursue the civil suit but requested she not consult a lawyer until the criminal trial was complete. Annette never said anything directly, but we speculated the medical and rehab bills were mounting, not to mention the psychiatric bills. Moreover, due to her head injury, Denise would have to remain on specialized medications for the rest of her life. I had Callan run Rizolli's financials. His legal holdings didn't add up to much more than half a million, but Callan was certain millions more were hidden in offshore accounts due to trails he'd established leading to the Cayman Islands. A savvy lawyer with deeper pockets could dig further and find the money. The knowledge Denise could bankrupt Rizolli, while he rotted in a prison cell, helped us all sleep well at night.

Dee's case also became the focus of my life. I continued to make deals and work on other cases, but J.J. wasn't piling as many new ones on my desk. The entire department knew how important this trial could turn out to be for the district attorney's office. I knew getting a conviction in this case could become a feather in my cap and skyrocket my career. Secretly, I started making plans to make a play for the Homicide or Crimes Against Persons Divisions.

When he had time, John continued to guide and mentor me through the pre-trial process. As opening arguments drew near, J.J. and John spoke regularly about the case and once in a while J.J. deigned to stray into the depths of the building to visit me in my shoebox office to be debriefed. J.J.'s support and belief in my skills meant a lot to me. Subtle hints were dropped regarding future career promotions should this case bring a successful conviction.

One afternoon about three weeks out from the trial, the DA stopped by to check on me just as Denise was gathering her things to leave. It was the first time J.J. had been available to meet her. "J.J. Stephenson, meet Denise Colquitt. Dee, J.J. is the district attorney and our fearless leader in the miasma of court systems here in Pittsburgh."

J.J. moved into politician mode, held out his hand and flashed his pearly whites. "It's nice to finally meet you, Ms. Colquitt. Cara is keeping me filled in on the case's progress. Thank you for being so helpful."

J.J. was a good-looking man, and his charm didn't fail to dazzle. Denise returned his warm smile. "It's a pleasure to meet you, Mr. Stephenson. Call me Denise."

"Dee, J.J. will be at the trial and may take the lead examining some of the witnesses." I'd explained how the two opposing lawyers would examine all the witnesses. However, I hadn't told her the district attorney might take the lead during trial since I was unsure of J.J.'s intentions.

Denise turned to me with wide begging eyes, her body stiff. "Oh, but you'll be asking me the questions we talked about on the stand, right? I mean, you'll be the one talking to me. Right?" Her voice pitched with panic.

My gaze flashed past her shoulder to meet J.J.'s. He gave a

slight nod.

I smiled with reassurance. "Yes, Dee. I'll be the one asking you questions in court. Okay?"

Her stance relaxed as relief flooded her system. She quickly turned back to J.J. "Don't be offended, Mr. Stephenson. I'm sure you're a good lawyer and all, it's just I've become so comfortable with Cara. I know I'll do much better if she's asking me the questions."

"Cara's one of my finest prosecutors. You're in good hands."

"Oh, I know. Cara's the best. I don't know what I would have done without her. She's helped me so much since taking this case. Don't worry. I'm sure she can use your help too." Denise patted J.J. on the shoulder as she passed him while exiting my office.

I had to bite my lip to keep from laughing. After all, J.J. was considered a top-notch prosecutor and was well respected by the staff. Even though he didn't spend as much time in court these days, his conviction rate was higher than any other DA in the state. It was one of the reasons he continued to be elected district attorney. Prior to becoming DA, J.J. played for the other team as a defense lawyer for a very old and highly respected law firm in Pittsburgh. My boss had seen all sides of the equation, which made for a strong ally or a formidable enemy, depending upon which side of the table you were sitting.

Once Denise was out of earshot, J.J. turned to me, his mien serious with warning. "Be careful what you tell her, Baker. If this case blows sideways, she's going to blame you. Don't let it get personal. This is business and you need to remember that. She's not your friend. She's the victim of a case you're prosecuting for the State. Don't forget."

"I won't, but this case is wrapped up in a bow like Christmas morning."

J.J. frowned and shook his head. "You're still young to the profession, Cara. Nothing's ever certain when it comes to juries."

I bit my lip and nodded. "I know."

This wasn't news to me. John had lectured me earlier about the same thing. It was just that, ever since Denise unloaded her story of the attack, we'd shared a bond, both of us driven: she to obtain revenge, and me to achieve justice to prove the system really worked.

Around four that afternoon Rizolli's lawyer, a rather green counselor named Ronald Jamieson, called. Our research showed Jamieson was only three years out of law school and up until now had dealt primarily with divorces, estate planning, child custody cases, and minor drug charges for white-collar kids. The weightiest court case he'd handled was defending a pair of middle-class teenagers charged with breaking and entering. They were convicted but Jamieson later got the conviction overturned on a technicality. It was clear the lawyer wasn't stupid, by any stretch of the imagination. However, the severity of this case was way out of his league. Callan provided me with a photo of Ronald exiting the courthouse. A thin man of average height, brown hair liberally sprinkled with gray and a long face with a dominant nose. Observing the photo made me finally realize what people meant when they said someone had a face like a horse.

Jamieson's license said he was twenty-eight, but the premature gray made him look older. I wondered if the gray hair got him the job as Rizolli's lawyer.

Jamieson called to discuss a deal. I suggested he come by my office, but he requested we meet at county lockup because his client wanted to speak to me directly. It was a big no-no for DAs to meet a defendant prior to court, and I couldn't believe Jamieson thought he had a chance in hell for it to happen. Generally, defense lawyers looking to make a deal approached an ADA in the hallways of the courthouse or the subtler ones cozied up to you at Sammy's dropping hints about how your client was a liar and the defendant was wrongly accused. Curiosity being what it was, an hour later I sat in an enclosed room across from Ronald Jamieson, Esq., and Tony "Thumbs" Rizolli shackled and cuffed to a metal table bolted to the floor. John was in court all day, and perhaps it was my own perverse nature that drove me to want to see this scumbag by myself.

Rizolli surprised me. His booking photo had been misleading. As a high-level mobster, I expected a tubby forty-something Italian with greasy slicked-back hair, not unlike Tony Soprano. A mid-thirties Italian, his black hair recently cropped short, deep-set brown eyes, high round cheeks and fleshy lips sat in front of me. He sported a beer gut. However his blue jumpsuit sleeves were rolled up to show dark, hair-covered muscles and, except for the gut, he seemed to be in good shape. He directed an intense glare at me and sported a smirk as though he knew something I didn't. A slight shudder ran through me. Rizolli was trying to intimidate me. I straightened my spine and clamped down on my anxiety. I refused to be intimidated by this brainless thug.

"Well, gentlemen, you requested this meeting. What is it you want?" I slapped my briefcase on the table, missing Rizolli's fingers by centimeters.

He didn't flinch, but his gaze sharpened and his smirk turned into a glower. The lawyer took the lead. "Mr. Rizolli would like to make a deal."

"The district attorney's office will not be making any deals with your client, Mr. Jamieson. I think that's been made clear. As you can see by the evidence, we have a strong case against your client. Either change to a guilty plea and move directly to sentencing or tighten your belt and get ready for trial," I threatened.

"Mr. Rizolli has information the DA's office might find interesting."

"What might that be?" I raised an eyebrow.

Rizolli sat forward, leaning over his hands, and his smirk returned. "I'm willing to provide information about certain high-level criminals." He spoke with a strong New Jersey accent.

"I'm sorry. You're going to have to be more specific. Give me a name." I showed little interest.

Rizolli shook his head. "Not without a deal on the table."

The fact Jamieson contacted me to make this deal either showed just how green he was, or his client was lying to him. I certainly had the authority to make deals for the DA's office; however, if Rizolli was alluding to the Barconi crime family, which I was pretty sure he was, New Jersey Mafia was out of my jurisdiction and dealt with Federal crimes. He should be talking to the FBI or attorney general's office, but I wasn't about to tell either of them that. As a matter of fact, it was stupid of me to come down here at all. I should have told Jamieson, "no deals" over the phone and been done with it. If Rizzoli dropped a name, I'd be ethically obligated to tell my boss, which could possibly put a deal in play, and that was the last thing I wanted for Denise Colquitt. J.J. would also be furious if he found out I was actually behind closed doors with a defendant and his attorney. Quite possibly he'd fire me.

Gathering my things, I got to my feet and ended the interview. "Let me make something very clear. We have everything we need to make this conviction. Only two things can change that, your client pleads guilty ... or he dies. Otherwise, I'll see you in court."

I glared directly into the criminal's eerie stare with gritted teeth and snarled. "Mr. Rizolli, I will be attending your sentencing since it'll be my pleasure to see you locked up for a very long time."

"Don't count on it, lady!" the mobster laughingly called after me.

With heart pounding agitation, I hightailed it out of the jail, putting as much distance between Rizolli and me as possible.

Chapter Twenty-Three

The little gas tank warning light brought me back to the present. I pulled off at the next exit ramp to fill up and take a restroom break. I bought myself a cup of cheap gas station coffee and debated purchasing a sad-looking banana. Common sense told me I should eat, but my stomach rebelled at the thought of swallowing actual food. While I waited for the tank to fill, my fingers dialed a number pattern memorized long ago.

"John Graham."

"John?" My voice wavered.

There was a pause. "Cara?"

"Yes."

A heavy breath blew across the phone line. "You heard about Denise." It was a statement, not a question. "Are you going to the funeral?"

"Yes." I waited, hoping he would tell me he was going too.

"I can't go, Cara. I'm due in court at one and there's no way it'll end in time. Alan and I attended the memorial service."

"I see." I'd have to face this on my own.

"I'm sorry."

I cleared my throat. "It's okay. I understand."

"Cara, it wasn't your fault. You did more than any other prosecutor would've done."

I nodded, and the silence drew out.

"Let's get together while you're here."

A voice in the background called John's name. "Sure. You need to go."

"Wait. I'll be with you in a minute." John's voice faded out, and then came back at me full force. "Cara…"

"I'll call you." I hung up knowing I had no intention of calling him back. Where I would have appreciated his presence and leaned on him for support at the funeral, I couldn't face a one-on-one.

I looked at the call history and found another missed call from Danny. He left no message. In the back of my mind, I knew I should talk to him, but I had no idea where to start or how to explain my role in what happened two years ago. Nor, did I want to drag him into my awful former life. He had enough to contend with in his own right. Mentally I'd put up a Chinese Wall, separating my life in Pittsburgh from the one in Denton. Heading back to Pittsburgh put me on the other side of that wall. Right now I couldn't organize my thoughts enough to figure out how to mesh to two worlds.

****

December, two years ago

It was a week before trial; John and I sat in his office discussing the strategy for opening arguments. J.J. hadn't revealed if he'd be presenting them, so I worked with John to prepare, in case I had to present. I'd watched John win over the jury within the first fifteen minutes of the case using his charisma and passion for justice. I took every detailed piece of advice he bestowed exceptionally serious.

"What the hell is this?" He stared past me.

Turning, I followed his gaze. "What is what?" Two men in dark suits, white shirts and conservative striped ties walked with a clipped gait past John's office.

"Feds." He spit out the word like a nasty taste was left in his mouth.

My stomach plummeted. "You think they're here about Rizolli?" I hadn't told John about my ill-advised visit to the slammer.

John shook his head. "I'm not sure."

It took less than ten minutes for the summons. John's

phone rang and, observing the caller display, he answered it on speakerphone. "Hi, Claudia. What can I do for you?"

"J.J. needs you and Baker to meet him in the boardroom."

"Does this have something to do with the two suits that just walked in?"

"I really couldn't say. He's in a mood, so don't make him wait." She hung up.

We gathered our files and trooped down the hall to a spacious meeting room located adjacent to J.J.'s office. It was dominated by a blond wooden table that seated ten and was considered the nicest meeting room in the building. Officially on the floor plan it was labeled "Conference Room C," but we all referred to it as the boardroom because it was used almost exclusively by J.J. for official meetings. A smaller meeting space was located in his office for more casual meetings.

Our boss wasn't in the room yet, so John and I settled ourselves facing the open door in order to watch the hallway. A few minutes later we were rewarded; J.J. came striding down the hall, the two suits in tow. John and I rose. Looking at the suits, he indicated the seats across from where John and I were then made his way around the table to stand next to me.

His voice harsh with barely controlled anger, J.J. introduced us. "Special Agent Bryant and Special Agent Hutchins meet Assistant District Attorneys John Graham and Cara Baker. They've been working the Colquitt case."

While J.J. made introductions, I studied Agent Bryant, thinking him remarkably handsome, with dark wavy hair and soft gray eyes. I barely registered Agent Hutchins, only that his handshake was firm but his hands cold. Both agents were tall, hovering right around six feet. What I didn't realize was the introductions were just the calm before the storm, and Bryant was a wolf in sheep's clothing.

"Agent Bryant, why don't you tell them what you just told me in my office?" J.J. took his seat.

The rest of us took our cue and sat. I regarded the two agents expectantly, while J.J. reclined with a guarded look and waited for the entertainment to begin.

Agent Bryant sat stiff in his high-backed tan leather chair. "The FBI is making a deal with Anthony Rizolli."

John leaned forward and ground out. "What kind of deal?"

"We're offering him immunity in exchange for his testimony against Carlo Barconi and about a dozen other known associates in the New Jersey Mafia."

I knew I shouldn't have been surprised but I felt blindsided. All these weeks we'd worked this case, waiting to hear something from the FBI, and now ... now when we had it in the bag ... ready to go ... practically a guaranteed conviction ... now the Feds decided to show up. I should have known this was coming after my little visit to see Rizolli and his lawyer. Jamieson was smarter than I initially gave him credit.

"This is bullshit!" John slammed his hand against the table so hard I jumped. "This case is sewn up. Rizolli's a criminal, and he's going to jail. What did you offer him, witness protection?"

"I'm afraid that information is above your pay grade." Hutchins responded calmly.

"What the hell took you so long? Rizolli's been rotting in jail for months. Why now?" John demanded.

"We made contact when he was initially booked, but he wasn't interested. His lawyer approached us yesterday. I guess the odds of beating this rap were dwindling and jail time wasn't looking so good." Bryant looked directly at me. "It seems Ms. Baker made quite an impression on Mr. Rizolli."

Both John and J.J. turned surprised looks at me. My stomach rolled over, and my mouth went arid.

I cleared my throat and licked my lips, breaking the stunned silence. "Mr. Bryant..."

"Special Agent Bryant," he responded.

"Special Agent Bryant," I mocked, "do you comprehend what kind of animal Tony Rizolli is? Is it the FBI's policy to allow rapists and murderers to roam free through the streets of innocent neighborhoods in Arizona and New Mexico?" I asked this with a sickly sweet smile.

"He won't be completely free. We'll be putting him on a tracking anklet and a short leash. Trust me, Ms. Baker. I probably know more about Tony Rizolli than you." His tone was curt.

"Really, Agent Bryant?" The anger took hold and I saw red. "Somehow I seriously doubt that." Whipping out one of my case file folders, I threw down 8 x 10 glossies of Denise Colquitt following the rape. Photos taken at the crime scene and in the hospital. Grotesque photos of her face, arms and chest torn and bleeding. Close-ups of her visage still bloodied, left eye swollen shut, a cut seeping through the bandage taped on by the EMTs, her knee swollen to the size of a grapefruit. The photos littered the table in front of the two agents.

"That monster you're talking about giving immunity to gruesomely assaulted an innocent woman and if you think for one moment I'm going to allow you to just let him walk out scot-free, you've got another think coming." My voice was sharp and indignant. Both hands splayed against the table. I towered like an avenging angel over the two men. My face burned with rage.

Agent Bryant seemed unruffled by my tirade. "Ms. Baker, I appreciate your candor and zeal to obtain justice. Unfortunately, it isn't up to you and this isn't a negotiation. Our coming here today was merely a courtesy."

"What the hell does that mean?" I glanced at J.J.

"The deal's been made," he rumbled.

That took the wind out of my sails, and I slumped back into my seat.

"So you see, Ms. Baker, there isn't anything to be done but finish the paperwork and have Rizolli transferred into FBI custody."

My head snapped up. "I'll go to the press and tell them exactly what kind of deals the FBI makes. Rizolli won't stand a chance as a snitch."

Before either of the agents could respond, J.J. thrust to his feet. "Baker," he barked, "in my office. Now!" Without a backward glance to see if I followed, he stalked down the hall.

I slammed the door behind me and waited for J.J. to chew me out for losing my cool in front of the Feds.

He turned to face me, let out a frustrated sigh, and pinched his nose between his thumb and forefinger. "Cara, it's over. The deal's been made."

"C'mon. Isn't there something we can do to prevent this gross injustice? Don't you have to sign off on it or something?"

"It's merely a formality. The attorney general is putting pressure on my office. There are other things at play here. Things above your pay grade."

I ground my teeth, hating that phrase "above your pay grade."

"If they can turn one fish loose to capture a dozen, they'll do it. The Barconi crime family is big fish with bigger crimes affecting more people, including bribery, drugs, racketeering, and human trafficking. The Feds are here to arrange for Rizolli's transfer into their custody in order to begin deposing him and to start the WITSEC proceedings."

Marching past the DA, I looked out his window onto the plaza below where pedestrians walked with purpose, going about their busy lives without realizing three floors up a tragedy was happening. "J.J., I promised Denise Colquitt justice," I whispered. "I promised we ... I ... would lock this bastard behind bars. I promised she'd have nothing to fear from him ever again."

"I know, Cara. Sometimes we can't keep our promises."

I sighed, rubbing my hands up and down my crossed arms. J.J. was too much a gentleman to say, I told you so. "How much longer can we keep him?"

"Not long. It can take up to twenty-four hours to process him once the ball starts rolling. What does it matter?"

I turned to face J.J. "Now she'll never be able to sue him in civil court. His immunity will see to that."

He nodded with sangfroid. "I know."

"How is she going to pay for her medical bills?"

"I don't know. I don't know." He sighed.

"How long can you stall the Feds?"

"Not long. Why?"

My mind started doing some fast thinking. "Callan found trails of money sitting in offshore accounts in the Caymans. Possibly millions of dollars."

"Yes. I recall John mentioning that. So?"

"Don't the Feds confiscate dirty money but allow legitimate dollars to move with the witness?"

"Something like that."

"If the Feds don't get their hands on the money in the Caymans, what's to stop Rizolli from taking it and disappearing for good, before Barconi comes to trial?"

"Nothing, I suppose, except for a tracking anklet. I imagine they'll make him wear one until the trial and maybe even afterwards."

"I want that money given to Denise Colquitt for her pain and suffering. I want Rizolli in a tracking anklet for twenty years." This was a bizarre request and I knew I skated on thin ice, but I refused to give up so easily. Someone needed to fight for Denise.

J.J. shook his head. "Cara, what you're proposing is quite a stretch. The Feds will never make a deal like that."

"But the FBI has the authority to freeze the accounts and seize the money, even overseas. What's going to happen to that cash? It sits around for years in some federal warehouse collecting dust, or as a number in some computer." I swooshed my hand in J.J.'s direction. "Am I right?"

J.J. nodded.

"I wasn't kidding when I threatened to go to the press, J.J." My ire was up. "How long do you think Rizolli will last in county lockup once Barconi hears about this? With twenty-four hour news and social media … the Feds won't be able to get to him fast enough." I pulled the cell phone out of my suit pocket and waggled it in the air.

"Cara," my boss' voice full of warning, "if you go to the press I'll have to fire you. The bar would investigate, and you'd lose your license. And that's the least of your worries. The FBI could bring you up on charges. You'd be charged as an accessory to murder. Your life, as you know it, would be over."

"I know." I stared him dead in the eye without flinching.

He considered me for a moment and apparently concluded that I wasn't bluffing. "All right. I'll let you make your little proposition to the FBI, but let me warn you, Cara, to temper your remarks. I don't want to have to fire you. If you make good on your threats, make no mistake ... I *will* do it."

We were startled by a quick knock. John opened the door. "Hey, boss, I think the Feds are getting antsy. You two ready to come back to the table?"

J.J. scrutinized me one more time; I could see the gears click into place. "Yes, I believe we are."

John had played host while we were gone; coffee mugs and stale donuts from the kitchen sat in front of the two agents and the photos had been returned to their file folder. I followed J.J. into the room and we took our seats.

"Gentlemen, thanks for waiting. I apologize for the delay," J.J. said. "We have a proposition for you."

Agent Hutchins leaned forward onto his elbow. "Mr. Stephenson—"

J.J. abruptly cut in. "That's District Attorney Stephenson, Special Agent Hutchins. And, I have not signed the exchange of custody papers ... yet."

Hutchins' head snapped back as though he'd been slapped. He cleared his throat. "As I was saying, I believe my partner made it clear we aren't here to negotiate."

I rushed in to start my groundwork. "Special Agents Bryant and Hutchins, please just listen for a moment. Look, I'm sorry for my outburst earlier. I don't know if you're fully aware of the ghastly things Rizolli has done to Ms. Colquitt and how she's suffered. However," I held up my hand to stop the denial I saw on the tip of Bryant's tongue, "I'm sure you are aware of many other heinous crimes committed by him, but you haven't had enough proof to bring to court. Am I right?"

Their well-trained faces remained expressionless, but I saw a flicker of understanding in Bryant's eyes. "That being said, I want to remind you Denise Colquitt is the victim here. What you're doing will make her a victim twice over and perpetrated by her own government, no less. A government that should provide her safety and justice. A government whose sworn duty it is to protect the innocent people of the United States. After all, we're working on the same team. Do you disagree?"

I could see my message was getting through. Hutchins remained poker-faced, but Bryant gave a slight shake of his head. "What are you getting at, Ms. Baker?"

"As you'll be taking away Ms. Colquitt's right to obtain justice and her right to sue the defendant for pain and suffering, I think the FBI owes Ms. Colquitt a settlement."

"You must be joking. Is this some sort of shakedown? You expect the government to pay Ms. Colquitt?" Bryant protested.

"No and yes. It's my understanding you'll be freezing all the defendant's assets, allowing him to take legitimately acquired money with him into the witness protection program. Is that correct?"

"I fail to see that's any of the DA's concern." Hutchins' deep ringing tones responded.

"Bear with me, Agent. Is that correct or not?"

"Perhaps," Bryant answered briefly.

I rolled my eyes. "We want a settlement for Ms. Colquitt from Rizolli's illegitimate assets you'll be confiscating."

Bryant decided to play along, with a snort he asked, "How much?"

"Five million."

Hutchins' eyebrows rose. Swiveling their chairs, the two agents shared grins, both probably thinking I was off my rocker.

"That's an interesting number, Ms. Baker. How on earth did you come up with it?" Agent Bryant snickered, while his partner masked a chuckle with a cough.

"Gentlemen," I stood and leaned over them. "You and I both know if Ms. Colquitt sued for pain and suffering, she'd win millions more. The photos speak for themselves." My eyes bored through them like daggers, effectively silencing their mirth.

Bryant had the decency to look ashamed, and he appeared to be pondering my suggestion. "What you're asking is preposterous, and I don't see any way to sell this idea to my superiors. You know if we agree, it could set a hell of a precedent."

"Five million and not a penny less." Returning to my seat, I crossed my arms and legs with a defiant expression and hid the dread I felt if the FBI didn't agree to this cockamamie scheme. "Oh, and I want Rizolli on a tracking anklet for the next twenty years." I was surprised neither John nor J.J. had spoken up, but I figured they were covering their own asses, leaving me out to tighten my own noose.

"I'm sorry to disappoint you," Bryant shook his head. "So far we've tracked less than a million. Our deal with Rizolli is five years after the trials … with convictions. Ten if he doesn't get us convictions."

"Don't jerk me around, Bryant. This thug's a high-level mobster, and I'm sure he's made millions in racketeering alone." I left the anklet issue be. The trials could take upwards of five years, possibly more. If they didn't get convictions, Rizolli would be in the anklet for a minimum of fifteen years. Longer than I originally thought we could negotiate.

"I can assure you we haven't found anything close to that much."

"I see." Suddenly I did see. The FBI knew nothing about the Cayman accounts, an oversight that needed to be brought to their attention. "Give me … seventy-two hours. If I can help the FBI find the money, do we have a deal?"

Bryant sat back, steepling his fingers. "Sure." He gave a patronizing smile. "But only forty-eight hours. If you can find five million in illegitimate funds, Ms. Colquitt can have it."

"Then I guess we'll see you back here in two days." John finally spoke up. "Shall we say three o'clock?"

"Three o'clock." Bryant confirmed then turned to J.J. "We'll need those papers signed, District Attorney Stephenson. Good luck on your wild goose chase, Ms. Baker." Bryant rose to his feet with a condescending grin.

I simply nodded and returned his pompous smile.

J.J. escorted the agents down the hall to the elevators. The minute the FBI was out of sight, I called Callan and asked him to join us. As providence would have it, he was in the building and soon arrived in the boardroom.

"What's up, counselors?"

"The FBI made a deal with Rizolli," John answered.

Callan whistled through his teeth and rocked back on his heels. John proceeded to fill the investigator in on our proposal to the FBI.

"So, can you find the money?" I asked.

"You said I only have forty-eight hours?"

"The FBI will be back on Friday at three."

Callan's face broke out into a broad grin. His eyes shifted back and forth between the two of us. "Well, then, I'd better get to work. I need to find five million dollars for Ms. Colquitt."

"Thanks, Callan." I sighed with relief. "I owe you one."

"I'll keep that in mind," He responded with a shrewd smile.

Once Callan left, John turned to me. "What the hell did the FBI agent mean when he said you made an impression on Rizolli?"

I sucked wind and confessed my little jailhouse visit. "I didn't know what Rizolli had told Jamieson, if anything, or if either one of them would go to the Feds, or if the Feds would be interested in making a deal. After all, Rizolli is up on felony charges."

John watched my confession with accusing eyes. Either Jamieson or Rizolli could have called the FBI, and clearly, the FBI was salivating to get a crack at the Barconi family no matter what the cost.

"Shit, Cara. You should have talked to me before trotting off to jail. That is the dumbest fucking thing you could have done. You realize that little visit could end your career." He rubbed a hand down his face.

I nodded. "I know. I'm sorry."

Chapter Twenty-Four

August

The car hummed quietly bringing me closer to the city I thought I'd left for good. I glanced down at my phone. A text message from Danny waited. Nothing else. No messages from Bryant. I didn't know if the lead Bryant mentioned would pan out, or if he was on a wild goose chase. I blamed the Marshals for losing Rizolli but was still angry with the FBI for originally granting the immunity. However, I'd been a fool to believe the move to Denton would be the fix I craved. It simply buried my deep-seated anger, guilt and resentment.

A small ray of hope wavered in the distance like a desert oasis shimmering in my subconscious, and, like a thirsty man, I yearned for it. If the Eagle was on the FBI's radar, I assumed his reputation was well deserved. Eagles were known for their predatory nature, and I hoped this one lived up to his moniker. That line of thinking didn't disturb me in the least. As a matter of fact, it'd be a relief if the Mafia took care of exterminating this particular rat.

You can run, Rizolli you rat, but you can't hide. I smiled evilly, as the miles sped by, relishing in my thoughts of justice and admittedly of revenge.

****

December, two years ago

Two days later at three, John, J.J., Callan and I sat in the same positions, facing the door, as Claudia escorted Agent Bryant down the hall to the boardroom. We all did the nice, shaking hands, and asked "How are you," without really meaning it or caring about the answer. J.J. introduced Callan and we took our seats.

My boss inclined his head to me.

"Special Agent Bryant, through our investigative efforts we were able to find three different offshore bank accounts in the Caymans, adding up to just over seven point two million. Two were set up under shell companies of shell companies and one under the name of Anthony Rizolli's dead grandmother. Mr. Callan was able to track the shell companies back to Rizolli." I placed three manila folders in front him.

Bryant kept his face from revealing his thoughts. However, I read disbelief in his eyes as he perused the research.

Callan leaned toward Bryant and, with his pen, pointed out connections as he explained his research. He laid down paper after paper, and at one point flipped up his lap top monitor to show off his hacking skills. It was clear by his reaction Bryant and the FBI were unprepared for our success. Everyone in that room knew from our findings the FBI had a hole in their investigation if they overlooked seven point two million. Moreover, Bryant seemed embarrassed to be caught with his pants down in front of a state district attorney and his "lowly" assistants. After about half an hour of explanations and review, Bryant excused himself and asked if there was somewhere he could make a phone call in private. J.J. showed him into the smaller conference room attached to his private office, and then he went to speak quietly to Claudia, whose desk was conveniently located near the closed door.

The rest of us sat wordlessly as we waited for Bryant's return. I fidgeted with my pencil, using my mind to will the FBI to stick to their agreement. John unhooked his iPhone from his belt and began tip-tapping messages. Callan, as skilled as the FBI Agent, sat in unmoving silence, waiting with a bland look on his face. I wished I could harness Callan's insouciance and offhand patience, but I knew of all the people working on this case, I was going to be the one to break the news to Denise. I prayed to God the news wouldn't break her.

Finally the door opened. J.J. looked up from Claudia's computer and followed Bryant's aggravated gait down the hall. His eyes swept across the three of us. "I assume you've prepared some paperwork?"

With a relieved smile, I pushed a dozen pages of legalese across the table at him. I was so thankful the FBI decided to play ball I couldn't even muster up a good gloat.

"Our legal department will have to review this before we sign anything." Bryant gathered the materials.

J.J. leaned across the wide table, placing his large hand on the manila envelope with the agreement. "I don't sign Rizolli's release forms until the papers are returned to us, signed. Are we clear?" His eyebrows rose in significance and his tone was curt but full of meaning. We weren't willing to release our ace in the hole until we got exactly what we were promised.

Bryant was nobody's fool. He responded with a brusque nod. "I'll be back by close of business Monday."

Chapter Twenty-Five

August

About an hour outside of Pittsburgh, I pulled off Interstate 79 at a rest stop to change into my funeral attire. The simple sleeveless black sheath dress and low-heeled pumps were pulled from the back of my closet, a remnant of my former life in the DA's office. Since the temperature was close to ninety, I dispensed with the matching black jacket. The red scarf I normally wore with it wouldn't be appropriate for today's venue. Instead, I tucked a gossamer black silk scarf into my handbag, intending to wear it over my head at the funeral. I completed the outfit with small silver earrings and a silver bracelet.

The fluorescent bulbs cast a greenish hue to my complexion, causing the circles under my eyes to stand out more than usual. Upon returning to the car, I drew out my makeup case and spent a solid quarter hour attempting to erase the ravages of the crying jag and sleepless night.

My reflection showed little improvement after applying the expensive crèmes and powders. I gave up and tossed everything back into the make-up case.

A glance at my phone showed no more messages, but once again a missed call from Danny, and nothing from Bryant. I motored back onto the highway for the remainder of the trip.

****

December, two years ago

My knuckles rapped resolutely on the weathered gray front door to Annette Colquitt's home, located in the working class neighborhood of McKee's Rocks. It was ten past seven and the sun had set. The front porch light threw a pathetically small orange glow across the wet concrete stoop. The dreary misty day was reflective of my mood, and I pulled my collar close to keep out the damp cold. A teenage girl with long dark brown hair and luminescent brown eyes answered the door. She tilted her head to one side. "Yes?"

This must be Natalie, Denise's younger sister who was still in high school. I smiled and introduced myself.

Natalie nodded in recognition. "Oh yeah. I've heard about you. You're Dee's lawyer. C'mon in." She stepped back and hollered over her shoulder in true teen fashion, "Mooom, Dee's lawyer is here."

I entered a miniscule foyer that opened into a small but neat living room with a slipcovered couch and recliner situated around a scratched oak coffee table circa 1960. To the left of the living room was a staircase that led up to the bedrooms. In the rear of the living room sat an informal dining table with textbooks and a blue spiral notebook lying open on top. A doorway led to the kitchen and back of the house. The aroma of pot roast and baked potatoes filled the air.

Annette walked out from the kitchen wiping her hands on a towel. "Hello, Cara. What a pleasant surprise."

I cringed inwardly, knowing how unpleasant the task in front of me loomed. "Hello, Annette."

"Come in and sit down." She indicated the couch. "Dinner will be ready in about twenty minutes. Would you like to join us?"

"No thank you. I was wondering if I could speak to you and Denise ... alone?" I felt no reason to drag Natalie into the ensuing disappointment, and if I was honest with myself, I wanted as few witnesses as possible to my perfidy. "There have been some developments in the case, and I have a few papers for her to sign."

"Sure. Why don't we sit at the table?" She turned to the

teen. "Natalie, go tell Dee Ms. Baker is here to see her, and you can finish up the rest of your homework in your room." Natalie gathered her notebooks and slowly trudged up the stairs.

"And, Natalie," called Annette, "keep the music down to a dull roar, please." Her gaze returned to mine with a proud motherly smile. "Would you like something to drink? I have Diet Coke or iced tea."

"Just a glass of water would be fine. Thanks." I feared my throat would close up over the awful words I had impart.

Denise, crutch-free but still sporting a knee brace, entered the dining area. She smiled shyly. "Hi, Cara." This was the first time I'd ever visited their home.

"Hello, Dee. Nice to see you. You're looking good." It was the truth. Denise had put on weight over the past weeks and her cheeks had filled out, changing the painfully angular face she possessed when we first met. The dark circles had receded, and her clothes seemed to fit better instead of sagging loose. Her hair, which hung limp at our first meeting, now looked thick and healthy and had recently been styled into a shoulder length bob that framed her features, setting off her pretty blue eyes, but hiding the ugly scar. The lump at the pit of my stomach twisted and roiled. The information I was here to divulge could devastate the immense improvements.

Annette came back into the room and suggested we sit. After taking a generous drink, I placed the glass next to my briefcase. Over the weekend, I'd spent most of my waking hours dreaming up a million different scenarios on how to break the news and what the Colquitts' reaction would be. Now the moment had arrived, I struggled to phrase the appropriate words. Technically, I knew my problem. I'd become too enmeshed in Denise Colquitt's pain and suffering. I made this case personal, instead of holding her and Annette at arm's length like John and J.J. were able to do. Moreover, I made her a promise I could no longer keep. Somewhere along the way, I stopped being a litigator doing my job and became her friend. Her confidant. It was wrong. I knew this case was going to be a hard lesson for me.

With great effort, I put on a detached mask. "Ladies, I have some bad news." They both froze. Fear leapt into Denise's eyes. Her pupils grew black.

"What kind of bad news?" Annette breathed.

I opened my mouth to tell the official story but … I couldn't lie to them. "Tony Rizolli has made a deal with the FBI."

Looks passed back and forth between the two women. Denise's gaze returned to me. "What does that mean?"

"It means the FBI has taken custody of Rizolli and will be granting him immunity in exchange for his testimony against Carlo Barconi and members of his Mafia crew."

Both ladies stared open-mouthed at me. Denise shook her head. "I don't get it."

I couldn't hold their gazes any longer. Looking down at the briefcase, I gripped the handle painfully. My speech came out slow and deliberate. "We won't be going to trial, Denise. Rizolli has signed a deal with the Feds and can no longer be prosecuted for any crimes he has committed in the past. He will provide testimony at upcoming Federal court trials and will be relocated in the witness protection program." Technically, I shouldn't have told them this much information, but I just didn't give a shit about technicalities right at this moment.

"How can the FBI do that? They can't just take the case away from me. They can't just pretend he didn't do this to me." Her body shook.

"Unfortunately, they can."

"Cara, you have to stop them." She reached out and placed her hand on mine. "Tell them they can relocate Rizolli after my trial. I want to testify. I have to testify." Tears rolled down her cheeks and the shaking became more violent.

"I tried. I'm sorry. It didn't work," I said miserably.

"You promised we'd get him," she accused with a martial light in her eyes. "You *promised*. You lied to me. You're a liar, Cara Baker. You never said the FBI could take him away like this. What kind of lawyer are you? How could you let this happen? I hate you!" She yelled. "You're no better than the monster who did this to me!"

I shook my head, unable to deny her denunciations. Unable to defend the complete and utter injustice being handed to her by someone she trusted to bring her abuser to justice.

"How can you let him get away with this? It's not fair. He almost killed me." She sobbed her voice cracking.

"I know. You're right," I murmured. The guilt already gnawing at me only worsened with her accusations. She was right. I had no business making those promises to her. It wasn't fair on any level and, as I told Bryant at our initial meeting, Denise Colquitt was now a victim twice over. I was angry Special Agent Bryant wasn't here to witness his devastation.

Annette moved, pulling her daughter to her chest. "Where is the justice, Ms. Baker?" she asked over Denise's head with quiet anguish.

I shook my head. Tears burned the backs of my lids. "I don't know."

We made a wretched tableau; Annette consoling and rocking her daughter, tortured tears running down her face. Denise wept into her mother's bosom, and me sniffling and refusing to allow the tears to fall; my face screwed up in grief.

Time passed and Denise's sobbing quieted.

Breathing deeply, I wiped my eyes with the back of my hand and gulped the rest of my water in an effort to swallow the lump in my throat.

I opened my mouth. Nothing came out. I cleared my throat and spoke with a raspy voice, "Because of his immunity deal, you won't be able to take Rizolli to civil court to sue for pain and suffering."

Annette shook her head. The hits just kept on coming. Blessedly, I knew there was one thing I'd done right, and it could, at least, alleviate the financial burden on the family. "The FBI agreed to give you some of the money they seized from Rizolli's accounts. I know it doesn't make up for the injustice, but it should pay for the doctors' bills and the continuing care." I spoke directly to Annette. I pulled an envelope containing the five million dollar check from my briefcase and gently laid it on the table. I didn't bother with the paper work. Snapping the lock shut, I stood and, in a zombie-like trance, let myself noiselessly out the door.

I called in sick the rest of the week and turned the ringer off on all my phones. I slid into depression, wandering aimlessly around my apartment, eating what was within easy reach, which consisted of a bag of popcorn, three apples, a quart of ice cream and very little else. I didn't shower and wore the same pajamas five days running. The lack of hygiene and stale air made the apartment smell like a gerbil cage, but I didn't care. I sat on the couch and watched bad soap operas and talk shows during the day and infomercials at night because I couldn't sleep. The scene at Dee's house ran over and over in my head. The guilt refused to lessen and as the days passed, it took root, festering in my thoughts and stomach. Months later it would be one of the contributing factors to my ulcers. On Sunday evening, I finally fell into an exhausted slumber and slept for sixteen hours straight, waking at six Monday morning with a renewed determination, ready to return to the trenches of my job.

I was one of the early birds in the office that morning, fueling myself with caffeine and resolve. Both J.J. and John were glad to see me back in the office looking bright-eyed and bushy tailed. J.J. specifically stopped by my office to congratulate me on my five-million-dollar coup with the FBI. He still couldn't believe they agreed to it. What my coworkers didn't realize, until months later—my bright-eyed look wasn't due to acceptance or sleep but rather a new drive. It was the beginning of the end for me at the DA's office.

During the week I spent drifting into depression and having a pity party at home; Annette Colquitt had contacted the office looking for me. Ultimately, John took her call. I don't exactly know what John told her, but she and her daughter left a few phone messages apologizing and thanking me for the money. Eventually, I received a thank you note that included an address and phone number change. I was pleased to note the address was located in a nice suburb called Cranberry Township with good schools. One morning I took a detour to work, driving by their new house, a white two-story Colonial style McMansion with black shutters and a red door. A tan Lexus sat in the driveway. Through the grapevine, I heard about the foundation Denise started for victims of violent crimes. I subscribed to their monthly e-newsletter to keep up with the foundation's activities in the community, and I made regular anonymous donations.

However, Denise and I never spoke again.

I requested to be moved into the crimes against persons division, which J.J. granted. I took on hard-core cases and stopped making deals for the lighter ones. Virtually every thug or crime that came across my desk I took to court, refusing to allow pleas to lesser charges.

Criminals either pled to the charge they were booked with or I took them to court. I became a tenacious and aggressive prosecutor, winning many of my cases. Instead of being the judges' favorite deal-making ADA, I became a thorn in their sides. Eventually J.J. started receiving complaints, and defense lawyers went over my head to request deals for their clients.

John took me aside and discussed the need to get back to making deals. "It's part of the job. It's what we do. We can't clog the court dockets with every case on your desk."

I nodded and assured him I understood and everything would be okay. Because I was winning my cases, J.J. had little justification to fire me. During the next year and a half, I made a name for myself as a dogged litigator and relentless opponent. I also received half a dozen proposals from assorted law firms, all of them offering to pay at least double my salary. I refused them all and drove myself harder, working sixteen hour days.

Because I was so focused on the job, my social life purposefully disappeared. I didn't date and rebuffed any invitations. In the past I'd been a regular at happy hour at Sammy's down the street from our offices, where other attorneys and office staff congregated on Friday nights. Not any longer. The only social activity in my life outside of work became the self-defense and martial arts classes I attended twice a week with my best friend Angela. Of course, the excessive work schedule and utter lack of a real life took its toll and led to the aforementioned ulcers and eventually a mammoth flame out, culminating in my move to South Carolina. After I collapsed in the middle of the courtroom during trial and was hospitalized for exhaustion, J.J. forced me to take a two-week vacation, from which I never returned. I faxed him my resignation.

Chapter Twenty-Six

August

Turning into the Northside Cemetery, across the river from McKee's Rocks, I stopped at the gatehouse to ask directions to the funeral. A kindly septuagenarian handed me a map and, with a shaky gnarled hand, indicated the way through a maze of sloping green hills and gravesites. I parked behind a blue SUV, the last in a line of cars. In the distance a small group of dark-clad mourners circled around Denise's grave, their heads bowed as the priest began his prayers. A large oak tree partially shaded the funeral-goers about ten feet away from the crowd, and it was where I took refuge; with the black scarf over my head and the large sunglasses, I doubted anyone would recognize me. In one hand I gripped a flower bunch I'd purchased from a street vendor, in the other a bundle of tissues which were immediately put to use. Over two dozen people formed the somber gathering at the grave site. I couldn't see Annette or Natalie and assumed they were seated somewhere in the front row of folding chairs. The day was sunny and hot, but there was no humidity and every so often a breeze kicked up, rustling the leaves in the trees above. My silky head covering billowed and danced lightly upon my cheeks.

The cleric droned on for about twenty minutes, the only interruption soft weeping. No one else spoke. I assumed the eulogies had been given at the memorial service on Saturday night. At the conclusion of the clergyman's sermon, two bagpipers stepped forward to play a somber dirge unknown to me but apt for the funeral. Then there was a rustling through the crowd and I watched the backs of two black-garbed women approach the mahogany casket—Natalie and her mother Annette. Each placed a yellow rose on the coffin, and as Natalie turned away, her head bowed, a high keening sob filled the air loud enough to be heard over the wail of the bagpipes.

Annette's shaking body collapsed over her daughter's casket. Her hands gripped the smooth wood, refusing to let go of the last physical piece of her daughter. My hands automatically reached forward in sympathy, but much too far away to be of any assistance. Natalie clutched her mother's shoulders trying, unsuccessfully, to pull her away. After what seemed like an eternity but was probably just a few moments, the priest came forward, spoke low and quick to the ladies and, with the help of another male attendee, propelled Annette away from the coffin along the grassy pathway to a waiting limousine.

The bagpipers came to a wheezing close as other mourners took turns laying flowers on the casket. I recognized Charlie Tanniger and Michael Finnigan from McCormack's as they stepped forward to bid adieu. Finally, one man who'd stood at a distance, similar to me, came forward and placed a beautiful purple iris on top of the many other offerings. His lips moved, but I was too far away to hear his last words to the deceased. He turned and I saw his profile. It seemed familiar. My brows crunched in concentration as I tried to place him when it hit me—the nose, jaw line, and lips were Denise's. This then must have been her absentee father. He shuffled away and at last, I remained the final mourner near the grave site.

Salty tears dried on my face as I advanced toward Denise's final resting place; the soft wind picked up and pulled the scarf from my head. Mixing my small offering in with the rest, I made sure to leave the iris undisturbed. I laid a hand on the glossy box.

My voice came out in a ragged whisper. "Good-bye, Dee. You were a beautiful person whose life was cut too short. I'm sorry I couldn't do more for you in your time of need. I'm sorry, I let you down." The tears started again, blurring my vision. My head bowed in grief, as I ineffectively blotted my face with dampened Kleenex and made my stumbling way back toward the Mini.

From close behind, I heard my name. "Mrs. Baker?"

I turned.

Natalie stood a few feet away. I froze, unable to move.

"Mrs. Baker, do you remember me? I'm Natalie, Dee's sister. We met once."

I nodded. My mind went blank, and the trite words of condolence wouldn't come forth.

"We're having a wake at the house, and my mom and I would like you to come." She said tentatively.

I stared. "Umm, I'm not really sure ..."

"It's just a small gathering. Please, say you'll come. My mom really wants to talk to you."

"I guess I could ... if you're sure it's all right with your mom." I hedged, glancing past her shoulder at the dark lines of the forbidding limousine.

"Absolutely. She's the one who recognized you when your scarf fell off and asked me to speak to you. We moved a while back. Do you know our new address?"

"Do you live in a white house with a red door up in Cranberry Township?"

"Yup," she nodded. "That's the place. So, we'll see you in a bit?" She tilted her head to the side with the question.

"Okay, I'll be there shortly."

Natalie turned and strode back to the waiting car, her long coltish legs quickly eating up the distance. The limousine lumbered out of its parking spot and took the lead; the quiet suddenly broke as other attendees cranked over their engines to follow.

I sat in the car for a good fifteen minutes after the blue SUV drove away, pulling myself together, gathering my thoughts. When I finally got a grip, I checked the mirror. The makeup I'd put on at the rest stop was a mess. Fortunately, I hadn't bothered with mascara or I would have had raccoon eyes on top of everything. It took a few more minutes to make myself presentable before driving over to Annette's home. When I arrived, the street was so full I had to park a block away, apparently everyone attending the funeral followed the limousine to the wake.

My stomach churned and my palms began to sweat as I approached the house, unsure of the type of reception awaiting me. With dragging feet, I plodded up the walkway and upon reaching the steps, the front door popped open.

A stocky red-haired man stepped out pulling a pack of cigarettes from his breast coat pocket. He gave me a faint smile and held the door. "You smoke?"

I shook my head.

"Me neither. Nasty habit, isn't it?" He stuck a butt in his mouth.

Smiling faintly at his little joke, I entered the foyer. A blast of cool air greeted me and a mixed aroma of coffee, perfume and homemade casseroles permeated the front hall. The rooms were large, and at least twenty-five mourners filled the living/dining room without making it feel stuffy or crowded, a distinct difference from the tiny house Denise used to reside in. People spoke softly in small groups or grazed from the overloaded buffet set up in the dining room. A throaty chuckle from the back of the house disturbed the solemnity. The mirth seemed out of place. I felt uncomfortable being here, and I debated whether I should turn around and head right back out the door when, once again, someone called my name.

"Cara Baker, right?" A male voice rumbled.

My shoulders hunched and I looked over to see who spoke.

A large pro-wrestler-looking fellow in a tight-fitting suit smiled his straight teeth at me. "Charlie Tanniger, from McCormack's."

I returned his delighted smile and his beefy handshake.

"I heard you moved down to Charleston." He scrutinized my face. "You look … tan." His eyes didn't miss the sleep deprivation. "When did you get into town?"

"Just as the funeral began. I left around four this morning."

He nodded with understanding. "Long trip."

"About ten hours." I shrugged with nonchalance.

"So, are you with a law firm down south or did you open up your own shop?"

I shook my head. "I'm not practicing law right now. I'm working at a library."

His eyes narrowed, trying to make the leap from lawyer to librarian. "You enjoy that?"

I laughed at his incredulous expression. "Yes, as a matter of fact, I do. A lot less stress."

"Humph." Charlie shook his shoulders. "Seems like a hell of a waste. Denise said you were a great lawyer. Said you really looked out for the little people when everyone else was trying to screw them."

"I don't know about that," I answered faintly.

"Well, she really appreciated that money you gave her. Said she didn't know how she would've paid all those medical bills. Her mom sure loves this house. I'm glad they moved here. It's a better place for them. Safer. Better schools for Natalie too."

I nodded blindly, shocked by his friendliness and honesty. I expected to be a pariah, not the savior of the little people. Apparently, the story Denise told Charlie didn't quite match up with the truth. Perhaps it had been less painful for Dee to tell people white lies.

Charlie continued, "And you know she never could've started that foundation without the money. Her work became really important to her."

"She was an amazing lady."

"Here you are." We were interrupted by Natalie. She peeked around Charlie's mammoth bicep. "I wasn't sure if you were going to make it."

I gulped. "Here I am."

"Sorry, Charlie, I need to steal Cara. Mom's been waiting to talk to her." Natalie took my hand.

"It was good seeing you again, Charlie," I said over my shoulder as Natalie led me away.

"You too, Cara. Get some rest. You look tired." He winked.

Natalie stopped for a moment to examine my face. "He's right. You do look tired."

I rolled my eyes. Did everyone have to point out, I looked like hell?

"Have you eaten yet?"

I shook my head, doubtful I could swallow anything. Natalie diverted from her current course and instead headed toward the buffet table.

She handed me a plate. "Here, try some of Mrs. Peterson's potato salad, a few veggies and hmmm, what's this?" She sniffed an orange colored salad filled with marshmallows, the only identifiable ingredient.

There was no way that was going down my gullet today.

Natalie winced and put the spoon back in the bowl. "Let's bypass that." She continued to pile food on the plate—cheese cubes, rolled up salami, a biscuit, coleslaw, a deviled egg and two petite pickles.

I laughed at the heaping plate. "Enough, Natalie. Enough."

"Hey, never say no to free food. That's one of the first things I learned at college. What do you want to drink? Wine, beer, soda?"

"A Diet Coke will be fine."

Natalie walked over to a side table covered with two-liter sodas, wine bottles and a tub of ice partially filled with beer.

"What college are you attending?"

"I'm starting my sophomore year at the University of Virginia. UVA all the way," she gave a discreet whoop.

"That's great." I tried to match her enthusiasm.

Natalie ducked her head and her expression turned sad. "Yeah, Denise was really proud of me for getting in. She and Mom were so excited I'd get a college degree."

"You should be proud. UVA is an excellent school." I spoke softly, sensing her sorrow.

"Yeah, Mom's driving me back down on Wednesday. Classes started last week." Her head popped up and she smiled shyly at me. "I should be thanking you, too. We'd never be able to afford college without the money you got for Denise. One of the first things she did was set up a college fund for me. Then she made me apply to all these crazy expensive schools, but my pick was UVA. I'm a big fan of Thomas Jefferson, and the campus is so pretty, don't you think?"

I nodded; once again Natalie left me speechless. I was thrilled the dirty Mafia money was having such a positive influence in so many people's lives—good people.

"C'mon, let's go. Mom's in the kitchen. You can sit at the table to eat."

I followed Natalie into a spacious gourmet kitchen with stainless steel appliances, black granite counter tops, and an enormous center island.

Natalie strode past the island to a tall kitchen table where Annette stood speaking with a short balding gentleman in an expensive dark suit. I estimated him to be in his early sixties.

"Mom, I found her," Natalie announced triumphantly, plunking my overfilled plate and diet soda on the table.

Annette turned at her daughter's announcement. Her face mirrored my own; lack of sleep, eyes tight with sorrow. I saw something else—strength and determination to carry on. Even though grief and aching pain were in her eyes, her stance was erect as if she refused to let it break her. When she glanced at Natalie, I realized she was staying strong for her daughter's sake, and I wondered if she was waiting to completely come apart once Natalie returned to college.

Would it be a relief for Natalie to leave, or would the silent house only make matters worse? The questions only furthered my own devastation. I never should have come.

Annette's stiff posture relaxed when she saw me. "Ms. Baker—"

"Cara."

"Cara," she nodded. "Thank you so much for coming."

To my utter astonishment, Annette walked forward, her arms held out.

I met her halfway. The hug was strong and tight. No weak fluttery society hugs for Annette.

"I'm so sorry for your loss, Annette," I whispered in her ear, my voice filled with emotion.

She stepped back, taking my hands in her calloused ones, and gave them a hard squeeze before releasing me. She introduced the bald man, "Cara Baker, this is Abraham Levy. He's Dee's lawyer. Abe, Cara's a lawyer too."

"Hello, Mr. Levy, it's nice to meet you." I shook his hand without bothering to correct Annette.

Natalie wandered off, leaving the three of us alone in the kitchen.

"Call me Abe. It's good to meet you, Cara." He pumped my hand. "I'm pleased you came today. It makes my job so much easier."

His statement confused me. "I'm sorry. Makes what easier?"

"You're listed in Denise's will. We're having a reading in about an hour, once the guests clear out. I'd appreciate it if you'd stay. That way I won't have to track you down later."

Even though he spoke perfect English, it wasn't computing. "I don't understand." I shook my head.

"Denise put you in her will."

My eyebrows went up in disbelief. "Umm, are you sure you have the right Cara?"

He chuckled. "Yes, I'm sure I have the right Cara."

Annette touched my shoulder, and I peered at her. She nodded.

I blew out a breath. "O-kay. If you want me to stay for the reading, I'm happy to oblige." What on earth could Denise have bequeathed to me? Maybe a mixed tape of songs crooning about how I done her wrong? This day was getting weirder by the minute.

"Why don't you sit down and eat something. You look like you need a pick-me-up. Abe, go mingle. I want to talk to Cara alone." She shooed the lawyer away and pulled out a chair for me.

Tentatively, I sat and took a fortifying drink in hopes the caffeine would give me enough boost to get through the rest of this day.

"Thank you again for coming."

Something clicked in my brain. "Did you send the news articles?"

Annette looked puzzled. "What news articles?"

"Someone mailed me Denise's obituary and the news articles. That's how I found out. I thought maybe you sent them."

She shook her head. "Actually I don't know where you moved. I was going to tell Abe to contact your former employer to track you down. I'm glad you came instead."

"Me too. I needed to say good-bye."

"This family owes you a debt of gratitude."

Unnerved I shook my head, disavowing her statement. "You don't owe me a thing."

"Yes!" Annette grabbed my right hand in both of hers, forcing me to look her in the eye. "Cara, I need you to listen and hear me. Things were said on that horrid, horrid night that need to be corrected. You've had the wrong impression for far too long. I see it in your eyes. I see the regret and guilt you've been living with for over two years, and you need to be released."

My mouth opened with a pop.

"I know," she stated.

"You know what?" My voice was gravelly.

"I know how you went to bat for Denise. I know how you stood up to the FBI. I know how you fought to make them give us the money. How you bargained for five million dollars when the Feds were telling you there wasn't more than five hundred thousand to be found. I know there was nothing you could do about Rizolli getting off. And I know how you threatened the FBI, putting your job in jeopardy."

I gulped, amazed by her revelations. "H-h-how do you know? When?"

"The next day, after you left, when things were calm again, I opened the envelope with the check. I almost passed out. Dee and I couldn't believe it. We thought it was some sort of mistake. So, I called your office, but you weren't there. After multiple calls, John Graham finally took my call and invited us out for coffee. He broke confidentiality and told me what transpired in your offices. He was angry on your behalf, for the way he thought we must have treated you since you'd gone into hiding. Denise felt awful for the horrible things she said to you that night …" She looked down, fidgeted with the coffee cup in front of her and whispered so softly I wasn't sure I heard her correctly. "I did too. I'll never forget your expression … so broken … when you left."

We were both crying; tears slid down our faces as the hurt and pain from that night so long ago resurfaced.

"I'm sorry, Cara. I'm so sorry. Dee was too. We wanted to tell you … but …" She choked, covering her mouth with her hand.

I turned away and grabbed a stray napkin on the table to blow my nose. When I could speak, I finished her thought. "But I never returned your calls."

Annette nodded. "Dee said awful things to you. Unforgivable. We figured you were too angry and hurt."

Closing my eyes, I dragged a hand down my face. "It was guilt. I felt so bad because I broke my promise to Denise. Everything she said was true. I was a coward. I couldn't face her again. I let you down."

"No! You didn't let us down," Annette's voice whipped out. "Your deal with the FBI probably saved us from living on the street, going homeless. The doctor bills were piling up. We never would have had the money to get through a civil suit without having to file for bankruptcy. We were already so close to the edge."

"But Denise didn't get her justice."

"She decided the money was going to be her justice. Her foundation became her justice." My brows drew together, my expression skeptical.

"Cara, you have to let go of the guilt." Annette's intense stare bore into me. "I watched it eat at you before you left and hoped you could find a happy life leaving this all behind. I checked in with John every few months to see how you were doing. He told me about your new insane work schedule and manic drive to put every criminal that came across your desk in jail. I heard about the long hours, the withdrawal from your friends and co-workers. I came to a few of your trials."

She nodded at my surprise. I never noticed her in the gallery.

"The quick wit and aura of lightness you had always exuded was gone. You became so hard and brittle—driven. No humor." She shook her head in despair. "I hoped getting away from here would help you forget. As I look at you today, it's all come back again. I can see it there in your eyes. In the way you hid from us at the funeral. The way you hesitated to come to my home today. You have to release it. You are forgiven, even though there isn't really anything to forgive. I'm so sorry you've been carrying it around for so long. We ... Dee and I ... didn't want that. We tried to contact you so we could tell you. We should have tried harder. I'm sorry for what was said ... and wasn't said that night. You have to let it go. Forgive me ... forgive Dee ... forgive yourself."

Annette's eloquent speech was such a relief, a balm to my conscience. The burden lifted from my shoulders as though it was a physical cross being removed.

"Thank you, Annette." My voice warbled low and gruff with emotion.

Her face lightened. "Thank you. For everything you did. God gave you lemons, and you made lemonade."

I gave a Mona Lisa smile at the reference. "No. Dee made lemonade. I just negotiated for the lemon grove."

My comment broke the tense atmosphere, and Annette let out a cough of laughter. I joined her, and before we knew it, we were having an emotional orgy. The pressure of the past week broke forth in over-the-top inappropriate laughter. A few of the stragglers wandered in from the front rooms, drawn by our outburst.

Natalie slid into the seat next to her mom. "Mom? What's so funny?" She seemed to sense our laughter running on the edge of hysteria.

Using the back of her hand, Annette wiped the tears away. "Nothing, dear. Cara and I ... we allowed our amusement to get away from us. That's all."

The other individuals that entered the kitchen with Natalie started making their excuses to leave.

Annette put on her good hostess manner and walked them to the door, saying all the right things and doing the pretty.

Natalie called her good-byes but remained in the kitchen with me. She seized a carrot stick off the untouched plate of food and crunched down on the orange veggie. "Hey, you haven't eaten anything I picked out for you."

"You're right." All of the sudden I was ravenous. "Let's remedy that, shall we." I started shoveling food in like it was going out of style.

"So, you and Mom had a pretty intense talk, huh?"

The creamy potato salad slid down my throat, and I nodded. "Yes. We had some things to catch up on."

"Yeah, I know. She and Dee felt really bad about that night you gave us the check." I cocked my head, surprised by her knowledge.

"I was hiding on the stairs. You didn't see me, but I heard everything and watched when you left. I didn't understand it all but felt really bad for you. Dee said some really harsh things."

With a shrug, I tried to make light of it. "She was upset. Sometimes we say things we don't mean."

"Natalie, come say good-bye to your cousins," Annette's voice scolded from the foyer.

Natalie wiggled her shoulders and jumped up, loping off with a resigned air. "Coming, Mom."

The kitchen remained quiet as I sat alone, finishing the snacks on my plate. The food felt good on my tender stomach; the knot I'd been carrying around finally released. For the first time in two years, the breath I took was blame free. My only regrets were it took Denise's death for me hear the truth. If only I'd returned a call or rung the doorbell that day I drove by to see the new house. My mind shuddered away from that line of thinking. Playing the "what if" game was dangerous and only led to more regret. Annette was right. It was time to move on. It was time to let go of the past. Forgive myself. Allow myself to move on with my life in South Carolina.

Crap. I needed to call Danny to explain and apologize. I knew we needed to talk, and a short phone conversation wasn't exactly the best way to go about explaining my recent impression of a sobbing lunatic. Now that the guilt over Denise had lifted, the guilt over my behavior toward Danny was starting to rear its ugly head. I looked under my seat, searching for my purse, so I could at least send a text assuring him of my safety, but I realized I'd left it in my car. I slid off the chair, planning to go out to retrieve it when Annette and Abe walked in.

"Good. You're still here." Abe smiled. "We were just about to get organized. Annette, where would you like to do this?"

"Right here at the kitchen table is fine." She eased herself into the seat across from me and let out a sigh. "Oh, that feels good. My back is killing me."

I retook my seat and Abe slid into a chair at the head of the table between Annette and me. Then Natalie came into the kitchen, carrying half a pie and a bottle of white wine.

"I thought we might need some fortification." She allowed the pie to slide off her hand onto the table. "Mr. Levy, would you like some pie?"

"I'd love some. Thank you, Natalie."

"Cara? Mom?" She wielded a pie server.

"Sure, sweetie. That sounds fine," Annette responded.

"I'll have some too. Thanks."

Natalie rooted through a kitchen cabinet, pulling out forks and paper plates, and proceeded to dole out pie to everyone. Annette found four wineglasses in the breakfront against the wall behind her, and I poured the wine. It seemed very surreal, as though we were having dessert after a nice dinner party, rather than gathered around the table to hear Denise's Last Will and Testament. Natalie sat next to her mother. She and Abe tucked into their slices of cherry pie. Annette took a few small bites but mostly just moved pieces around the plate with her fork and drank sparingly. I took a few bites of the tasty pie, but my focus was on the wine.

Unlike Annette, I finished half the glass with three gulps in quick succession. In combination with my lack of sleep, the alcohol very quickly went to work relaxing me.

Abe finished his pie and set the plate aside. He pulled a sheaf of papers from the briefcase sitting at his elbow and a glasses case out of his breast pocket. Adjusting his Cheaters, he began, "Okay, ladies. Here we go."

Abe turned on his lawyer mode and began reading all the dry legalese contained in most wills. He started with Denise's requests regarding the foundation. It received a million dollars to be spent or invested as Annette saw fit. Both Annette and Natalie were members of the foundation's board of directors, and they were directed to work with the rest of the board to determine the foundation's course. There were pages of paperwork concerning the foundation which Annette would have to review and sign at a time when she could concentrate. Denise split her assets between her mother and sister. Annette got the house and half the money. Natalie had a college fund, which would take her as far as she wanted. She received the Lexus and a trust fund with the other half of the money, which she could access upon her twenty-fifth birthday. I zoned out somewhere during the long discussion surrounding the foundation and was brought back to reality when my name was mentioned.

"And to Cara Baker, I hereby bequeath two hundred and fifty thousand dollars, to be spent on herself, in a manner that will make her happy. She is not allowed to donate any of the money."

I knocked a fork to the floor as my jaw dropped and my eyebrows flew high. Abe lowered his reading glasses and looked significantly at me.

"I-I ... can't accept that money, Abe. It needs to go to Natalie and Annette." I avoided their eyes.

"Ms. Baker—"

"Call me Cara," I corrected.

"Denise was quite clear on this point. She left a letter for you." He reached into his briefcase and pulled out a plain white envelope. My name was scrawled across the center in Denise's spiky handwriting.

With shaky hands, I took the letter and stared at it.

"Cara?"

My eyes flashed up to Annette's.

She met my gaze. "It's okay, sweetie. Natalie and I have more than enough, and I think this is Dee's way of setting things right."

I shook my head. "I don't think I can take the money."

"Let's look at this a different way." Natalie sat forward. "Let's say we hired a lawyer and filed suit and we won. How much money would the lawyer have taken from the settlement?"

I shrugged, looking at Abe for guidance. "I don't know, maybe thirty percent?"

Abe nodded in agreement. "Sometimes more."

"So, thirty percent of five million is …" Natalie's eyes stared off as she figured the amount in her head.

"One point five million," Annette finished for her.

"So, you see, just think of the money as Dee's payment for services rendered." Natalie turned to her mom. "Hey, we got off cheap. Just think how much money we would have had to give away to a slimy lawyer, no offense, Abe and Cara, if we'd had to go to court."

Annette still watched me. "I'm not sure we would have made it to the civil suit. We might have been homeless before then. The medical bills were piling up."

Natalie looked surprised. Clearly, Denise and Annette had kept her in the dark to protect her. A breath whistled out between Natalie's teeth. "Oh, Mom. I had no idea things were that bad."

Annette turned to her daughter and threw an arm around her shoulders. "You were still in high school, kiddo, and we were protecting you. I didn't want you to realize how desperate things were getting."

Moisture formed in Natalie's eyes as she turned to me. "See, you really are a savior to this family. I think you'd better take the money."

I didn't agree but instead made a grunting noise.

Abe carried on reading the will. Since emotions were riding high, I didn't want to rock the boat. I figured I'd visit Abe privately at his office to see what could be done with the money so I could return it or perhaps give it to Denise's foundation, where it belonged. Abe's voice hummed in the background while I stared, unseeing, at the envelope in front of me. What in the world would I do with two hundred and fifty thousand dollars? I could take a trip to Morocco and Egypt, two places I'd always wanted to visit. I could take a balloon ride or go skydiving. I could buy a car to rival Danny's Maserati. I could open my own practice. My mind skittered to a stop.

My own practice. There weren't any lawyers in Denton. Residents had to travel into Charleston to find one. As much I enjoyed my time at the library, truthfully I didn't see myself doing it for the rest of my career. I knew from experience Jackie used lawyers from Charleston for all her closings. Danny told me Jerome used to work out of his home for folks in the community, but since he'd passed away, everyone had to go farther afield for any kind of legal advice. The idea had merit, and, even though I wouldn't get rich, I could probably comfortably support myself. Food for thought.

Chapter Twenty-Seven

"Do you think you could forgive a friend for being so monumentally stupid?"

It was around half past eight, and I stood in the hallway of an older remodeled brick apartment building in Shady Side. I had moved beyond utter exhaustion into numbness. My head bobbled and didn't quite feel attached to the rest of my body. When I left Annette's home, I drove on autopilot and wound up outside the apartment complex of my best friend, Angela Washington. One of the few people who continued to stay connected to me during my crash and burn at the DA's office. One of the people I'd given my new Denton address to and to whom I'd become a terrible friend. I took forever to answer her e-mails and never returned any of the phone messages in the beginning. The phone messages ceased a few months ago and the e-mails were sporadic at best. I took full blame for the communication dearth.

Angela was a corporate lawyer who worked for one of the big pharmaceutical companies in Pittsburgh. She and I had the "displeasure" (as she would put it) of interning together at the DA's office during law school, and she determined, upon graduation, her life was not headed in the direction of working for the "underbelly of the Pittsburgh legal system." Instead, Angela's job focused on contract law and research of federal and state codes, a job she enjoyed but would have bored me to tears within a month. She knew bits and pieces about my work in the DA's office, and I'm sure the grapevine provided loads of gossipy information. Angela never pried—instead she was a stable friend during a difficult time.

Her stiff inscrutable demeanor relaxed, and a grin spread across her café au lait features as warm arms came around my shoulders. My body went limp with relief as I returned the hug. Her familiar pear-flavored scent enveloped me. I was so relieved by her reception I didn't want to let go.

Angela extended her arms and stood back, looking at me with her liquid chocolate eyes. She wore a black skirt with an orange wrap top and tall black wedge sandals, which made her at least four inches taller than me. Her face was full of compassion. "Did you come up for the funeral?"

I nodded.

"I wondered. Well, you look warn to a nub. Come on in and take a load off. I'll pour us some drinks." She drew me into the clean lines of her contemporary living room where I collapsed on a brown leather couch.

Angela returned, carrying a tray with two glasses of soda and a plate of cookies, which she placed on the shiny black-lacquered coffee table. She sat in a leather chair directly across from me. My body flopped willy-nilly on the couch and couldn't produce enough energy to sit up to retrieve my drink off the tray. Angela watched me, bouncing her foot, patiently waiting for whatever bits of information I was willing to drop. Unfortunately for her, I was ready to offload everything, and as a good friend, I thought it was about time Angela heard it all.

The words tumbled forth, somewhat in order of events, although I only had a vague recollection of what I said. Angela asked few questions and generally they were only for clarification. At some point she produced a bottle of wine and after my first glass, I must have fallen asleep because when I woke, it was seven in the morning and I was stiff from having slept curled up on a short couch. The afghan draped over me slid to the floor as I sat up. A dull throb pounded behind my eyes. My dress was a twisted, wrinkled mess and I stumbled, trying to unwind it, on my way to the kitchen in search of aspirin and coffee.

Some things never changed. Coffee, already made, sat warming in the pot, and the aspirin was still located on the lower right shelf next to the mugs. After downing three of the lifesaving little pills with water, which I drank directly from the tap, I poured a large mug of Angela's vanilla bean coffee. If I could have mainlined it directly into an artery, I would have. Angela's shower turned off and I made my way back to the couch to drink my caffeine and wait.

She walked out of her room looking tall and elegant, wearing a silky red robe and a towel wrapped around her head. "Yo, girl, you look like something the cat dragged in. How do you feel?"

"Like hell, but the coffee is starting to help."

"You bring any luggage on this trip?"

I nodded while I sipped from the cup, holding it like a lifeline. "It's in the car."

"Go down and fetch your stuff so you can shower. I've called Bernie, my boss, to tell him I'm coming in late this morning. We'll go to IHOP and get ourselves a big breakfast. You still have more to tell me."

I looked at her innocently, raising my eyebrows high on my forehead.

"I want to hear about Danny."

"Did I mention him last night?" The last few days were starting to blur together. I couldn't get a handle on our conversation last night.

"After the glass of wine. Just before you conked out. And I want to hear the rest." She pointed an imperious finger in my direction.

With a sigh, I hauled my butt off the couch and trudged downstairs to retrieve my overnight bag.

Catching my reflection in the window of the car had me gasping. The hairstyle I currently sported could best be described as rooster afro gone bad, and my face had red lines of jungle rot that crisscrossed the left side of my cheek. I snatched my things from the trunk and hustled back to Angela's apartment, hoping no one I knew saw me.

Forty-five minutes later I squeezed the Mini into the last parallel parking spot in front of IHOP. The joint was crowded, but we were lucky a table opened up as we walked in. After giving the waitress our order, Angela looked at me with her patient face.

I fidgeted with the straw's wrapper in an effort to ignore my friend's calm anticipation. It wasn't that I didn't want to tell her. It was just … there were sensitive issues surrounding Danny's story, and as she waited, I sifted through my thoughts, trying to decide what parts of the truth I could divulge. I decided to play it safe and went with the germaphobe tale Mandy and Jackie knew. So, over a Rooty Tooty Fresh 'N Fruity breakfast, I spilled my guts about the past months in small-town South Carolina.

When I finished, Angela's brown eyes assessed me. "You know, you owe that man an explanation, besides that sad little text you sent him—what? Twenty-four hours ago?"

I agreed.

"You planning to drive back home today?"

"I hadn't really thought about it but, yes, I suppose I'll head back home today." I sighed. "I need to make sure I haven't ruined everything with him." With downcast eyes, I pushed the remains of the eggs around my plate, my appetite vanished.

"Girl, cheer up. If he cares for you as much as I think he does, he'll forgive you. You may have to beg, but a little beggin' never hurt anyone."

I looked up with a smile. "No. You're right. A little begging never hurt." I tilted my head, "Angela, have I ever told you you're the best friend a girl could have?"

"Don't you forget it, sister." She snapped her fingers thrice in a Z formation.

"I won't."

"Do you have a picture of this fine specimen?"

"I do. Where's my phone." I pulled it out of the bottom of my purse but couldn't get it to turn on. "Damn. The battery's dead, and I forgot the charger."

"You better call that boy. He's probably going nuts wondering what you're up to." Angela whipped out her phone and pushed it across the table at me.

Angela was right, but I shook my head and held up my hand. "No. I'll see him tonight. I need time to think about what I'm going to say. I have a feeling our next conversation is going to be a long one and should be done face-to-face." Changing the subject I asked, "By the way when are you going to come down and visit me?"

Angela retrieved her phone and began tapping away. "How does next month look?"

"It looks fine to me. Tell me when, and I'll be sure to stock up on the wine."

"Oh, I'm not coming down for wine. I'm coming to check out this fine young thing living above you. So, you better fix this before I get there. After all, I need to make sure he meets my standards and is good enough for my best friend."

A belly laugh rolled out. "We'll be sure to kiss and make up before your arrival."

It was late morning by the time Angela and I said our goodbyes and shared hugs with promises to stay in touch until her visit next month. I had every intention of keeping that promise. Since Denise's demise, it had become crystal clear that friends like Angela were a blessing, and it was up to me to maintain our friendship. I'd make it a priority.

Chapter Twenty-Eight

Darkness had fallen by the time I arrived home and my hands were full as I staggered into the entryway. I dropped the keys, along with my handbag, on the foyer table and was in the process of lowering my duffle bag to the floor when I spotted movement out of the corner of my eye. My stomach plummeted. My heart started jackrabbiting as a scream crawled up my throat. A lamp in the front parlor clicked on.

"Geez!" A hand went to my chest as I stumbled back, knocking my purse and keys off the table. "You scared the bejeezus out of me."

Danny remained silent. The lamp behind him threw his stiffly postured silhouette into relief. His eyes were shadowed, but his ominous glare bore into me.

My gaze flicked down to the papers spread across the coffee table. Denise's obituary lay on top of the heap of files I recognized as copies of the Colquitt case I'd illegally taken with me when I moved.

"How l-long have you been s-sitting there?"

"Hours," he replied harshly.

Oops. He was pissed and probably hurt too. As he had every right to be. I'd shut him out of my life, and I'd lied to him by omission. What seemed like an easy task at the IHOP ten hours ago was looking a heck of a lot more difficult in the glower of this angry stranger. This week was turning into an exhausting emotional roller coaster, and, even though all I wanted to do was crawl into bed, I owed Danny so much more. My time of reckoning had arrived. Taking a deep breath, I walked tentatively into the parlor, seizing a footstool along the way, and placed it in front of my silent, seething boyfriend. Gingerly, I took a seat and faced his angry countenance.

"Saddle up, buddy, because I'm going to touch you."

Surprise flickered.

I placed one hand on each knee, just below his shorts. The soft blond hair tickled my hands. "I'm sorry I didn't ... couldn't tell you before." I indicated the mess of papers. "But I'm here now and I'd like to tell you my story. Will you listen?"

He gave a stiff nod.

"This weekend has opened my eyes to things I wished I'd known before. Will you hear what I have to say with an open mind and perhaps try to forgive me?"

His posture relaxed and he placed his large warm callused hands upon mine. "You sneak out in the wee hours of the morning. You don't answer your phone. You send me a bizarre and disturbing text." He sighed. "I've been going out of my mind trying to figure out what's going on with you. You scared the hell out of me."

"I know. I'm sorry."

He gestured with his chin toward the littered coffee table. "Does that have something to do with where you've been?"

"Yes."

"Why don't you tell me where you fit into all of this?"

So, I told him about my life as Assistant District Attorney Cara Baker. It was clear he'd spent the past twenty-four hours doing research. As my story unraveled, Danny asked detailed questions about the case against Tony Rizolli and about Denise Colquitt. At one point, he clutched my arms and pulled me onto his lap, and the remainder of the tale was told in the tender comfort of his embrace, with his warm breath tickling my scalp. When, at last, I wound down, he sat silent.

"So, where did the U.S. Marshals stick this bastard?"

"Oh, yeah. That's the kicker. I don't know where they placed him, but they've gone and lost him."

"What? How the hell did that happen?"

"He cut his tracking anklet and took off. Agent Bryant has

been in touch with me. As a matter of fact, he called while I was driving up to the funeral. He said they were following up on a lead."

"What happens if they don't find him?"

"The US Attorney's office is screwed. He's the key witness in their case against the Barconi crime family. I'm beginning to wonder if there was more money hidden elsewhere and Rizolli's sitting on a beach somewhere in Sicily."

Danny's chin rubbed against my hair as he shook his head and gave a disgusted snort. "That animal really screwed up a bunch of lives, didn't he?"

"Oh, I don't know. I mean, don't get me wrong. This guy's a boil on the butt of the universe, but I can't help thinking Denise's foundation helped lots of women, families and children. And maybe I wasn't really supposed to be a DA for all my life. On the drive home, I was thinking of using Denise's money to open my own practice here in Denton. Something small. Estate planning, wills, real estate, contracts. You know, small things that come up in a town like this. Jackie's realty company holds all their closings in Charleston. And with Jerome gone … Do you think Denton could support a small-town lawyer?" Twisting, I looked to see Danny's reaction.

For the first time, since the night of the auction, I watched a smile spread across his features. "I think this town could support a lawyer. I'll be your first client. One of my contracts is up for negotiation in October, and I could use some legal advice." He leaned down and kissed my forehead. Then my nose. Then he nibbled on my lips, starting a slow-burning flame. By the time we broke away from the kiss, I was panting.

I switched positions. Straddling him, I nibbled on his earlobe and a zing ran down my spine as a low moan escaped his mouth. My hands slipped under his T-shirt and ran up his hard muscled chest. I moved my mouth to his, allowing him access to plunder the hot recesses.

"Cara," he rasped. "At this rate, I'm not sure I can make it upstairs."

I let out a slow, sexy laugh. "What's wrong with right here?"

I ran little kisses along his neck.

"Do you have condoms hiding in the coffee table?"

I sat back on my haunches. "Uh, no. You're right."

In one fluid motion, that took an incredible amount of strength, Danny stood with both hands cupping my bottom. I wrapped my legs around his waist as he carried me upstairs to the bedroom. I continued my assault on his neck, face and ears, and I was damn lucky he didn't drop me on the way. Soon enough, I felt the soft comforter beneath me as Danny pulled the shirt over my head and then stripped off his.

Chapter Twenty-Nine

I woke refreshed but to an empty bed. A situation I was starting to get used to since my sweetie pie seemed to be a morning person. Stretching out the kinks, I sat up and looked around the room. For the first time in too long, my heart was filled with happiness and excitement about my life.

The guilt dragging at me for the past two and a half years had lifted. And, for the first time in over a week, I woke without the need for more sleep. The weary exhaustion was finally gone. I felt strong. I felt loved. I climbed out of bed and pulled on a tank top and a pair of shorts. On my way to the stairs, I noticed the connecting door to Danny's apartment stood ajar. I figured he was catching up on work lost by the past forty-eight hours of worry I'd put him through and decided to leave him alone and instead lumbered down to the kitchen for the necessary cup of coffee. My favorite blue mug sat next to the warm pot, along with an orange multi-vitamin. Danny knew me so well. I stared at the little pill nestled in my palm.

I really love this man.

Hold up. I paused and ran that thought through my head again. *I love Danny.*

Yup, that's what I thought you said. I said it out loud. "I love Danny."

Hm. My lips pursed. I liked it. No fear. Nothing. Just a zippy little thrill running through my bones. *I'll be damned.* Danny and I hadn't reached the stage of professing our love in so many words, but our relationship seemed to be moving in that direction. I supposed when Danny came up for air today, I should mention this little tidbit to him.

A smile spread across my face. *He might like that.*

In the meantime, while I drank the warm brew, I detached my cell phone from its charger. Danny, that adorable man, must have plugged it in for me this morning. Nine messages awaited me. The first three were from Danny. The fourth, from Agent Bryant, asked me to call him after the funeral. Two more from Danny, one from Angela telling me the dates she could come to visit, one from my mom and one more from Agent Bryant. I hummed as the messages played, only half-listening when something caught my attention and I replayed Bryant's message again.

"Cara, we've lost Rizolli's trail. We tracked him down to the South Carolina border. He seems to be heading south on the I-95 corridor. I'm calling in a favor. An agent's going to check on you."

Bryant picked up on the second ring. "It's Cara. What's the four-one-one?"

"Where the hell have you been?"

"I told you. I went to the funeral in Pittsburgh. I'm sorry I didn't get back to you. My phone died and I didn't have my charger with me."

"Where are you now?"

"Home. Why? Where are you?"

"Hutchins and I are headed to Charleston."

My stomach did a flip-flop.

"We're following up at a possible sighting at one of the motels in the area. I had a field agent check on your house this morning. He said everything looked fine. Is everything fine?"

"Seems fine to me."

"I don't like this. After we check the motel, I'm going to swing by your house. Will that be a problem?" Tension and concern filled his voice.

"No. That's fine. I'm not going to work today, so anytime is okay."

"Good. Stay home and lock your doors. Do you have an alarm system?"

I laughed. "No, Agent Bryant. We're in small-town America here. I don't think most people lock their doors at night, much less install security systems."

"That fills me with confidence," he replied sarcastically.

"Don't worry. I'm not going anywhere."

"I'll see you in about an hour."

I closed my phone and stuffed it back into the bottomless depths of my purse. The envelope Abe had given me lay innocently on the counter. The letter had been tucked alongside the phone in my handbag, which was also on the island. I picked up the letter and turned it over. It was sealed. Weighing the white envelope in my hands, I waged a mental debate, ultimately dropping it back on the countertop. Of course, the note would have to be opened, but reading it held no appeal to me today. I stared out into my back yard; it had been far too long since I'd wandered the pathways replete with late summer blooms.

Last night's thunderstorm left behind a gentle breeze lifting some of the hot southern summer weather but still leaving a humid dampness in the air. I slipped into my red rubber polka dot gardening shoes and wandered down the trail, pulling a few weeds here and there as I walked, enjoying the peacefulness. Leaves rustled and birds twittered in their nests, and the crunching of the gravel beneath my feet sounded loud to my ears in the quiet garden. I approached the gazebo and saw a flash of blond hair. I must have been mistaken. Danny wasn't working; he was relaxing out here. Probably waiting for me to join him.

Out of the gloom, he came to stand in the gazebo doorway. Leaves shifted and the sun lit up his features. Even with the bad bleached surfer dye job and twenty pounds of weight loss, recognition flared immediately. My heart skittered, and I froze. The smile melted off my face and bit by bit turned to revulsion.

He wore a blue jogging suit with black shoes. Sunlight glinted off the steel blade he held nonchalantly in his right hand. His dark piggy eyes were alight with evil pleasure as he smirked at my reaction.

Dropping a cigarette, he ground it out on the wooden floor.

His rough smoker's voice broke the silence. "It's good to see you again, Counselor."

I swallowed twice and tried to collect a coherent thought from my reeling brain. "Rizolli," I croaked and then cleared my throat. "I heard you left the WITSEC program. I was hoping you were taking a dirt nap." I used as much frost as I could muster, in an effort to keep the fear from leaking out and sending my system into hysteria.

He chuckled. "I just bet you were, sweet cheeks. I could tell you were a feisty one when we met in jail."

I didn't respond, stoically standing my ground.

"Did you enjoy your little friend's funeral?" Rizolli sneered.

The air whistled through my teeth and my eyes narrowed. "Did you have something to do with her death?"

A malevolent smile broke across his swarthy features as he played with the knife. "Maybe." Flick, flick, flick, the knife closed. "Maybe not," he said with evil glee. Flick, flick, flick, the knife opened. "Did you get the envelope I sent?"

I gasped and my heart dropped. Did he kill her? Have her killed? Or was he messing with my head, and taking credit for an accident? He'd obviously been in Pittsburgh around the time of her death. How?

He loved watching my reaction. It was part of his game. He swished the knife around. "I thought it was a nice touch, sending the obituary to you. But, you surprised me. I didn't expect you to go rushing off to the funeral. I figured slashing your tires would keep you around longer. Small towns work quicker than I thought." He waited for my reaction.

Refusing to give him the satisfaction, I clamped my teeth together and stared blandly over his shoulder.

Flick, flick, flick went the knife. "So, how was the funeral? Last I heard you weren't seeing much of that Colquitt bitch."

Anger replaced fear. "Get to the point, Rizolli. What are you doing here?"

His cocky smile turned into a sinister sneer. "I want my money."

"What?" I was confused.

"The money you and the FBI stole from my Cayman accounts. Seven point two million to be exact." He ground between his teeth.

Uncontrollable laughter burst forth from my lips. I knew Rizolli was here to torture and kill me. The situation was bad, and my mirth was a reaction to the tension. If I screamed, Danny would come running and be put in danger too. My only chance was to keep Rizolli talking and hope Bryant and Hutchins showed up in time.

I clamped down on my anxiety, ready to ride him out. "I don't have any of that money. It all went to Denise."

"I know."

The short answer frightened me. "So, if you know I don't have the money, what the hell are you doing here, Rizolli? You have to know it's a dangerous move. The FBI is on to you. They've been tracking you since Virginia and should be here any moment."

His eyes narrowed, studying me, trying to decide if I was bluffing. "I seriously doubt the FBI is on its way here. You're grasping at straws."

He didn't believe me. I didn't know if that was good news or bad.

"In answer to your question, I'm here to tidy up loose ends. You see ... nobody steals from Tony Rizolli." He held the knife at eye level with the point facing up to the sky, his face an evil mask. "First, I'm going to cut you, just like I did to that slut in the back alley. I'm looking forward to making you scream. Ever since your little visit to the jailhouse, I've been thinking about teaching you a lesson." His voice was eerily calm. "You really should have been more respectful."

A kick of adrenaline raced through my body, and it took only seconds to make the decision of fight or flight. With a lunge, I threw the coffee at his eyes and made a direct hit. Rizolli roared, putting his free hand up to his face. I chucked the coffee cup at him, aiming for his head. Unfortunately, it beaned one of his upraised arms, doing little damage. I turned and fled down the garden path.

The gravel did nothing to hide the sounds of my flight and soon, over the pounding in my ears, I heard his pursuit. In my haste, I took a wrong turn, heading deeper into the garden rather than closer to the house. Rizolli followed. He was gaining and I decided to take a calculated risk, something we'd been taught in one of my defense classes. Whipping around a corner, I paused and hid behind a tree to wait. Tony was only a few seconds behind me but probably couldn't hear my halt over the hammering of his own steps. I flung out my arm and clotheslined him, catching him directly in the throat. The move was so unexpected I hit him at full speed. Pain arced down my arm and into my hand, but Rizolli went down hard, banging his head against the ground and knocking the wind out of him. He dropped the knife and, with a sweep of my foot, it flew deep into a flower bed. Hoping to decommission him, I kicked him once in the ribs and twice in the kidneys. My rubber boots softened the blows, and I wasn't achieving the type of damage I wanted, so I took to my heels and retraced my steps, bolting toward the house.

Stumbling into the kitchen, I slammed the back door. My right arm throbbed and my hand tingled painfully; it took a few precious seconds to flip the lock. Laden with panic, I hopped around, searching for the phone.

"Shit, shit, shit, shit," I whimpered over and over again, my mind spinning like a hamster in its wheel. The cordless wasn't sitting on its charger where it was supposed to be.

"*Shit.*"

My handbag still sat on the kitchen island, and I snatched it off the counter with my good arm. The zipper was open and everything went flying. I watched in horror as my cell phone arched up into the air, hit the refrigerator then smacked against the floor and broke apart in three different directions.

Now what? My mind went blank and, for a few precious moments, I stared at the busted cell phone, mentally willing it not to be broken. When my brain unfroze and I realized that wasn't going to happen, my eyes frantically searched the kitchen for answers. I remembered the page button on my charger stand. Slapping the button, I heard the phone give a beep-beep-beep and traced the sound under the table. The missing cordless phone innocently sat on a kitchen chair.

I was standing upright, the phone in my hand, when three gunshots fired in quick succession through my French doors. Rizolli made a stunningly spectacular entrance. Glass flew everywhere. He looked left, then right and saw me next to the kitchen table. Two walls cornered me giving me nowhere to run.

He jerked the muzzle of a deadly looking 9 mm in my direction. "Drop the phone, bitch!"

Eyes wide, my hand went slack and the phone clattered to the floor.

He stalked around the kitchen table. The gun remained steady, sighted directly at my head. His black running shoes crunched on the broken glass. He stopped in front of me, his face full of anger and hatred.

Since there was no place for flight, without a conscious decision, my body determined to make one last stand and fight. With my left foot, I took a step forward, closing the distance between Rizolli and me, and swung my right leg back to get momentum.

Three things happened in such quick succession it was almost simultaneous. I planted my left foot and powering with my right leg, I kicked Rizolli as hard as humanly possible in the nuts. The contact reverberated up my leg. My boots, still slippery from the dampness outside, had my left leg sliding out from beneath me. As I felt myself falling backward against the wall, I registered two sounds—a gunshot and a feral animalistic yell. The bullet breezed past my head so close it lifted my hair. Just as I hit the ground, a white light flashed, blinding me. Then there was silence.

It took a few moments of repetitive blinking before my eyes readjusted from the flash. When I was able to focus, the strangest scene met my eyes. Rizolli, still upright, had dropped the gun. But, instead of having folded into a fetal position grasping the family jewels, as I expected, he clutched at his chest, gasping for air. It looked like he was trying to emit a scream. He stumbled back a step, then his eyes rolled up, and he fell, hitting his head on the edge of the counter before crashing to the floor.

Needless to say, I was dazed and disoriented. My thought processes were overloaded and my brain had shut down. A rushing sound filled my ears, which I soon realized was my own harsh breathing. The kitchen looked like a hurricane had blown through—broken glass littered the room, the contents of my handbag were strewn across the floor, and blood from where Rizolli cut himself on the glass seeped out of his arms and legs. I caught a slight movement in my peripheral vision and slowly turned my neck, feeling each sinew and muscle shift. Danny, his eyes a bright neon green, shook and emanated an unnatural glow. I must have sat there gawking, my mouth agape, for two full minutes, while Danny stared with a look of what I can only describe as shock and horror at the prone body on my kitchen floor.

Returning my gaze to the carnage, I spotted Rizolli's gun a few inches from my foot. With a flick, I slid it farther away from the body. My movement awoke Danny from his trance.

He fell to his knees, placing his hands on his thighs, his eyes still bright, locked onto me. "Christ, I thought he shot you." He croaked in a ragged voice then bowed his head, his shoulders shuddering from his own heavy breaths.

I shook my head and attempted to clear the confusion. The adrenaline started to ebb, and I began to feel my body again. A dull pain throbbed in my right arm. Little cuts from flying glass were bleeding on my left arm and leg. Something uncomfortable was lodged beneath my rear. Reaching under my leg, I pulled out the cordless phone. Amazingly, it remained intact.

I started to dial but paused midway. "Danny?"

He looked up.

"I have to make some phone calls. You're going to have about ten minutes to pull it together before this place is swarming. Do you understand?"

Danny nodded and closed his eyes tight.

First, I dialed the FBI. It took a few tries because the

adrenaline had receded and my fingers shook as I made an effort to press the correct buttons.

"Agent Bryant."

"Tom, I've found Rizolli."

"Where?"

My teeth began chattering. Reaction was setting in. "He's d-dead on my k-kitchen floor. You and Hutchins better get your asses here quick. My n-next call is to n-nine-one-one." In the background I heard the acceleration of a car just before I hung up.

True to my word, my next call was to nine-one-one. "Nine-one-one, what is your emergency?"

I clamped down on my chattering teeth and spoke slow and clear. "My name is Cara Baker. I live at twenty-one twelve Poplar Place in Denton. There's been a shooting. Send the police, an ambulance and notify the medical examiner." I hung up before the operator could ask any more questions. My hand dropped to the side.

Danny's glow faded as he struggled to pull the swirling emotions into himself. "D-Danny," I said softly around the chattering.

His eyes opened, their color fading into a bright grass green. Still a bit above normal, but not too far off.

"The FBI and p-police will be here soon. L-listen to me. You came d-down after the gunshots. You didn't see anything. W-when you arrived, Rizolli was dead on the floor and you found me here. Do y-you understand?"

Danny shook his head.

"Danny, trust me on this. I d-don't know what the hell just happened here, but it w-won't do anyone any good if you're in the m-middle of this. You're just a bystander. Are we clear?"

"I touched him. My handprint is burned onto his flesh."

I blinked. Gradually getting to my knees, I crawled over to Rizolli's body. Sure enough, the flesh on his left wrist was ringed with red-blistered burn markings. If you looked closely, it resembled three fingers and a thumb. I swallowed back the bile that arose in my throat, "Holy shit."

My head swiveled back to Danny. "L-let me see your hand."

He held out both palms for my inspection. Nothing but pink, healthy skin.

"They'll never b-be able to explain it." Very deliberately, I reiterated. "You were not here. Do you understand?"

Danny finally nodded.

I scooted back to my previous position and flopped my head against the wall. My eyes closed as I waited, putting all my effort into controlling my rolling stomach, shaking body, and ringing ears. I made a conscious effort to breathe. In and out, the air whistled through my nostrils. *Do not throw up. Do not throw up. Do not throw up.*

A blanket dropped over me, and Danny wrapped his arms around my shoulders, "You're going into shock."

Warmth seeped into my limbs and the ringing in my ears lessened. Footsteps sounded out back. My eyes flashed to the door. Stealthily, with gun drawn, Agent Bryant stepped through the broken entrance. His eyes darted around the room, taking in the wreckage, Rizolli's dead body, and Danny and I huddled in the corner. He crouched and placed two fingers on Rizolli's neck.

Bryant holstered his gun and spoke into his hand. "We're clear. You'd better get in here." Then he turned to me. He hadn't changed over the past few years. He wore the requisite FBI uniform—dark suit and tie, although the white shirt was wrinkled. His face, drawn and tired, sported a five o'clock shadow and red-rimmed eyes. However, unlike our last meeting, the agent looked at me with worry and compassion.

"Are you okay, Baker?"

I nodded and answered through chattering teeth, "I th-think so. Just some s-scrapes and bruises."

Bryant scrutinized me. "You look pale."

Danny still hugged the blanket around me. "She's going into shock."

"Have you called for an ambulance?" Bryant shifted his glance to Danny.

"I d-did after I phoned you." I looked up as Hutchins

walked through the back door. My gaze returned to Bryant. "I'm okay. I told them to send the p-police, ME, and an ambulance."

"What happened?" he asked with concern and crouched down to my level.

Shaking loose from Danny's hold, I sat up, took a lungful of air, and tensed my muscles to control the shivering. "He was waiting for me out in the garden with a knife. I threw my coffee at him and ran. When I got inside, I locked the door behind me. He shot the door to hell and followed me. I kicked him in the nuts, fell down, and the bullet missed me by millimeters." I pointed to the bullet hole on the wall.

Bryant squinted at me. "Not quite." His hand touched my left ear and came away with blood. "Looks like he barely nicked you."

"I don't know what happened after that. He dropped the gun, grabbed his chest, and fell to the floor. I didn't realize if you junk-punched a fellow hard enough you could cause him to have a heart attack."

Hutchins coughed.

Bryant jerked his head toward Danny. "Where were you during all of this?"

I reached out from under the blanket to squeeze Danny's hand. "Danny's my tenant. He lives in the apartment on the third floor."

"I heard the shots and came down to see what was going on." He paused.

I squeezed again.

"By the time I got downstairs, Cara was lying here and the stiff was over on the floor there. My main concern was Cara. She insisted on making some phone calls. Then her color turned bad, she started to shake and it looked like she might be sick. I got a blanket and then you showed up." He gave a casual shrug.

Purposefully, I changed the subject. "Will the FBI take over the investigation?"

Bryant gazed around the kitchen. "Hell, I don't know if this is an FBI, U.S. Marshal, or local law enforcement mess." He rubbed a hand through his thick hair.

Hutchins' soft voice interjected, "It might be easier if the FBI takes over the investigation."

Bryant stared at Rizolli and nodded. The doorbell rang. Hutchins went to answer it.

"I'd like to move Cara out of here," Danny stated.

"Good idea. Hold on just a sec." Bryant whipped out his cell phone and took a couple of snapshots, a close-up where the bullet grazed my head, my position on the floor and the cuts littering my body. "Let's move her over to the couch."

"It's all right, Danny. I can walk if someone can just help me up." I held up my hand.

Bryant reached down, but Danny ignored the two of us. Without a by-your-leave, he scooped me into his arms, walked deliberately around the dead body and debris and into the family room where he tenderly placed me on the couch. After that, everything revved into overdrive.

Hutchins brought the police in to play the, "whose jurisdiction will the case fall under" game. Bryant got on the phone to talk to his people. Then the ambulance showed up. When the EMTs realized there wasn't much to do with the body on the floor, Bryant sent them over to me.

A very nice man pulled some glass out of my left arm and leg. My right arm was still mobile and, after an examination, the EMT reckoned I'd pinched a nerve and the tingling pain was due to swelling around the funny bone. He gave me ice to reduce the swelling and recommended ibuprofen. The side of my head where the bullet whizzed past was only a scratch, but they wanted to take me in and have a doctor examine me. The EMT felt some of the deeper cuts could use stitching and the arm an x-ray. I declined a trip to the ER and asked the EMT to bandage the deeper cuts. I told him I'd see a doctor later, after things settled down. I was not going to leave my house. The EMT started to press his point when Danny and Bryant took him aside. I didn't pay attention to their conversation, but a few moments later the EMT came back to finish patching me up and said nothing further about the hospital.

Someone in a suit showed up with cameras and took photos

of the crime scene and me before heading out back. Another suit showed up and started bagging evidence. A U.S. Marshal, named McTumis, arrived and tried to take over the situation. Things got pretty tense for a bit while Bryant and McTumis held a standoff. Phoning their bosses, they strutted like peacocks endeavoring to determine who was going to be the head honcho on this investigation. In the end, the Marshal lost out when it was brought to his superior's attention they were responsible for losing Rizolli in the first place, which almost got a former ADA killed.

Somewhere during the time the EMT was patching me up, the medical examiner arrived with the meat wagon. I don't know what arrangements the FBI made with the local ME, but they were able to come to an agreement because eventually the EMTs helped bag and load Rizolli's body onto the truck.

While Bryant and Hutchins dealt with the local police and ME, McTumis decided to push his luck. He parked himself across from the couch, sat on my coffee table and asked me to tell him what happened.

Unfortunately, for him, I was a seasoned lawyer well aware of the arts of interrogation. Secondly, since the FBI won the pissing contest I knew I didn't owe the Marshal any sort of statement. And finally, I was livid at the Marshals Service for telling Rizolli about the money taken from his offshore accounts, thereby putting him on this rampage, which may have eventually led to Dee's death. I was in no mood to have any story cajoled out of me, so needless to say McTumis' move to try and have a "sit down" with me was not a smart one.

"Look, pal, I'd appreciate it if you'd get your ass off my coffee table. I don't know where you learned your manners, but where I grew up, we sit in chairs, on couches, or on the floor if need be. Not on tables."

McTumis was taken aback by my attack, and at first I thought he was going to respond in kind. However, I guess he decided to turn on the charm to try and get his way. He moved to a chair. "I'm sorry about that. This has been a great shock to you, but I must say you're handling it very well." He looked over at the body and gave an exaggerated shudder. "You're lucky to be alive, Ms. Baker."

"No thanks to you."

He coughed and cleared his throat. "Yes, we deeply regret that. Tell me, why do you think Rizolli came after you? This seems rather drastic. After all, you're not even a prosecutor anymore. And you never actually took him to court. So, why all this?" He indicated the carnage.

Clearly this guy wasn't getting the hint, and his arrogance only served to fire me up. My jaw hardened, and I squinted my eyes. "McTumis, I'm not really sure why you're here or what you think you're planning to accomplish by trying to question a former district attorney, but let me clarify a few things for you. Since Special Agent Bryant is running this investigation, I'm under no obligation to provide a bumbling Marshal any sort of statement. You all have fucked up big time. Some paper pusher of yours let confidential information slip to Rizolli regarding the seizing of his offshore assets, providing him with enough information to know Denise Colquitt was the recipient of a large portion of that money. Then you went and lost him. You didn't bother to seriously search for him and simply assumed he'd been whacked by the Mafia crime boss you were supposed to be protecting him from. Those two screw-ups, put together, allowed Rizolli to go to Pittsburgh and finish the job I was originally prosecuting him for. Now you have the gall to stroll into my home and start asking me asinine questions about why Rizolli might hold a grudge against me. Don't waste my time asking me questions you can read in a damn file. And furthermore, since I believe you've been dismissed from this case, you're no longer welcome in my home. Get the hell out!" I was screeching at the poor man by the time I finished my tirade, and the silence in the room was deafening.

Someone snickered behind me. McTumis sat red-faced and speechless.

Hutchins stepped into the breach. "Marshal McTumis, perhaps you could step outside with me so we can see where Ms. Baker was originally attacked."

McTumis took the olive branch and, excusing himself, hustled out to follow Hutchins into the backyard. Glancing over my shoulder, I found Bryant staring at me with a wide grin. I rolled my eyes and shook my head with a grimace.

At some point, Charleston's local news station got wind that a New Jersey mobster had been killed in Denton, and they showed up with their trucks to take some B-roll and vie for a statement from someone involved. Bryant had the local officers outline my entire yard with crime scene tape to keep them off the property. I felt terrible as the voracious media vultures swooped down. Ringing doorbells, they hounded my neighbors for sound bites. Once the media circus began, my phone didn't stop ringing. At first it was people important to me—Jackie, then Mandy, then Eric. To my surprise, John Graham got wind of the situation and called on behalf of the DA's office. He offered to help in any way he could, going so far as to provide me with the name of a lawyer in Charleston, should I need one.

Hours later, things started to wind down. Bryant arranged to have the local sheriff provide an official statement to the press and had them set up near the village green. Of course, the media people flocked to the center of town to get the scoop, which moved them away from my property and made me eternally grateful to the FBI. After all the photos had been taken, bullets dug out of the walls, evidence accumulated, bagged and numbered, a crime scene cleaning crew showed up to scour my bloody glass-strewn floor. At some point, Beau called Danny on his cell and asked what he could do to help. Danny told him to pick up some plywood from the local hardware store. So, while the crew cleaned, Danny and Beau hammered plywood over the broken French door. That was the only time during the entire ordeal that Danny left my side.

It was late evening when Danny and I sat on the love seat in the front parlor as Bryant closed the door behind the cleaning crew. He checked his phone and then joined us, collapsing in a chair.

He placed his elbows on his knees, hung his hands between them and regarded me. "I'm sorry to have to do this to you,

Cara, especially after the circus you've just endured, but you know I need to get your official statement. Normally, I'd take you in to the local field office. However, this entire situation has turned into a SNAFU of epic proportions. I'm sure that lawyer mind of yours is dreaming up ways to sue the pants off me, the FBI, the U.S. Marshals and everyone else involved. I wouldn't even blame you. So, I'm leaving the choice up to you. I can either take your statement here or you can come to the field office tomorrow."

I gave a wan smile. "I know, Tom. Let's get this over with." I glanced at Danny. "Are you ready to do this?"

He nodded. "If you're sure you are."

"Then we'll do it here. Thanks for the courtesy."

Bryant set a digital recorder on the table between us and pressed play. I explained my story, omitting Danny's involvement. I brought him into the tale after Rizolli was dead on the floor. I included Rizolli's brag about murdering Denise Colquitt, which deepened Tom's frown. When I finished, the FBI agent turned to Danny and asked him if he had anything to add to the story.

I squeezed his hand and Danny shook his head.

Tom shut off the recorder. He'd gone easy on me. If I was in a field office with a camera and other FBI field agents watching, he would have been forced to grill me for an hour or more.

"It's strange how he just collapsed like that," Bryant threw out with nonchalance.

I made a conscious effort not to react. Instead, I shrugged with indifference and didn't meet his eyes. "Probably too much hard living. You know, they say smoking will kill you."

"Do you know how he got the burn marks on his wrist?"

Danny tensed.

I forced myself to remain loose and calm. I quirked an eyebrow. "Not a clue."

With a sharp nod, he stood and gathered his recorder and phone. "I'll be in touch if we need anything else." He paused; his intelligent blue eyes regarded me then flicked to Danny.

Tom wasn't dumb. He knew, I knew, more than I was telling, but for whatever reason, he didn't push it. "If the ME comes up with a reason for death beyond a heart attack, the FBI will label this incident self-defense."

Relief flooded me. Bryant may not have known how Rizolli died on my floor, but he knew I put up a fight and if that bullet had come one inch closer, it would be my body he would've scraped off the kitchen floor.

I escorted him to the door. "Thanks, Tom. I appreciate it."

He gripped the hand I offered and gave it a gentle pump. "No problem. I'm sorry it came to this. I'll do whatever I can to clear the investigation up quickly."

With little hope of a quick resolution, I nodded.

He walked off my front porch shaking his head. "By the way," he turned with a smirk, "I enjoyed the ass chewing you gave McTumis. I think the videographer caught some of it."

My face burned with embarrassment.

"Don't worry. That prick deserved it. I can't wait to tell the guys at the office. They're gonna love it."

His laughter faded into the night as I closed the door behind him.

Chapter Thirty

Danny, my shadow, had followed the two of us to the door and now stood warily at the bottom of the stairs. Waiting.

"Sorry to put you through all that."

"I don't really think it was your fault." Eyeing me, he remained, stiff and tense, but I wasn't ready to start the questions.

"Look, I need a shower." I waved a hand at the dried blood and general mess. "I'm beginning to disgust myself."

He frowned. "You're supposed to go to the hospital to get some of those cuts taken care of. I promised the EMTs I'd take you after the FBI left."

"Tomorrow. Why don't you go up to your apartment and see if you can find us something to eat? I don't know about you, but I'm starved. I'll meet you in about half an hour?"

He stood with his arms crossed looking stern. I imagined the mental debate going in his head. *Should I argue with her, or just sling her over my shoulder and haul her to the hospital?*

"I need some time. Alone. Then we'll talk." I wasn't up for the hospital tonight. He gave a sharp nod and allowed me to pass.

Once in the bathroom, I stripped down and threw the clothes directly into the trash.

Frankly, it surprised me they weren't taken in for evidence. I had a feeling Bryant and Hutchins were going to work with the Marshals to make this go away as quickly as possible. This disaster made everyone look bad. With Rizolli dead, the FBI's case against Carlo Barconi was screwed. Moreover, the Marshals looked like fools for losing Rizolli. Undoubtedly, there'd be a lot of finger pointing and blame would be passed around at all levels. Eventually there would be a sacrificial scapegoat. I hoped it would be McTumis.

I removed the bandages and looked in the mirror to review the damage. Scratches and abrasions littered the left side of my body; the deeper gashes were held together with medical glue. The bleeding had stopped and the glue seemed to be holding, so I figured they'd be fine. The bullet grazed the left side of my head, just above my ear. The scrape could easily be covered with simple hair styling. As I gazed at the cut, the reality of how close I came to death swamped me. My stomach recoiled. I flipped up the toilet lid and got sick.

Hot water sluiced over my sore body, easing the aches and pains. I stood under the shower's spray for a long time to get my equilibrium back. When I was done, I re-bandaged the worst of the cuts and put on a loose pair of pink cotton lounge pants and a baggy T-shirt.

Danny's apartment was empty when I arrived. A glass of red wine sat on the kitchen counter next to a frozen pizza box. I took the wine and wandered over to the balcony where Danny's silhouette showed against the darkened sky. He didn't turn at my approach, so I snaked my arms around his waist and laid my head against his strong back. Tension emanated from his spine. His warm hands covered mine.

"Tell me about it," I whispered.

Danny turned in my embrace and hugged me close. "For a few of the most awful moments of my life, I thought I'd lost you. I wanted the world to stop spinning and just freeze. To keep the truth away. When I saw him aim that gun at your head …" Taking a step back, he released me.

I gazed up at him. "Tell me."

"In my gut, I knew exactly who was holding you at gunpoint. I was frightened by what he was about to do. And furious. I've never felt so blazing angry at another human being in my entire life." He paused. "When I grabbed him, I was funneling my own anger and fear, but it was nothing compared to the emotional hurricane going on inside his body. There was so much hatred. It was like a black evil oozing out of his pores. Instead of absorbing those feelings, I turned them back on him. All that rage and fury must have overloaded his system." He shook his head. "I don't understand how I burned him. I didn't feel the heat coming from my hands. It was more like I turned back fiery heat *he* was emanating."

"Did you know you could do that?"

"God, no." He turned away from me to gaze out over the yard.

"Listen, Cara, you've gone through so much ... so much ..." Danny scrubbed his hands through his hair in frustration. "The past week ... I understand if you'd rather not have me in your life right now ... I mean, this is a lot to take in ... and I know it's ... shocking. I'm shocked by it ... shocked and disgusted."

"So, what you're saying is ... if you'd had a gun in your hand, you wouldn't have shot him to save my life?"

His face whipped back to me. "Of course not! If I'd had a gun in my hand, he wouldn't have had time to take aim at you. I would have put him down immediately!"

"Good. Just making sure." I grinned.

"But listen, I'm dangerous. I've warned you before." His voice was intense. "Today you witnessed just how dangerous I can be. You've been fighting what I've been telling you for weeks. *I can hurt you.*" He made a disgusted noise in the back of this throat. "And now you've lied to the FBI to protect me."

I clicked my tongue. "The FBI can take a flying leap. If it weren't for them, Rizolli would have been locked away, rotting in a jail cell. Frankly, I have no earthly idea how we could have explained what really happened. Death by emotion?"

"Cara ..." he ground out.

I held up my hand. "I have something to say." I spoke with slow deliberation. "I am not afraid of you. You will not hurt me, and you may not break up with me. You just saved my life."

Danny rolled his eyes. "I don't know about that. You looked like you were handling the situation. That kick to the cajones was vicious. Remind me never to piss you off." He winced.

"I'm not done."

He bowed his head contrite.

"I'm in love with you." I poked my finger into his chest to emphasize my point.

He grimaced. "Cara, this is like … some sort of 'hero' worship. Like in that movie *Speed* with Sandra Bullock. I saved your life and your emotions are all in a whirl, and…"

I socked him in the shoulder, hard. "I am not under some sort of delusional 'hero' worship and I'm *not* Sandra Bullock in *Speed*! What is with you and that chick?"

"Ow!" He rubbed his arm.

"I was going to tell you out in the gazebo this morning … only it wasn't you … and he tried to kill me … and the day pretty much went down the crapper after that. But we're here now, and I just thought I should tell you." My voice became quiet. "I've fallen in love with you."

He stared, unfathomable, silent. His smile gone.

Uh, oh. Awkward. My cheeks heated. "Ah, hey, look, umm, I'm not expecting you to say it back. Okay? As a matter of fact, I don't want you to, because, ah … I don't want you to feel like you have to lie to me. I know uh … you care about me and … that's enough for now. You know, maybe you'll eventually grow to … ah…" I rambled feeling more and more like an idiot when Danny silenced my blathering with a slow sensual kiss, taking me under deep. My legs turned to jelly before we came up for air.

He held my face between his hands, jade-colored eyes soft and warm looked down upon me. "Sweetheart, I've been in love with you since you baked me that first pan of pasta."

"Why didn't you say something?" I whispered.

"I didn't want to push you." He used hushed tones. "I've been deathly afraid of scaring you off ever since Jeff brought you up to my apartment."

"Pshaw. It takes more than that to scare me off." Stretching up on my tiptoes, I wrapped my arms around Danny's neck and fused my lips to his. The kiss made my toes curl and started a fire in my belly. "Take me to bed." I laid my head against his shoulder.

Danny's loving eyes searched my face. I could tell questions whirled through his mind, but I didn't have any more answers.

"Make love to me. Make me forget. Tonight I don't want to think. I just want to feel." He didn't have to be asked twice. He scooped me up, nudged the door open with his hip, and carried me down the hall to his bedroom.

Epilogue

Christmastime

"It's listing to the left."

Dad pulled the tree farther to the left. "No, no. My left. Your right."

My father readjusted while Danny, buried under the branches, fiddled with the screws to tighten the eight-foot fir in place.

"How's that?" came Danny's muffled voice.

"I think it's okay," I said uncertain. "Mom!" I hollered. "Come tell me if the tree looks okay."

My mother wandered into the parlor, wiping her hands on a red-checkered kitchen towel. "It looks lovely. What a beautiful Christmas tree you boys picked out."

Dad came to stand next to Mom while Danny scooted out from beneath the greens. Both of them stood, hands on hips, admiring their manly handiwork when the doorbell rang.

I checked my watch. "That's my three o'clock appointment."

Mom and Dad retreated into the kitchen.

Danny gave me a chaste peck on the cheek. "We'll decorate it tonight after dinner." He took the steps two at a time as he hurried up to his office.

While my parents visited, we observed the proprieties, Danny slept in his apartment and I slept alone, one floor below. My parents planned to stick around until after my New Year's Eve party. Danny's sister and his parents were planning to arrive together, just after Christmas, to attend the party. The three of them were so excited to see Danny I received phone calls on a daily basis, asking all sorts of bizarre questions—from what the weather would be like to what flavor of coffee I preferred. Danny's sister, Rebecca, would be staying in my other guest room and his parents would stay in the guest room in Danny's apartment. Danny's withdrawal from the world had been so complete, he'd cut himself off from his family. I could tell by his recent behavior that he was getting nervous with anticipation. It had been eight years since he'd seen any of them in person.

I opened the front door to reveal my client, a petite, white-haired lady wearing a lavender sweat suit and white tennis shoes. I smiled. "Hello, Mrs. Simkins. How are you doing today?"

Bright pink lipstick smiled back at me. "I'm fine, dear." Her eyes lit on the tree in the parlor. "Oh, what a nice tree."

"Thank you. Why don't you come into my office? Can I get you something to drink?" I led her into the study and closed the door to ensure privacy.

"No, thanks."

Mrs. Simkins sat in the navy guest chair, while I rounded my desk and picked up a manila folder labeled, Gladys Simkins, Last Will and Testament. I passed it across to her. "Here's the Will with the changes you requested. Why don't we go over it together to make sure it's exactly what you want?"

About a month after Rizolli's death, I quit my job at the library and acquired a license to practice law in South Carolina. A small plaque hung from the front porch and read, *Cara S. Baker, Esq. Attorney-at-Law*. Much to my surprise, news of a lawyer in Denton spread like wildfire through the small community and surrounding areas. For the past months, I'd gathered a steady stream of clients. If it continued to grow at this pace, I'd soon need to rent office space and hire help. Both Jackie and Beau immediately brought their business to me. I managed Jackie's real estate transactions, and became their personal attorney.

Denise's money allowed me to live comfortably while I got the new business off the ground. Unfortunately, I was never able to read the final words she wrote. Rizolli saw to that when he landed on the letter and bled all over it. I would like to believe it contained forgiveness and kind words. The FBI bagged it for evidence. About a month after the incident, Bryant mailed me a box of personal affects taken, along with notification Rizolli's death was officially due to a brain aneurism and massive heart failure, an unusual combination. I found the letter, stained brown with dried blood, inside a plastic evidence bag. It was unsalvageable and the thought of touching Rizolli's blood gave me the jeepers. Regretfully, I threw it in the trash.

My parents arrived mid-month to spend the Christmas holidays with me. They hadn't changed much in the year since I'd last seen them. Mom sported a few more gray hairs, while Dad had lost some weight around the middle and gained more real estate on his balding dome. Their RV was parked in the back alley along the fence line, while their small SUV was parked next to the Mini in the carport.

Actually, this was my mother's second visit to my South Carolina home. Less than forty-eight hours after Rizolli died on my kitchen floor, Mom showed up at the front door. The local news story about the strange death of a Mafia member in a small town outside of Charleston was quickly picked up by the national twenty-four hour news media outlets. Unbeknownst to me, Danny took it upon himself to contact my parents to let them know I was okay. They were traveling the Pacific Northwest at the time, and Mom made Dad drive her to the closest airport, which turned out to be Portland, where she hopped the first flight heading east. When I opened the door to find her standing on my front porch, I was so thankful I burst into tears. She pulled me into a lavender-scented hug, and I was home.

Mom stayed for a week—doing my laundry, cooking delicious meals to tempt my non- existent appetite, and most importantly, listening. Initially, she was hurt I'd hidden so much from her, but because I was her daughter, she forgave me. Since Danny was the one who called my parents to reassure them, his presence as my tenant was gratefully accepted. A few days in to her visit, I revealed our romantic relationship. Mom wasn't surprised. She said she knew Danny cared for me when he called, and she was pleased I was dating such a nice, handsome young man. Fortunately, Mom accepted him at face value.

In the weeks following Mom's visit, my life slowly returned to normal. My celebrity among the local population waned, and the latest Hollywood starlet overdose captured the media's attention, removing the remnants of paparazzi hanging around the Denton area.

Therefore, I was surprised when I arrived home one evening to find a black Navigator with dark shaded windows and a shiny red Lincoln sedan parked in front of my house. When I got out of my car, an overweight dark-haired man, wearing black jeans and a black leather jacket, heaved himself out of the Navigator. Alarm bells went off in my head. He looked out of place. Frankly, he looked like a Mafia thug.

"Cara Baker?"

Skittish, I remained where I was, keeping the car between us. My eyes bounced between the driver in the Navigator and the thug on my lawn. Twice I cleared my throat. "Yes?"

The thug waddled across the lawn and held out his hand toward me. "Compliments of Carlo Barconi," he said with a Jersey accent.

I stared confused.

The thug stood opposite me, on the passenger side of the Mini, and held out a set of keys over the roof. He jiggled them. "Lady."

Cautiously, I held out my hand, and he dropped the keys.

"I don't get it." I swallowed.

The thug reached into his coat pocket. My mind screamed *gun*! I dropped to the ground on my hands and knees.

"Let's just say Mr. Barconi was appreciative ... lady? Where'd you go?" Footsteps came around the car. "You drop something?"

I looked up.

The thug, his bulky weight leaning down toward me, held a packet of papers.

"What do you want?"

"I don't want nothin', lady. Here are the papers for the car. You bein' a lawyer and all, Mr. Barconi figured you'd want the bill of sale. Just to show that it's legit and all."

I got to my feet and he handed me the papers. Unfolding them, I found a sales slip for a brand new Lincoln MKS, paid in full, along with a car title carrying my name.

The thug chatted at me while I reviewed the paperwork.

"It's a nice car, and Mr. Barconi thought you'd like red. Which I sees you do since you're already driving a red car." He tapped the Mini with a fat forefinger. "But this is too little. You get into an accident with a car like this, and SPLAT!"

I jumped.

"You get squished like a bug. You need a nice luxury car, like that one. Much safer, you know?" He pointed to the red sedan.

"I'm sorry. I didn't catch your name."

"Everybody calls me Bobby V." The thug gave a greasy grin.

"Okay, Bobby. Why is Carlo Barconi giving me a car?" I was still confused.

"Like I said before, Mr. Barconi likes to show his appreciation when someone does him a favor." Bobby V. winked.

A lightbulb finally clicked on. Rizolli was dead. Carlo knew the Feds' strongest witness against him would never testify. In my discussions with Agent Bryant, I'd read between the lines. Their case was falling apart and Barconi hadd been released from custody. Carlo also knew Rizolli died in my house. The Feds did a fairly good job of keeping a lid on Rizolli's death. However, Barconi probably figured it was a cover-up and that I had actually killed Rizolli and no one was going to prosecute me because of my connections to the DA's office. A shudder of disgust ran down my spine.

My attention was momentarily diverted when Danny burst through the front door like a wary bear. "What's going on out here?"

I waved a hand at him. "We're fine, Danny."

Bobby V. stood with his hands up in the air mumbling,

"Whoa, whoa, whoa."

The driver in the Navigator got out. A kid. He looked to be in his early twenties, tall and wiry, with light brown hair, and wearing a dark brown leather jacket. I didn't want to speculate what was hidden under the jacket.

"Who's this?" Danny shoved out his chin, hands on his hips, legs spread shoulder width.

Bobby put his pudgy palms down. "We're all good here." He glanced over at the driver and jerked his head at him. The kid got back into the car. Bobby's voice was congenial to diffuse the tension. "As I was telling Ms. Baker here, my name's Bobby V. We was just delivering a gift to the lady." He waved in the direction of the shiny red Lincoln.

Danny's eyebrows rose. I wasn't sure if it was at the Jersey accent or the car. "Mr. V." I stepped between Danny and Bobby.

"Bobby. Everyone calls me Bobby."

"Bobby." I spoke gently, handling the situation with kid gloves. "It's very generous ... and ... and thoughtful of Mr. Barconi to provide such a lovely gift. But ... uh ... truly it's too much. I couldn't accept such generosity." I held the paperwork and keys toward him.

Bobby backed away, throwing his hands up. "Mr. Barconi was quite clear. He said I was to leave the car with you. He said to say that if you don't like the car, you can sell it and buy yourself a mink coat or a diamond bracelet. You know, whatever you like."

"Bobby, it's not that this isn't a nice car." I tried to reason with him. "I'm sure it's very nice. It just isn't appropriate for me to accept a gift like this from a stranger. I really think it would be best if you returned the car to Mr. Barconi. Besides, gifts like this tend to come with strings."

Bobby shook his head.

"Strings, Bobby. I don't think I want to know what's attached to the other end of those strings."

Danny had come to stand beside me and now put a comforting arm around my shoulders. Suddenly, the back door of the Navigator popped open. Out stepped a man wearing black trousers, a gray button-down shirt and a black sport coat. He was of medium height and medium build with more salt than pepper in his graying hair. His eyes were dark and deep-set. I recognized him immediately from FBI photos and my shoulders tensed beneath Danny's hands. The newcomer waved at the kid, who hopped out of the car at the same time as his boss. The kid's head bobbed back and forth between Danny, Bobby and Carlo Barconi, unsure what to do.

"It's okay, Marco. Stay with the car." Mr. Barconi spoke softly as he approached us. "Ms. Baker, I assume you know who I am."

I gulped and nodded.

Barconi's gaze shifted to Danny. "And you must be Daniel Johnson, tenant, boyfriend," he took in the possessive arm around me, "… watchdog?" A black eyebrow winged up.

Danny's arm tightened. "And you would be?" He asked in a barely friendly tone.

"Danny, this is Carlo Barconi." I clarified.

"I see," Danny hissed through his teeth and lightened his grip, removing his hand from skin contact.

Barconi threw back his head and laughed. "Down boy! I assure you I'm not here to hurt Ms. Baker. Actually, I've become quite a fan. You did me a favor. You saved me a lot of trouble and money."

"That wasn't my intent."

Carlo smirked. "No, I'm sure it wasn't." He eyeballed me up and down. "Tony was a fighter. I'm impressed you were able to take him down."

I didn't respond.

"Let me assure you, there are no strings attached to this gift."

I started to shake my head but paused under the Mafia boss' steely glare.

"And I always pay my debts. Let me also assure you I've let it be known should any harm come to you … someone will answer to me." Carlo's silky voice gave me goose bumps.

"Was there supposed to be retaliation over Rizolli?" I crossed my arms.

Barconi shook his head. "Not that I know of. Anthony burned his bridges when he became a snitch. It's just a precaution on my part."

I nodded, judging Carlo, trying to decide if there was real danger here.

"Bobby, let's not bother this pretty lady any further." His gaze swept by Danny. "Mr. Johnson, it was nice to meet you. Keep her safe."

"That's my plan," Danny responded through a clenched jaw.

We watched, wary, as Carlo and Bobby V. clambered back into the Navigator. Marco turned the ignition, and the big car rumbled to life. Before pulling away, Barconi's back window slid down. "Tell Agent Bryant I said hello."

We didn't move until the car rounded the corner out of sight. Danny shook his head and whistled through his teeth. "Jesus, babe, you sure do attract some crazy people. Is that guy really a mob boss?"

"Yes, he is." I pulled my cell phone out of my purse.

Eventually, I sold the car and donated the proceeds to Denise Colquitt's foundation. That is, after the FBI was through with it. When I called Bryant to explain the unusual gift, he warned me not to touch the car. Field agents arrived within ten minutes with a bomb-sniffing dog, a drug-sniffing dog and a fingerprinting kit. The car was as clean as the sale and title, just as Bobby V. had guaranteed.

However, if this episode in my life taught me anything; there are no guarantees. As I moved forward, I didn't know where life would lead me, or if it would be tranquil, but I'd hold to these two simple truths—the law fulfilled my career aspirations, and my heart lay with Danny at Poplar Place.

Acknowledgements

Poplar Place is my first novel and I couldn't have written it without help. Thanks to Lotta Crabtree for her medical and legal knowledge and for being my inspiration for making my main character a Pittsburgh ADA. I also thank her for the introduction to Kevin Lee whose knowledge of the politics of the Pittsburgh legal system I found invaluable. Thanks, Kevin, for answering endless questions about the halls of justice in the Allegheny County court system, for providing me with interesting character development, and giving me an excellent feel for neighborhoods surrounding downtown Pittsburgh. Denton and some of the locations mentioned in Pittsburgh are fictional. I did take some literary liberties with our legal system and inaccuracies no way reflect information provided to me by others. To Betsy Gilbert, thank you for editing and providing feedback, and being my chief cheerleader. Finally, thanks to my family for their love and support.

Mirror Touch Synesthesia

The question I have been asked the most often by interviewers, readers and book clubs is about Danny's condition. What is it? When I originally conceived this story in the early part of 2000, I wanted to give Danny a sixth sense that would provide him a viable reason for becoming a reclusive hermit. During my college years I'd done research on supernatural phenomenon such as ESP, telekinesis and astral projection. Some would call Danny an empath, something that we only see in fictional television or movie characters. However, since the first publication of *Poplar Place*, it has been brought to my attention that Danny is not alone.

In 2011 psychologists Michael Banissy and Jamie Ward published a paper in the *Journal of Neuroscience*, documenting their research on a newly recognized condition called mirror-touch synesthesia. A synesthete, as they are called, can feel when another person is physically touched. In addition, some synesthetes are so perceptive they, much like Danny, absorb the person's feelings and mental states. Highly sensitive synesthetes have to struggle on a daily basis to cope with the intrusion of people's emotions; it has forced some to become as reclusive as my character. In *Poplar Place* Danny needed physical contact to absorb emotions of another, in real life a synesthete does not need the contact. Visually witnessing the touch is enough for a synesthete to feel it themselves. There have even been reports of synesthetes being affected by seeing violence on television. Imagine being a synesthete on a crowded rush hour subway train, feeling every brush, touch or pressure on the dozen or so people within ten-foot radius. Overwhelming.

When I created Danny's character and his sixth sense, I added the physical changes to increase the reasons for him to become a recluse. My research has found no evidence of this phenomenon in real life or of the ability to impose feelings onto other people as Danny does. Those characteristics seem to remain a fictional creation.

About the Author

Ellen Butler is a bestselling and award-winning novelist living in the Virginia suburbs of Washington, DC. She holds a Master's Degree in Public Administration and Policy, and her history includes a long list of writing and editing for dry but illuminating professional newsletters and windy papers on public policy. The leap to novel writing was simply a creative outlet for Ellen's overactive and romantic imagination to run wild. Professionally, she belongs to the Virginia Writer's Club, the OSS Society, International Thriller Writers, and Sisters in Crime.

Stalk Ellen at:
Website: ellenbutler.net
Twitter & Instagram: @EButlerBooks
Facebook: facebook.com/EllenButlerBooks
Goodreads: goodreads.com/EllenButlerBooks

Guided Reading Questions
Guided Reading Questions for Book Clubs can be found on Ellen's Website at:
www.ellenbutler.net/book-clubs

Novels by Ellen Butler
Suspense/Thriller
Isabella's Painting (A Karina Cardinal Mystery)
The Brass Compass
Contemporary Romance
Love, California Style Trilogy
Heart of Design (book 1)
Planning for Love (book 2)
Art of Affection (book 3)
Second Chance Christmas

The Brass Compass Excerpt

Chapter One

Into the Night

February 1945
Germany

"*Was ist sein Name?*" What is his name? The SS officer's backlit shadow loomed over his victim as he yelled into the face of the shrinking man on the third-story balcony. "We know you've been passing messages. Tell us, who is your contact?" he continued in German.

Lenz's gray-haired head shook like a frightened mouse. With his back to me, I was too far away to hear the mumbled response or the Nazi's next question. I pulled my dark wool coat tighter and sank deeper into the shadow of the apartment building's doorway across the street from where my contact underwent interrogation. The pounding of my heart pulsated in my ears, and I held my breath as I strained to listen to the conversation. In front of Lenz's building stood a black Mercedes-Benz with its running lights aglow, no doubt the vehicle that brought the SS troops. None of the neighboring buildings showed any light, as residents cowered behind locked doors praying the SS wouldn't come knocking. This was a working-class neighborhood, and everyone knew it was best to keep your mouth shut and not stick your nose in the business of the Schutzstaffel.

Their presence at Lenz's home explained why my contact at the bakery was absent from our assignation earlier today. I dreaded to imagine what they had done to Otto for him to give up Lenz's name ... or worse, mine. Even though I'd never told Otto my name, a description of me could easily lead the SS to their target.

"*Lügner!*" Liar!

I flinched as the officer's ringing accusation bounced off the brick buildings. A young SS Stormtrooper stepped out onto the balcony and requested his superior look at something in his hand. I should have taken their distraction to slip away into the darkness and run; instead I stayed, anxiously listening, to hear if Lenz would break under the SS grilling and reveal my identity. Clearly, they suspected he was involved in spying and would take him away. They probably also knew he had information to spill and would eventually torture it out of him, which was the only reason he hadn't been shot on sight. It was only a matter of time before he gave me away. My friends in the French Resistance had been directed to hold out for two days before releasing names to allow the spies to disband and disappear. I wasn't sure if the German network applied the same rules, so I remained to see if he would break before they took him.

"Where did you find this?" the officer asked.

The trooper indicated inside the apartment.

"*Zeig es mir.*" Show me. He followed his subordinate through the doorway into the building.

Lenz turned and braced himself against the balcony. I watched in horror as he climbed atop the railing.

"*Halt!*" a bellow from inside rang out.

Lenz didn't hesitate, and I averted my eyes, biting down hard on my cold knuckles, as he took his final moments out of the hands of the Nazis. Sounds of shattering glass and buckling metal ripped through the darkness as his body slammed into the SS vehicle. In my periphery, a neighboring blackout curtain shifted.

"*Scheisse!*" the SS officer swore as he and his subordinate leaned over the railing to see Lenz's body sprawled across their car. "Search the apartment. *Tear it apart!*"

The moment they crossed the threshold, I sprinted into the night.

My breath puffed out in small plumes of smoke as I dodged through alleys, in and out of darkened doorways, moving on the balls of my feet. Silently, I cursed the cloudless sky as the moonlight bounced off the cobblestones, its brightness clear enough to land a plane. Unless waiting at midnight at a drop zone for needed supplies, a spy preferred the inky blackness of cloudy skies. Especially when escaping the enemy.

A few kilometers from Lenz's apartment, I paused behind the brick rubble of a bombed-out building. My gaze searched the area for any sign of movement. Standing alert, I held my breath, attuning my senses to the nighttime sounds, and listened for the whisper of cloth, the click of a boot heel, or heaven forbid, the cock of a gun. The thundering of my heartbeat slowed, and I balled my fists to stop my shaking hands. All seemed quiet … for the moment.

My fingers curled around the tiny film cartridge, filled with information vital to the Allied cause, nestled in my coat pocket. Dropping down to one knee, I slipped the heel of my right boot aside and tucked it into the hidden cavity. The coded message I'd planned to pass to Lenz would have to be burned, but I couldn't take the chance of lighting a fire right now. It would have to wait until morning.

The Brass Compass Now Available.
Visit *ellenbutler.net* to get your copy today.